Golden The Fairy Book

By **Andrew Lang**

Copyright © 2017 by Success Park Publishers.
All rights reserved.
Beta release 0.2 edition

Author: Andrew Lang (1844-1912)
Published: 1906

Table of Contents

Preface..1

The Story of the Hero Makoma...2

The Magic Mirror..6

Story of the King Who Would See Paradise.......................10

How Isuro the Rabbit Tricked Gudu..................................12

Ian, the Soldier's Son..15

The Fox and the Wolf...23

How Ian Direach Got the Blue Falcon...............................27

The Ugly Duckling..32

The Two Caskets..38

The Goldsmith's Fortune..45

The Enchanted Wreath..47

The Foolish Weaver...52

The Clever Cat...53

The Story of Manus...60

Pinkel the Thief..64

The Adventures of a Jackal..70

The Adventures of the Jackal's Eldest Son.......................73

The Adventures of the Younger Son of the Jackal............76

The Three Treasures of the Giants..78

The Rover of the Plain..84

The White Doe..89

The Girl-Fish...100

The Owl and the Eagle...106

The Frog and the Lion Fairy..109

The Adventures of Covan the Brown-Haired........................120

The Princess Bella-Flor..127

The Bird of Truth...132

The Mink and the Wolf..138

Adventures of an Indian Brave..141

How the Stalos Were Tricked..144

Andras Baive..148

The White Slipper..150

The Magic Book...157

- **Children's Classics**
- **Self-Help/Philosophy/Motivational Classics**
- **Timeless Classic Novels and Novellas**

Timeless Classics for Your Collection

Classic Books for Your Inspiration and Entertainment

**Visit Us at:
goo.gl/U8oLCr**

Books by:
Jane Austen
Brontë Sisters
Elizabeth Gaskell
Arthur Conan Doyle
Jack London
Louisa May Alcott
Edith Nesbit
L Frank Baum
Mark Twain
James Allen
Stephen Crane
Charles F. Haanel
Lewis Carroll
Jules Verne
Charles Dickens
and Others!

Preface

The children who read fairy books, or have fairy books read to them, do not read prefaces, and the parents, aunts, uncles, and cousins, who give fairy books to their daughters, nieces, and cousins, leave prefaces unread. For whom, then, are prefaces written? When an author publishes a book 'out of his own head,' he writes the preface for his own pleasure. After reading over his book in print—to make sure that all the 'u's' are not printed as 'n's,' and all the 'n's' as 'u's' in the proper names—then the author says, mildly, in his preface, what he thinks about his own book, and what he means it to prove—if he means it to prove anything—and why it is not a better book than it is. But, perhaps, nobody reads prefaces except other authors; and critics, who hope that they will find enough in the preface to enable them to do without reading any of the book.

This appears to be the philosophy of prefaces in general, and perhaps authors might be more daring and candid than they are with advantage, and write regular criticisms of their own books in their prefaces, for nobody can be so good a critic of himself as the author—if he has a sense of humour. If he has not, the less he says in his preface the better.

These Fairy Books, however, are not written by the Editor, as he has often explained, 'out of his own head.' The stories are taken from those told by grannies to grandchildren in many countries and in many languages—French, Italian, Spanish, Catalan, Gaelic, Icelandic, Cherokee, African, Indian, Australian, Slavonic, Eskimo, and what not. The stories are not literal, or word by word translations, but have been altered in many ways to make them suitable for children. Much has been left out in places, and the narrative has been broken up into conversations, the characters telling each other how matters stand, and speaking for themselves, as children, and some older people, prefer them to do. In many tales, fairly cruel and savage deeds are done, and these have been softened down as much as possible; though it is impossible, even if it were desirable, to conceal the circumstance that popular stories were never intended to be tracts and nothing else. Though they usually take the side of courage and kindness, and the virtues in general, the old story-tellers admire successful cunning as much as Homer does in the Odyssey. At least, if the cunning hero, human or animal, is the weaker, like Odysseus, Brer Rabbit, and many others, the story-teller sees little in intellect but superior cunning, by which tiny Jack gets the better of the giants. In the fairy tales of no country are 'improper' incidents common, which is to the credit of human nature, as they were obviously composed mainly for children. It is not difficult to get rid of this element when it does occur in popular tales.

The old puzzle remains a puzzle—why do the stories of the remotest people so closely resemble each other? Of course, in the immeasurable past, they have been carried about by conquering races, and learned by conquering races from vanquished peoples. Slaves carried far from home brought their stories with them into captivity. Wanderers, travellers, shipwrecked men, merchants, and wives stolen from alien tribes have diffused the stories; gipsies and Jews have passed them about; Roman soldiers of many different races, moved here and there about the Empire, have trafficked in them. From the remotest days men have been wanderers, and wherever they went their stories accompanied them.

The slave trade might take a Greek to Persia, a Persian to Greece; an Egyptian woman to Phoenicia; a Babylonian to Egypt; a Scandinavian child might be carried with the amber from the Baltic to the Adriatic; or a Sidonian to Ophir, wherever Ophir may have been; while the Portuguese may have borne their tales to South Africa, or to Asia, and thence brought back other tales to Egypt. The stories wandered wherever the Buddhist missionaries went, and the earliest French voyageurs told them to the Red Indians. These facts help to account for the sameness of the stories everywhere; and the uniformity of human fancy in early societies must be the cause of many other resemblances.

In this volume there are stories from the natives of Rhodesia, collected by Mr. Fairbridge, who speaks the native language, and one is brought by Mr. Cripps from another part of Africa, Uganda. Three tales from the Punjaub were collected and translated by Major Campbell. Various savage tales, which needed a good deal of editing, are derived from the learned pages of the 'Journal of the Anthropological Institute.' With these exceptions, and 'The Magic Book,' translated by Mrs. Pedersen, from 'Eventyr fra Jylland,' by Mr. Ewald Tang Kristensen (Stories from Jutland), all the tales have been done, from various sources, by Mrs. Lang, who has modified, where it seemed desirable, all the narratives.

The Story of the Hero Makoma

From the Senna (Oral Tradition)

Once upon a time, at the town of Senna on the banks of the Zambesi, was born a child. He was not like other children, for he was very tall and strong; over his shoulder he carried a big sack, and in his hand an iron hammer. He could also speak like a grown man, but usually he was very silent.

One day his mother said to him: 'My child, by what name shall we know you?'

And he answered: 'Call all the head men of Senna here to the river's bank.' And his mother called the head men of the town, and when they had come he led them down to a deep black pool in the river where all the fierce crocodiles lived.

'O great men!' he said, while they all listened, 'which of you will leap into the pool and overcome the crocodiles?' But no one would come forward. So he turned and sprang into the water and disappeared.

The people held their breath, for they thought: 'Surely the boy is bewitched and throws away his life, for the crocodiles will eat him!' Then suddenly the ground trembled, and the pool, heaving and swirling, became red with blood, and presently the boy rising to the surface swam on shore.

But he was no longer just a boy! He was stronger than any man and very tall and handsome, so that the people shouted with gladness when they saw him.

'Now, O my people!' he cried, waving his hand, 'you know my name—I am Makoma, "the Greater"; for have I not slain the crocodiles into the pool where none would venture?'

The Orange Fairy Book - 3

Then he said to his mother: 'Rest gently, my mother, for I go to make a home for myself and become a hero.' Then, entering his hut he took Nu-endo, his iron hammer, and throwing the sack over his shoulder, he went away.

Makoma crossed the Zambesi, and for many moons he wandered towards the north and west until he came to a very hilly country where, one day, he met a huge giant making mountains.

'Greeting,' shouted Makoma, 'you are you?'

'I am Chi-eswa-mapiri, who makes the mountains,' answered the giant; 'and who are you?'

'I am Makoma, which signifies "greater,"' answered he.

'Greater than who?' asked the giant.

'Greater than you!' answered Makoma.

The giant gave a roar and rushed upon him. Makoma said nothing, but swinging his great hammer, Nu-endo, he struck the giant upon the head.

He struck him so hard a blow that the giant shrank into quite a little man, who fell upon his knees saying: 'You are indeed greater than I, O Makoma; take me with you to be your slave!' So Makoma picked him up and dropped him into the sack that he carried upon his back.

He was greater than ever now, for all the giant's strength had gone into him; and he resumed his journey, carrying his burden with as little difficulty as an eagle might carry a hare.

Before long he came to a country broken up with huge stones and immense clods of earth. Looking over one of the heaps he saw a giant wrapped in dust dragging out the very earth and hurling it in handfuls on either side of him.

'Who are you,' cried Makoma, 'that pulls up the earth in this way?'

'I am Chi-dubula-taka,' said he, 'and I am making the river-beds.'

'Do you know who I am?' said Makoma. 'I am he that is called "greater"!'

'Greater than who?' thundered the giant.

'Greater than you!' answered Makoma.

With a shout, Chi-dubula-taka seized a great clod of earth and launched it at Makoma. But the hero had his sack held over his left arm and the stones and earth fell harmlessly upon it, and, tightly gripping his iron hammer, he rushed in and struck the giant to the ground. Chi-dubula-taka grovelled before him, all the while growing smaller and smaller; and when he had become a convenient size Makoma picked him up and put him into the sack beside Chi-eswa-mapiri.

He went on his way even greater than before, as all the river-maker's power had become his; and at last he came to a forest of bao-babs and thorn trees. He was astonished at their size, for every one was full grown and larger than any trees he had ever seen, and close by he saw Chi-gwisa-miti, the giant who was planting the forest.

Chi-gwisa-miti was taller than either of his brothers, but Makoma was not afraid, and called out to him: 'Who are you, O Big One?'

'I,' said the giant, 'am Chi-gwisa-miti, and I am planting these bao-babs and thorns as food for my children the elephants.'

'Leave off!' shouted the hero, 'for I am Makoma, and would like to exchange a blow with thee!'

The Orange Fairy Book - 4

The giant, plucking up a monster bao-bab by the roots, struck heavily at Makoma; but the hero sprang aside, and as the weapon sank deep into the soft earth, whirled Nu-endo the hammer round his head and felled the giant with one blow.

So terrible was the stroke that Chi-gwisa-miti shrivelled up as the other giants had done; and when he had got back his breath he begged Makoma to take him as his servant. 'For,' said he, 'it is honourable to serve a man so great as thou.'

Makoma, after placing him in his sack, proceeded upon his journey, and travelling for many days he at last reached a country so barren and rocky that not a single living thing grew upon it—everywhere reigned grim desolation. And in the midst of this dead region he found a man eating fire.

'What are you doing?' demanded Makoma.

'I am eating fire,' answered the man, laughing; 'and my name is Chi-idea-moto, for I am the flame-spirit, and can waste and destroy what I like.'

'You are wrong,' said Makoma; 'for I am Makoma, who is "greater" than you—and you cannot destroy me!'

The fire-eater laughed again, and blew a flame at Makoma. But the hero sprang behind a rock—just in time, for the ground upon which he had been standing was turned to molten glass, like an overbaked pot, by the heat of the flame-spirit's breath.

Then the hero flung his iron hammer at Chi-idea-moto, and, striking him, it knocked him helpless; so Makoma placed him in the sack, Woro-nowu, with the other great men that he had overcome.

And now, truly, Makoma was a very great hero; for he had the strength to make hills, the industry to lead rivers over dry wastes, foresight and wisdom in planting trees, and the power of producing fire when he wished.

Wandering on he arrived one day at a great plain, well watered and full of game; and in the very middle of it, close to a large river, was a grassy spot, very pleasant to make a home upon.

Makoma was so delighted with the little meadow that he sat down under a large tree and removing the sack from his shoulder, took out all the giants and set them before him. 'My friends,' said he, 'I have travelled far and am weary. Is not this such a place as would suit a hero for his home? Let us then go, to-morrow, to bring in timber to make a kraal.'

So the next day Makoma and the giants set out to get poles to build the kraal, leaving only Chi-eswa-mapiri to look after the place and cook some venison which they had killed. In the evening, when they returned, they found the giant helpless and tied to a tree by one enormous hair!

'How is it,' said Makoma, astonished, 'that we find you thus bound and helpless?'

'O Chief,' answered Chi-eswa-mapiri, 'at mid-day a man came out of the river; he was of immense statue, and his grey moustaches were of such length that I could not see where they ended! He demanded of me "Who is thy master?" And I answered: "Makoma, the greatest of heroes." Then the man seized me, and pulling a hair from his moustache, tied me to this tree—even as you see me.'

Makoma was very wroth, but he said nothing, and drawing his finger-nail across the hair (which was as thick and strong as palm rope) cut it, and set free the mountain-maker.

The three following days exactly the same thing happened, only each time with a different one of the party; and on the fourth day Makoma stayed in camp when the others went to cut poles, saying that he would see for himself what sort of man this was that lived in the river and whose moustaches were so long that they extended beyond men's sight.

So when the giants had gone he swept and tidied the camp and put some venison on the fire to roast. At midday, when the sun was right overhead, he heard a rumbling noise from the river, and looking up he saw the head and shoulders of an enormous man emerging from it. And behold! right down the river-bed and up the river-bed, till they faded into the blue distance, stretched the giant's grey moustaches!

'Who are you?' bellowed the giant, as soon as he was out of the water.

'I am he that is called Makoma,' answered the hero; 'and, before I slay thee, tell me also what is thy name and what thou doest in the river?'

'My name is Chin-debou Mau-giri,' said the giant. 'My home is in the river, for my moustache is the grey fever-mist that hangs above the water, and with which I bind all those that come unto me so that they die.'

'You cannot bind me!' shouted Makoma, rushing upon him and striking with his hammer. But the river giant was so slimy that the blow slid harmlessly off his green chest, and as Makoma stumbled and tried to regain his balance, the giant swung one of his long hairs around him and tripped him up.

For a moment Makoma was helpless, but remembering the power of the flame-spirit which had entered into him, he breathed a fiery breath upon the giant's hair and cut himself free.

As Chin-debou Mau-giri leaned forward to seize him the hero flung his sack Woronowu over the giant's slippery head, and gripping his iron hammer, struck him again; this time the blow alighted upon the dry sack and Chin-debou Mau-giri fell dead.

When the four giants returned at sunset with the poles, they rejoiced to find that Makoma had overcome the fever-spirit, and they feasted on the roast venison till far into the night; but in the morning, when they awoke, Makoma was already warming his hands to the fire, and his face was gloomy.

'In the darkness of the night, O my friends,' he said presently, 'the white spirits of my fathers came upon me and spoke, saying: "Get thee hence, Makoma, for thou shalt have no rest until thou hast found and fought with Sakatirina, who had five heads, and is very great and strong; so take leave of thy friends, for thou must go alone."'

Then the giants were very sad, and bewailed the loss of their hero; but Makoma comforted them, and gave back to each the gifts he had taken from them. Then bidding them 'Farewell,' he went on his way.

Makoma travelled far towards the west; over rough mountains and water-logged morasses, fording deep rivers, and tramping for days across dry deserts where most men would have died, until at length he arrived at a hut standing near some large peaks, and inside the hut were two beautiful women.

'Greeting!' said the hero. 'Is this the country of Sakatirina of five heads, whom I am seeking?'

'We greet you, O Great One!' answered the women. 'We are the wives of Sakatirina; your search is at an end, for there stands he whom you seek!' And they pointed to what Makoma had thought were two tall mountain peaks. 'Those are his legs,' they said; 'his body you cannot see, for it is hidden in the clouds.'

Makoma was astonished when he beheld how tall was the giant; but, nothing daunted, he went forward until he reached one of Sakatirina's legs, which he struck heavily with Nu-endo. Nothing happened, so he hit again and then again until, presently, he heard a tired, far-away voice saying: 'Who is it that scratches my feet?'

And Makoma shouted as loud as he could, answering: 'It is I, Makoma, who is called "Greater"!' And he listened, but there was no answer.

Then Makoma collected all the dead brushwood and trees that he could find, and making an enormous pile round the giant's legs, set a light to it.

This time the giant spoke; his voice was very terrible, for it was the rumble of thunder in the clouds. 'Who is it,' he said, 'making that fire smoulder around my feet?'

'It is I, Makoma!' shouted the hero. 'And I have come from far away to see thee, O Sakatirina, for the spirits of my fathers bade me go seek and fight with thee, lest I should grow fat, and weary of myself.'

There was silence for a while, and then the giant spoke softly: 'It is good, O Makoma!' he said. 'For I too have grown weary. There is no man so great as I, therefore I am all alone. Guard thyself!' and bending suddenly he seized the hero in his hands and dashed him upon the ground. And lo! instead of death, Makoma had found life, for he sprang to his feet mightier in strength and stature than before, and rushing in he gripped the giant by the waist and wrestled with him.

Hour by hour they fought, and mountains rolled beneath their feet like pebbles in a flood; now Makoma would break away, and summoning up his strength, strike the giant with Nu-endo his iron hammer, and Sakatirina would pluck up the mountains and hurl them upon the hero, but neither one could slay the other. At last, upon the second day, they grappled so strongly that they could not break away; but their strength was failing, and, just as the sun was sinking, they fell together to the ground, insensible.

In the morning when they awoke, Mulimo the Great Spirit was standing by them; and he said: 'O Makoma and Sakatirina! Ye are heroes so great that no man may come against you. Therefore ye will leave the world and take up your home with me in the clouds.' And as he spake the heroes became invisible to the people of the Earth, and were no more seen among them.

The Magic Mirror

[Native Rhodesian Tale.]

From the Senna

A long, long while ago, before ever the White Men were seen in Senna, there lived a man called Gopani-Kufa.

One day, as he was out hunting, he came upon a strange sight. An enormous python had caught an antelope and coiled itself around it; the antelope, striking out in despair with its horns, had pinned the python's neck to a tree, and so deeply had its horns sunk in the soft wood that neither creature could get away.

'Help!' cried the antelope, 'for I was doing no harm, yet I have been caught, and would have been eaten, had I not defended myself.'

'Help me,' said the python, 'for I am Insato, King of all the Reptiles, and will reward you well!'

Gopani-Kufa considered for a moment, then stabbing the antelope with his assegai, he set the python free.

'I thank you,' said the python; 'come back here with the new moon, when I shall have eaten the antelope, and I will reward you as I promised.'

'Yes,' said the dying antelope, 'he will reward you, and lo! your reward shall be your own undoing!'

Gopani-Kufa went back to his kraal, and with the new moon he returned again to the spot where he had saved the python.

Insato was lying upon the ground, still sleepy from the effects of his huge meal, and when he saw the man he thanked him again, and said: 'Come with me now to Pita, which is my own country, and I will give you what you will of all my possessions.'

Gopani-Kufa at first was afraid, thinking of what the antelope had said, but finally he consented and followed Insato into the forest.

For several days they travelled, and at last they came to a hole leading deep into the earth. It was not very wide, but large enough to admit a man. 'Hold on to my tail,' said Insato, 'and I will go down first, drawing you after me.' The man did so, and Insato entered.

Down, down, down they went for days, all the while getting deeper and deeper into the earth, until at last the darkness ended and they dropped into a beautiful country; around them grew short green grass, on which browsed herds of cattle and sheep and goats. In the distance Gopani-Kufa saw a great collection of houses all square, built of stone and very tall, and their roofs were shining with gold and burnished iron.

Gopani-Kufa turned to Insato, but found, in the place of the python, a man, strong and handsome, with the great snake's skin wrapped round him for covering; and on his arms and neck were rings of pure gold.

The man smiled. 'I am Insato,' said he, 'but in my own country I take man's shape—even as you see me—for this is Pita, the land over which I am king.' He then took Gopani-Kufa by the hand and led him towards the town.

On the way they passed rivers in which men and women were bathing and fishing and boating; and farther on they came to gardens covered with heavy crops of rice and maize, and many other grains which Gopani-Kufa did not even know the name of. And as they passed, the people who were singing at their work in the fields, abandoned their labours and saluted Insato with delight, bringing also palm wine and green cocoanuts for refreshment, as to one returned from a long journey.

'These are my children!' said Insato, waving his hand towards the people. Gopani-Kufa was much astonished at all that he saw, but he said nothing.

The Orange Fairy Book - 8

Presently they came to the town; everything here, too, was beautiful, and everything that a man might desire he could obtain. Even the grains of dust in the streets were of gold and silver.

Insato conducted Gopani-Kufa to the palace, and showing him his rooms, and the maidens who would wait upon him, told him that they would have a great feast that night, and on the morrow he might name his choice of the riches of Pita and it should be given him. Then he was away.

Now Gopani-Kufa had a wasp called Zengi-mizi. Zengi-mizi was not an ordinary wasp, for the spirit of the father of Gopani-Kufa had entered it, so that it was exceedingly wise. In times of doubt Gopani-Kufa always consulted the wasp as to what had better be done, so on this occasion he took it out of the little rush basket in which he carried it, saying: 'Zengi-mizi, what gift shall I ask of Insato to-morrow when he would know the reward he shall bestow on me for saving his life?'

'Biz-z-z,' hummed Zengi-mizi, 'ask him for Sipao the Mirror.' And it flew back into its basket.

Gopani-Kufa was astonished at this answer; but knowing that the words of Zengi-mizi were true words, he determined to make the request. So that night they feasted, and on the morrow Insato came to Gopani-Kufa and, giving him greeting joyfully, he said:

'Now, O my friend, name your choice amongst my possessions and you shall have it!'

'O king!' answered Gopani-Kufa, 'out of all your possessions I will have the Mirror, Sipao.'

The king started. 'O friend, Gopani-Kufa,' he said, 'ask anything but that! I did not think that you would request that which is most precious to me.'

'Let me think over it again then, O king,' said Gopani-Kufa, 'and to-morrow I will let you know if I change my mind.'

But the king was still much troubled, fearing the loss of Sipao, for the mirror had magic powers, so that he who owned it had but to ask and his wish would be fulfilled; to it Insato owed all that he possessed.

As soon as the king left him, Gopani-Kufa again took Zengi-mizi, out of his basket. 'Zengi-mizi,' he said, 'the king seems loth to grant my request for the Mirror—is there not some other thing of equal value for which I might ask?'

And the wasp answered: 'There is nothing in the world, O Gopani-Kufa, which is of such value as this Mirror, for it is a Wishing Mirror, and accomplishes the desires of him who owns it. If the king hesitates, go to him the next day, and the day after, and in the end he will bestow the Mirror upon you, for you saved his life.'

And it was even so. For three days Gopani-Kufa returned the same answer to the king, and, at last, with tears in his eyes, Insato gave him the Mirror, which was of polished iron, saying: 'Take Sipao, then, O Gopani-Kufa, and may thy wishes come true. Go back now to thine own country; Sipao will show you the way.'

Gopani-Kufa was greatly rejoiced, and, taking farewell of the king, said to the Mirror:

'Sipao, Sipao, I wish to be back upon the Earth again!'

Instantly he found himself standing upon the upper earth; but, not knowing the spot, he said again to the Mirror:

'Sipao, Sipao, I want the path to my own kraal!'

And behold! right before him lay the path!

When he arrived home he found his wife and daughter mourning for him, for they thought that he had been eaten by lions; but he comforted them, saying that while following a wounded antelope he had missed his way and had wandered for a long time before he had found the path again.

That night he asked Zengi-mizi, in whom sat the spirit of his father, what he had better ask Sipao for next?

'Biz-z-z,' said the wasp, 'would you not like to be as great a chief as Insato?'

And Gopani-Kufa smiled, and took the Mirror and said to it:

'Sipao, Sipao, I want a town as great as that of Insato, the King of Pita; and I wish to be chief over it!'

Then all along the banks of the Zambesi river, which flowed near by, sprang up streets of stone buildings, and their roofs shone with gold and burnished iron like those in Pita; and in the streets men and women were walking, and young boys were driving out the sheep and cattle to pasture; and from the river came shouts and laughter from the young men and maidens who had launched their canoes and were fishing. And when the people of the new town beheld Gopani-Kufa they rejoiced greatly and hailed him as chief.

Gopani-Kufa was now as powerful as Insato the King of the Reptiles had been, and he and his family moved into the palace that stood high above the other buildings right in the middle of the town. His wife was too astonished at all these wonders to ask any questions, but his daughter Shasasa kept begging him to tell her how he had suddenly become so great; so at last he revealed the whole secret, and even entrusted Sipao the Mirror to her care, saying:

'It will be safer with you, my daughter, for you dwell apart; whereas men come to consult me on affairs of state, and the Mirror might be stolen.'

Then Shasasa took the Magic Mirror and hid it beneath her pillow, and after that for many years Gopani-Kufa ruled his people both well and wisely, so that all men loved him, and never once did he need to ask Sipao to grant him a wish.

Now it happened that, after many years, when the hair of Gopani-Kufa was turning grey with age, there came white men to that country. Up the Zambesi they came, and they fought long and fiercely with Gopani-Kufa; but, because of the power of the Magic Mirror, he beat them, and they fled to the sea-coast. Chief among them was one Rei, a man of much cunning, who sought to discover whence sprang Gopani-Kufa's power. So one day he called to him a trusty servant named Butou, and said: 'Go you to the town and find out for me what is the secret of its greatness.'

And Butou, dressing himself in rags, set out, and when he came to Gopani-Kufa's town he asked for the chief; and the people took him into the presence of Gopani-Kufa. When the white man saw him he humbled himself, and said: 'O Chief! take pity on me, for I have no home! When Rei marched against you I alone stood apart, for I knew that all the strength of the Zambesi lay in your hands, and because I would not fight against you he turned me forth into the forest to starve!'

And Gopani-Kufa believed the white man's story, and he took him in and feasted him, and gave him a house.

In this way the end came. For the heart of Shasasa, the daughter of Gopani-Kufa, went forth to Butou the traitor, and from her he learnt the secret of the Magic Mirror. One night, when all the town slept, he felt beneath her pillow and, finding the Mirror, he stole it and fled back with it to Rei, the chief of the white men.

So it befell that, one day, as Gopani-Kufa was gazing up at the river from a window of the palace he again saw the war-canoes of the white men; and at the sight his spirit misgave him.

'Shasasa! my daughter!' he cried wildly, 'go fetch me the mirror, for the white men are at hand.'

'Woe is me, my father!' she sobbed. 'The Mirror is gone! For I loved Butou the traitor, and he has stolen Sipao from me!'

Then Gopani-Kufa calmed himself, and drew out Zengi-mizi from its rush basket.

'O spirit of my father!' he said, 'what now shall I do?'

'O Gopani-Kufa!' hummed the wasp, 'there is nothing now that can be done, for the words of the antelope which you slew are being fulfilled.'

'Alas! I am an old man—I had forgotten!' cried the chief. 'The words of the antelope were true words—my reward shall be my undoing—they are being fulfilled!'

Then the white men fell upon the people of Gopani-Kufa and slew them together with the chief and his daughter Shasasa; and since then all the power of the Earth has rested in the hands of the white men, for they have in their possession Sipao, the Magic Mirror.

Story of the King Who Would See Paradise

Once upon a time there was king who, one day out hunting, came upon a fakeer in a lonely place in the mountains. The fakeer was seated on a little old bedstead reading the Koran, with his patched cloak thrown over his shoulders.

The king asked him what he was reading; and he said he was reading about Paradise, and praying that he might be worthy to enter there. Then they began to talk, and, by-and-bye, the king asked the fakeer if he could show him a glimpse of Paradise, for he found it very difficult to believe in what he could not see. The fakeer replied that he was asking a very difficult, and perhaps a very dangerous, thing; but that he would pray for him, and perhaps he might be able to do it; only he warned the king both against the dangers of his unbelief, and against the curiosity which prompted him to ask this thing. However, the king was not to be turned from his purpose, and he promised the fakeer always to provided him with food, if he, in return, would pray for him. To this the fakeer agreed, and so they parted.

Time went on, and the king always sent the old fakeer his food according to his promise; but, whenever he sent to ask him when he was going to show him Paradise, the fakeer always replied: 'Not yet, not yet!'

After a year or two had passed by, the king heard one day that the fakeer was very ill—indeed, he was believed to be dying. Instantly he hurried off himself, and found that it was really true, and that the fakeer was even then breathing his last. There and then the king besought him to remember his promise, and to show him a glimpse of Paradise. The dying fakeer replied that if the king would come to his funeral, and, when the grave was filled in, and everyone else was gone away, he would come and lay his hand upon the grave, he would keep his word, and show him a glimpse of Paradise. At the same time he implored the king not to do this thing, but to be content to see Paradise when God called him there. Still the king's curiosity was so aroused that he would not give way.

Accordingly, after the fakeer was dead, and had been buried, he stayed behind when all the rest went away; and then, when he was quite alone, he stepped forward, and laid his hand upon the grave! Instantly the ground opened, and the astonished king, peeping in, saw a flight of rough steps, and, at the bottom of them, the fakeer sitting, just as he used to sit, on his rickety bedstead, reading the Koran!

At first the king was so surprised and frightened that he could only stare; but the fakeer beckoned to him to come down, so, mustering up his courage, he boldly stepped down into the grave.

The fakeer rose, and, making a sign to the king to follow, walked a few paces along a dark passage. Then he stopped, turned solemnly to his companion, and, with a movement of his hand, drew aside as it were a heavy curtain, and revealed—what? No one knows what was there shown to the king, nor did he ever tell anyone; but, when the fakeer at length dropped the curtain, and the king turned to leave the place, he had had his glimpse of Paradise! Trembling in every limb, he staggered back along the passage, and stumbled up the steps out of the tomb into the fresh air again.

The dawn was breaking. It seemed odd to the king that he had been so long in the grave. It appeared but a few minutes ago that he had descended, passed along a few steps to the place where he had peeped beyond the veil, and returned again after perhaps five minutes of that wonderful view! And what WAS it he had seen? He racked his brains to remember, but he could not call to mind a single thing! How curious everything looked too! Why, his own city, which by now he was entering, seemed changed and strange to him! The sun was already up when he turned into the palace gate and entered the public durbar hall. It was full; a chamberlain came across and asked him why he sat unbidden in the king's presence. 'But I am the king!' he cried.

'What king?' said the chamberlain.

'The true king of this country,' said he indignantly.

Then the chamberlain went away, and spoke to the king who sat on the throne, and the old king heard words like 'mad,' 'age,' 'compassion.' Then the king on the throne called him to come forward, and, as he went, he caught sight of himself reflected in the polished steel shield of the bodyguard, and started back in horror! He was old, decrepit, dirty, and ragged! His long white beard and locks were unkempt, and straggled all over his chest and shoulders. Only one sign of royalty remained to him, and that was the signet ring upon his right hand. He dragged it off with shaking fingers and held it up to the king.

'Tell me who I am,' he cried; 'there is my signet, who once sat where you sit —even yesterday!'

The king looked at him compassionately, and examined the signet with curiosity. Then he commanded, and they brought out dusty records and archives of the kingdom, and old coins of previous reigns, and compared them faithfully. At last the king turned to the old man, and said: 'Old man, such a king as this whose signet thou hast, reigned seven hundred years ago; but he is said to have disappeared, none know whither; where got you the ring?'

Then the old man smote his breast, and cried out with a loud lamentation; for he understood that he, who was not content to wait patiently to see the Paradise of the faithful, had been judged already. And he turned and left the hall without a wor, and went into the jungle, where he lived for twenty-five years a life of prayer and and meditation, until at last the Angel of Death came to him, and mercifully released him, purged and purified through his punishment.

How Isuro the Rabbit Tricked Gudu

[A Pathan story told to Major Campbell.]

Far away in a hot country, where the forests are very thick and dark, and the rivers very swift and strong, there once lived a strange pair of friends. Now one of the friends was a big white rabbit named Isuro, and the other was a tall baboon called Gudu, and so fond were they of each other that they were seldom seen apart.

One day, when the sun was hotter even than usual, the rabbit awoke from his midday sleep, and saw Gudu the baboon standing beside him.

'Get up,' said Gudu; 'I am going courting, and you must come with me. So put some food in a bag, and sling it round your neck, for we may not be able to find anything to eat for a long while.'

Then the rabbit rubbed his eyes, and gathered a store of fresh green things from under the bushes, and told Gudu that he was ready for the journey.

They went on quite happily for some distance, and at last they came to a river with rocks scattered here and there across the stream.

'We can never jump those wide spaces if we are burdened with food,' said Gudu, 'we must throw it into the river, unless we wish to fall in ourselves.' And stooping down, unseen by Isuro, who was in front of him, Gudu picked up a big stone, and threw it into the water with a loud splash.

'It is your turn now,' he cried to Isuro. And with a heavy sigh, the rabbit unfastened his bag of food, which fell into the river.

The road on the other side led down an avenue of trees, and before they had gone very far Gudu opened the bag that lay hidden in the thick hair about his neck, and began to eat some delicious-looking fruit.

'Where did you get that from?' asked Isuro enviously.

'Oh, I found after all that I could get across the rocks quite easily, so it seemed a pity not to keep my bag,' answered Gudu.

'Well, as you tricked me into throwing away mine, you ought to let me share with you,' said Isuro. But Gudu pretended not to hear him, and strode along the path.

By-and-bye they entered a wood, and right in front of them was a tree so laden with fruit that its branches swept the ground. And some of the fruit was still green, and some yellow. The rabbit hopped forward with joy, for he was very hungry; but Gudu said to him: 'Pluck the green fruit, you will find it much the best. I will leave it all for you, as you have had no dinner, and take the yellow for myself.' So the rabbit took one of the green oranges and began to bite it, but its skin was so hard that he could hardly get his teeth through the rind.

'It does not taste at all nice,' he cried, screwing up his face; 'I would rather have one of the yellow ones.'

'No! no! I really could not allow that,' answered Gudu. 'They would only make you ill. Be content with the green fruit.' And as they were all he could get, Isuro was forced to put up with them.

After this had happened two or three times, Isuro at last had his eyes opened, and made up his mind that, whatever Gudu told him, he would do exactly the opposite. However, by this time they had reached the village where dwelt Gudu's future wife, and as they entered Gudu pointed to a clump of bushes, and said to Isuro: 'Whenever I am eating, and you hear me call out that my food has burnt me, run as fast as you can and gather some of those leaves that they may heal my mouth.'

The rabbit would have liked to ask him why he ate food that he knew would burn him, only he was afraid, and just nodded in reply; but when they had gone on a little further, he said to Gudu:

'I have dropped my needle; wait here a moment while I go and fetch it.'

'Be quick then,' answered Gudu, climbing into a tree. And the rabbit hastened back to the bushes, and gathered a quantity of the leaves, which he hid among his fur, 'For,' thought he, 'if I get them now I shall save myself the trouble of a walk by-and-by.'

When he had plucked as many as he wanted he returned to Gudu, and they went on together. The sun was almost setting by the time they reached their journey's end and being very tired they gladly sat down by a well. Then Gudu's betrothed, who had been watching for him, brought out a pitcher of water—which she poured over them to wash off the dust of the road—and two portions of food. But once again the rabbit's hopes were dashed to the ground, for Gudu said hastily:

'The custom of the village forbids you to eat till I have finished.' And Isuro did not know that Gudu was lying, and that he only wanted more food. So he saw hungrily looking on, waiting till his friend had had enough.

In a little while Gudu screamed loudly: 'I am burnt! I am burnt!' though he was not burnt at all. Now, though Isuro had the leaves about him, he did not dare to produce them at the last moment lest the baboon should guess why he had stayed behind. So he just went round a corner for a short time, and then came hopping back in a great hurry. But, quick though he was, Gudu had been quicker still, and nothing remained but some drops of water.

'How unlucky you are,' said Gudu, snatching the leaves; 'no sooner had you gone than ever so many people arrived, and washed their hands, as you see, and ate your portion.' But, though Isuro knew better than to believe him, he said nothing, and went to bed hungrier than he had ever been in his life.

Early next morning they started for another village, and passed on the way a large garden where people were very busy gathering monkey-nuts.

'You can have a good breakfast at last,' said Gudu, pointing to a heap of empty shells; never doubting but that Isuro would meekly take the portion shown him, and leave the real nuts for himself. But what was his surprise when Isuro answered:

'Thank you; I think I should prefer these.' And, turning to the kernels, never stopped as long as there was one left. And the worst of it was that, with so many people about, Gudu could not take the nuts from him.

It was night when they reached the village where dwelt the mother of Gudu's betrothed, who laid meat and millet porridge before them.

'I think you told me you were fond of porridge,' said Gudu; but Isuro answered: 'You are mistaking me for somebody else, as I always eat meat when I can get it.' And again Gudu was forced to be content with the porridge, which he hated.

While he was eating it, however a sudden thought darted into his mind, and he managed to knock over a great pot of water which was hanging in front of the fire, and put it quite out.

'Now,' said the cunning creature to himself, 'I shall be able in the dark to steal his meat!' But the rabbit had grown as cunning as he, and standing in a corner hid the meat behind him, so that the baboon could not find it.

'O Gudu!' he cried, laughing aloud, 'it is you who have taught me to be clever.' And calling to the people of the house, he bade them kindle the fire, for Gudu would sleep by it, but that he would pass the night with some friends in another hut.

It was still quite dark when Isuro heard his name called very softly, and, on opening his eyes, beheld Gudu standing by him. Laying his finger on his nose, in token of silence, he signed to Isuro to get up and follow him, and it was not until they were some distance from the hut that Gudu spoke.

'I am hungry and want something to eat better than that nasty porridge that I had for supper. So I am going to kill one of those goats, and as you are a good cook you must boil the flesh for me.' The rabbit nodded, and Gudu disappeared behind a rock, but soon returned dragging the dead goat with him. The two then set about skinning it, after which they stuffed the skin with dried leaves, so that no one would have guessed it was not alive, and set it up in the middle of a lump of bushes, which kept it firm on its feet. While he was doing this, Isuro collected sticks for a fire, and when it was kindled, Gudu hastened to another hut to steal a pot which he filled with water from the river, and, planting two branches in the ground, they hung the pot with the meat in it over the fire.

'It will not be fit to eat for two hours at least,' said Gudu, 'so we can both have a nap.' And he stretched himself out on the ground, and pretended to fall fast asleep, but, in reality, he was only waiting till it was safe to take all the meat for himself. 'Surely I hear him snore,' he thought; and he stole to the place where Isuro was lying on a pile of wood, but the rabbit's eyes were wide open.

'How tiresome,' muttered Gudu, as he went back to his place; and after waiting a little longer he got up, and peeped again, but still the rabbit's pink eyes stared widely. If Gudu had only known, Isuro was asleep all the time; but this he never guessed, and by-and-bye he grew so tired with watching that he went to sleep himself. Soon after, Isuro woke up, and he too felt hungry, so he crept softly to the pot and ate all the meat, while he tied the bones together and hung them in Gudu's fur. After that he went back to the wood-pile and slept again.

In the morning the mother of Gudu's betrothed came out to milk her goats, and on going to the bushes where the largest one seemed entangled, she found out the trick. She made such lament that the people of the village came running, and Gudu and Isuro jumped up also, and pretended to be as surprised and interested as the rest. But they must have looked guilty after all, for suddenly an old man pointed to them, and cried:

'Those are thieves.' And at the sound of his voice the big Gudu trembled all over.

'How dare you say such things? I defy you to prove it,' answered Isuro boldly. And he danced forward, and turned head over heels, and shook himself before them all.

'I spoke hastily; you are innocent,' said the old man; 'but now let the baboon do likewise.' And when Gudu began to jump the goat's bones rattled and the people cried: 'It is Gudu who is the goat-slayer!' But Gudu answered:

'Nay, I did not kill your goat; it was Isuro, and he ate the meat, and hung the bones round my neck. So it is he who should die!' And the people looked at each other, for they knew not what to believe. At length one man said:

'Let them both die, but they may choose their own deaths.'

Then Isuro answered:

'If we must die, put us in the place where the wood is cut, and heap it up all round us, so that we cannot escape, and set fire to the wood; and if one is burned and the other is not, then he that is burned is the goat-slayer.'

And the people did as Isuro had said. But Isuro knew of a hole under the wood-pile, and when the fire was kindled he ran into the hole, but Gudu died there.

When the fire had burned itself out and only ashes were left where the wood had been, Isuro came out of his hole, and said to the people:

'Lo! did I not speak well? He who killed your goat is among those ashes.'

Ian, the Soldier's Son

[Mashona Story.]

There dwelt a knight in Grianaig of the land of the West, who had three daughters, and for goodness and beauty they had not their like in all the isles. All the people loved them, and loud was the weeping when one day, as the three maidens sat on the rocks on the edge of the sea, dipping their feet in the water, there arose a great beast from under the waves and swept them away beneath the ocean. And none knew whither they had gone, or how to seek them.

Now there lived in a town a few miles off a soldier who had three sons, fine youths and strong, and the best players at shinny in that country. At Christmastide that year, when families met together and great feasts were held, Ian, the youngest of the three brothers, said:

'Let us have a match at shinny on the lawn of the knight of Grianaig, for his lawn is wider and the grass smoother than ours.'

But the others answered:

'Nay, for he is in sorrow, and he will think of the games that we have played there when his daughters looked on.'

'Let him be pleased or angry as he will,' said Ian; 'we will drive our ball on his lawn to-day.'

And so it was done, and Ian won three games from his brothers. But the knight looked out of his window, and was wroth; and bade his men bring the youths before him. When he stood in his hall and beheld them, his heart was softened somewhat; but his face was angry as he asked:

'Why did you choose to play shinny in front of my castle when you knew full well that the remembrance of my daughters would come back to me? The pain which you have made me suffer you shall suffer also.'

'Since we have done you wrong,' answered Ian, the youngest, 'build us a ship, and we will go and seek your daughters. Let them be to windward, or to leeward, or under the four brown boundaries of the sea, we will find them before a year and a day goes by, and will carry them back to Grianaig.'

In seven days the ship was built, and great store of food and wine placed in her. And the three brothers put her head to the sea and sailed away, and in seven days the ship ran herself on to a beach of white sand, and they all went ashore. They had none of them ever seen that land before, and looked about them. Then they saw that, a short way from them, a number of men were working on a rock, with one man standing over them.

'What place is this?' asked the eldest brother. And the man who was standing by made answer:

'This is the place where dwell the three daughters of the knight of Grianaig, who are to be wedded to-morrow to three giants.'

'How can we find them?' asked the young man again. And the overlooker answered:

'To reach the daughters of the knight of Grianaig you must get into this basket, and be drawn by a rope up the face of this rock.'

'Oh, that is easily done,' said the eldest brother, jumping into the basket, which at once began to move—up, and up, and up—till he had gone about halfway, when a fat black raven flew at him and pecked him till he was nearly blind, so that he was forced to go back the way he had come.

After that the second brother got into the creel; but he fared no better, for the raven flew upon him, and he returned as his brother had done.

'Now it is my turn,' said Ian. But when he was halfway up the raven set upon him also.

'Quick! quick!' cried Ian to the men who held the rope. 'Quick! quick! or I shall be blinded!' And the men pulled with all their might, and in another moment Ian was on top, and the raven behind him.

'Will you give me a piece of tobacco?' asked the raven, who was now quite quiet.

'You rascal! Am I to give you tobacco for trying to peck my eyes out?' answered Ian.

'That was part of my duty,' replied the raven; 'but give it to me, and I will prove a good friend to you.' So Ian broke off a piece of tobacco and gave it to him. The raven hid it under his wing, and then went on; 'Now I will take you to the house of the big giant, where the knight's daughter sits sewing, sewing, till even her thimble is wet with tears.' And the raven hopped before him till they reached a large house, the door of which stood open. They entered and passed through one hall after the other, until they found the knight's daughter, as the bird had said.

'What brought you here?' asked she. And Ian made answer:

'Why may I not go where you can go?'

'I was brought hither by a giant,' replied she.

'I know that,' said Ian; 'but tell me where the giant is, that I may find him.'

'He is on the hunting hill,' answered she; 'and nought will bring him home save a shake of the iron chain which hangs outside the gate. But, there, neither to leeward, nor to windward, nor in the four brown boundaries of the sea, is there any man that can hold battle against him, save only Ian, the soldier's son, and he is now but sixteen years old, and how shall he stand against the giant?'

'In the land whence I have come there are many men with the strength of Ian,' answered he. And he went outside and pulled at the chain, but he could not move it, and fell on to his knees. At that he rose swiftly, and gathering up his strength, he seized the chain, and this time he shook it so that the link broke. And the giant heard it on the hunting hill, and lifted his head, thinking—

'It sounds like the noise of Ian, the soldier's son,' said he; 'but as yet he is only sixteen years old. Still, I had better look to it.' And home he came.

'Are you Ian, the soldier's son?' he asked, as he entered the castle.

'No, of a surety,' answered the youth, who had no wish that they should know him.

'Then who are you in the leeward, or in the windward, or in the four brown boundaries of the sea, who are able to move my battle-chain?'

'That will be plain to you after wrestling with me as I wrestle with my mother. And one time she got the better of me, and two times she did not.'

So they wrestled, and twisted and strove with each other till the giant forced Ian to his knee.

'You are the stronger,' said Ian; and the giant answered:

'All men know that!' And they took hold of each other once more, and at last Ian threw the giant, and wished that the raven were there to help him. No sooner had he wished his wish than the raven came.

'Put your hand under my right wing and you will find a knife sharp enough to take off his head,' said the raven. And the knife was so sharp that it cut off the giant's head with a blow.

'Now go and tell the daughter of the king of Grianaig; but take heed lest you listen to her words, and promise to go no further, for she will seek to help you. Instead, seek the middle daughter, and when you have found her, you shall give me a piece of tobacco for reward.'

'Well have you earned the half of all I have,' answered Ian. But the raven shook his head.

'You know only what has passed, and nothing of what lies before. If you would not fail, wash yourself in clean water, and take balsam from a vessel on top of the door, and rub it over your body, and to-morrow you will be as strong as many men, and I will lead you to the dwelling of the middle one.'

Ian did as the raven bade him, and in spite of the eldest daughter's entreaties, he set out to seek her next sister. He found her where she was seated sewing, her very thimble wet from the tears which she had shed.

'What brought you here?' asked the second sister.

'Why may I not go where you can go?' answered he; 'and why are you weeping?'

'Because in one day I shall be married to the giant who is on the hunting hill.'

'How can I get him home?' asked Ian.

'Nought will bring him but a shake of that iron chain which hangs outside the gate. But there is neither to leeward, nor to westward, nor in the four brown boundaries of the sea, any man that can hold battle with him, save Ian, the soldier's son, and he is now but sixteen years of age.'

'In the land whence I have come there are many men with the strength of Ian,' said he. And he went outside and pulled at the chain, but he could not move it, and fell on his knees. At that he rose to his feet, and gathering up his strength mightily, he seized the chain, and this time he shook it so that three links broke. And the second giant heard it on the hunting hill, and lifted his head, thinking—

'It sounds like the noise of Ian, the soldier's son,' said he; 'but as yet he is only sixteen years old. Still, I had better look to it.' And home he came.

'Are you Ian, the soldier's son?' he asked, as he entered the castle.

'No, of a surety,' answered the youth, who had no wish that this giant should know him either; 'but I will wrestle with you as if I were he.'

Then they seized each other by the shoulder, and the giant threw him on his two knees. 'You are the stronger,' cried Ian; 'but I am not beaten yet.' And rising to his feet, he threw his arms round the giant.

Backwards and forwards they swayed, and first one was uppermost and then the other; but at length Ian worked his leg round the giant's and threw him to the ground. Then he called to the raven, and the raven came flapping towards him, and said: 'Put your hand under my right wing, and you will find there a knife sharp enough to take off his head.' And sharp indeed it was, for with a single blow, the giant's head rolled from his body.

'Now wash yourself with warm water, and rub yourself over with oil of balsam, and to-morrow you will be as strong as many men. But beware of the words of the knight's daughter, for she is cunning, and will try to keep you at her side. So farewell; but first give me a piece of tobacco.'

'That I will gladly,' answered Ian breaking off a large bit.

He washed and rubbed himself that night, as the raven had told him, and the next morning he entered the chamber where the knight's daughter was sitting.

'Abide here with me,' she said, 'and be my husband. There is silver and gold in plenty in the castle.' But he took no heed, and went on his way till he reached the castle where the knight's youngest daughter was sewing in the hall. And tears dropped from her eyes on to her thimble.

'What brought you here?' asked she. And Ian made answer:

'Why may I not go where you can go?'

'I was brought hither by a giant.'

'I know full well,' said he.

'Are you Ian, the soldier's son?' asked she again. And again he answered:

'Yes, I am; but tell me, why are you weeping?'

'To-morrow the giant will return from the hunting hill, and I must marry him,' she sobbed. And Ian took no heed, and only said: 'How can I bring him home?'

'Shake the iron chain that hangs outside the gate.'

And Ian went out, and gave such a pull to the chain that he fell down at full length from the force of the shake. But in a moment he was on his feet again, and seized the chain with so much strength that four links came off in his hand. And the giant heard him in the hunting hill, as he was putting the game he had killed into a bag.

'In the leeward, or the windward, or in the four brown boundaries of the sea, there is none who could give my chain a shake save only Ian, the soldier's son. And if he has reached me, then he has left my two brothers dead behind him.' With that he strode back to the castle, the earth trembling under him as he went.

'Are you Ian, the soldier's son?' asked he. And the youth answered:

'No, of a surety.'

'Then who are you in the leeward, or the windward, or in the four brown boundaries of the sea, who are able to shake my battle chain? There is only Ian, the soldier's son, who can do this, and he is but now sixteen years old.

'I will show you who I am when you have wrestled with me,' said Ian. And they threw their arms round each other, and the giant forced Ian on to his knees; but in a moment he was up again, and crooking his leg round the shoulders of the giant, he threw him heavily to the ground. 'Stumpy black raven, come quick!' cried he; and the raven came, and beat the giant about the head with his wings, so that he could not get up. Then he bade Ian take out a sharp knife from under his feathers, which he carried with him for cutting berries, and Ian smote off the giant's head with it. And so sharp was that knife that, with one blow, the giant's head rolled on the ground.

'Rest now this night also,' said the raven, 'and to-morrow you shall take the knight's three daughters to the edge of the rock that leads to the lower world. But take heed to go down first yourself, and let them follow after you. And before I go you shall give me a piece of tobacco.'

'Take it all,' answered Ian, 'for well have you earned it.'

'No; give me but a piece. You know what is behind you, but you have no knowledge of what is before you.' And picking up the tobacco in his beak, the raven flew away.

So the next morning the knight's youngest daughter loaded asses with all the silver and gold to be found in the castle, and she set out with Ian the soldier's son for the house where her second sister was waiting to see what would befall. She also had asses laden with precious things to carry away, and so had the eldest sister, when they reached the castle where she had been kept a prisoner. Together they all rode to the edge of the rock, and then Ian lay down and shouted, and the basket was drawn up, and in it they got one by one, and were let down to the bottom. When the last one was gone, Ian should have gone also, and left the three sisters to come after him; but he had forgotten the raven's warning, and bade them go first, lest some accident should happen. Only, he begged the youngest sister to let him keep the little gold cap which, like the others, she wore on her head; and then he helped them, each in her turn, into the basket.

Long he waited, but wait as he might, the basket never came back, for in their joy at being free the knight's daughters had forgotten all about Ian, and had set sail in the ship that had brought him and his brothers to the land of Grianaig.

At last he began to understand what had happened to him, and while he was taking counsel with himself what had best be done, the raven came to him.

'You did not heed my words,' he said gravely.

'No, I did not, and therefore am I here,' answered Ian, bowing his head.

'The past cannot be undone,' went on the raven. 'He that will not take counsel will take combat. This night, you will sleep in the giant's castle. And now you shall give me a piece of tobacco.'

'I will. But, I pray you, stay in the castle with me.'

'That I may not do, but on the morrow I will come.'

And on the morrow he did, and he bade Ian go to the giant's stable where stood a horse to whom it mattered nothing if she journeyed over land or sea.

'But be careful,' he added, 'how you enter the stable, for the door swings without ceasing to and fro, and if it touches you, it will cause you to cry out. I will go first and show you the way.'

'Go,' said Ian. And the raven gave a bob and a hop, and thought he was quite safe, but the door slammed on a feather of his tail, and he screamed loudly.

Then Ian took a run backwards, and a run forwards, and made a spring; but the door caught one of his feet, and he fell fainting on the stable floor. Quickly the raven pounced on him, and picked him up in his beak and claws, and carried him back to the castle, where he laid ointments on his foot till it was as well as ever it was.

'Now come out to walk,' said the raven, 'but take heed that you wonder not at aught you may behold; neither shall you touch anything. And, first, give me a piece of tobacco.'

Many strange things did Ian behold in that island, more than he had thought for. In a glen lay three heroes stretched on their backs, done to death by three spears that still stuck in their breasts. But he kept his counsel and spake nothing, only he pulled out the spears, and the men sat up and said:

'You are Ian the soldier's son, and a spell is laid upon you to travel in our company, to the cave of the black fisherman.'

So together they went till they reached the cave, and one of the men entered, to see what should be found there. And he beheld a hag, horrible to look upon, seated on a rock, and before he could speak, she struck him with her club, and changed him into a stone; and in like manner she dealt with the other three. At the last Ian entered.

'These men are under spells,' said the witch, 'and alive they can never be till you have anointed them with the water which you must fetch from the island of Big Women. See that you do not tarry.' And Ian turned away with a sinking heart, for he would fain have followed the youngest daughter of the knight of Grianaig.

'You did not obey my counsel,' said the raven, hopping towards him, 'and so trouble has come upon you. But sleep now, and to-morrow you shall mount the horse which is in the giant's stable, that can gallop over sea and land. When you reach the island of Big Women, sixteen boys will come to meet you, and will offer the horse food, and wish to take her saddle and bridle from her. But see that they touch her not, and give her food yourself, and yourself lead her into the stable, and shut the door. And be sure that for every turn of the lock given by the sixteen stable lads you give one. And now you shall break me off a piece of tobacco.'

The next morning Ian arose, and led the horse from the stable, without the door hurting him, and he rode across the sea to the island of the Big Women, where the sixteen stable lads met him, and each one offered to take his horse, and to feed her, and to put her into the stable. But Ian only answered:

'I myself will put her in and will see to her.' And thus he did. And while he was rubbing her sides the horse said to him:

'Every kind of drink will they offer you, but see you take none, save whey and water only.' And so it fell out; and when the sixteen stable-boys saw that he would drink nothing, they drank it all themselves, and one by one lay stretched around the board.

Then Ian felt pleased in his heart that he had withstood their fair words, and he forgot the counsel that the horse had likewise given him saying:

'Beware lest you fall asleep, and let slip the chance of getting home again'; for while the lads were sleeping sweet music reached his ears, and he slept also.

When this came to pass the steed broke through the stable door, and kicked him and woke him roughly.

'You did not heed my counsel,' said she; 'and who knows if it is not too late to win over the sea? But first take that sword which hangs on the wall, and cut off the heads of the sixteen grooms.'

Filled with shame at being once more proved heedless, Ian arose and did as the horse bade him. Then he ran to the well and poured some of the water into a leather bottle, and jumping on the horse's back rode over the sea to the island where the raven was waiting for him.

'Lead the horse into the stable,' said the raven, 'and lie down yourself to sleep, for to-morrow you must make the heroes to live again, and must slay the hag. And have a care not to be so foolish to-morrow as you were to-day.'

'Stay with me for company,' begged Ian; but the raven shook his head, and flew away.

In the morning Ian awoke, and hastened to the cave where the old hag was sitting, and he struck her dead as she was, before she could cast spells on him. Next he sprinkled the water over the heroes, who came to life again, and together they all journeyed to the other side of the island, and there the raven met them.

'At last you have followed the counsel that was given you,' said the raven; 'and now, having learned wisdom, you may go home again to Grianaig. There you will find that the knight's two eldest daughters are to be wedded this day to your two brothers, and the youngest to the chief of the men at the rock. But her gold cap you shall give to me and, if you want it, you have only to think of me and I will bring it to you. And one more warning I give you. If anyone asks you whence you came, answer that you have come from behind you; and if anyone asks you whither you are going, say that you are going before you.'

So Ian mounted the horse and set her face to the sea and her back to the shore, and she was off, away and away till she reached the church of Grianaig, and there, in a field of grass, beside a well of water, he leaped down from his saddle.

'Now,' the horse said to him, 'draw your sword and cut off my head.' But Ian answered:

'Poor thanks would that be for all the help I have had from you.'

'It is the only way that I can free myself from the spells that were laid by the giants on me and the raven; for I was a girl and he was a youth wooing me! So have no fears, but do as I have said.'

Then Ian drew his sword as she bade him, and cut off her head, and went on his way without looking backwards. As he walked he saw a woman standing at her house door. She asked him whence he had come, and he answered as the raven had told him, that he came from behind. Next she inquired whither he was going, and this time he made reply that he was going on before him, but that he was thirsty and would like a drink.

'You are an impudent fellow,' said the woman; 'but you shall have a drink.' And she gave him some milk, which was all she had till her husband came home.

'Where is your husband?' asked Ian, and the woman answered him:

'He is at the knight's castle trying to fashion gold and silver into a cap for the youngest daughter, like unto the caps that her sisters wear, such as are not to be found in all this land. But, see, he is returning; and now we shall hear how he has sped.'

At that the man entered the gate, and beholding a strange youth, he said to him: 'What is your trade, boy?'

'I am a smith,' replied Ian. And the man answered:

'Good luck has befallen me, then, for you can help me to make a cap for the knight's daughter.'

'You cannot make that cap, and you know it,' said Ian.

'Well, I must try,' replied the man, 'or I shall be hanged on a tree; so it were a good deed to help me.'

'I will help you if I can,' said Ian; 'but keep the gold and silver for yourself, and lock me into the smithy to-night, and I will work my spells.' So the man, wondering to himself, locked him in.

As soon as the key was turned in the lock Ian wished for the raven, and the raven came to him, carrying the cap in his mouth.

'Now take my head off,' said the raven. But Ian answered:

'Poor thanks were that for all the help you have given me.'

'It is the only thanks you can give me,' said the raven, 'for I was a youth like yourself before spells were laid on me.'

Then Ian drew his sword and cut off the head of the raven, and shut his eyes so that he might see nothing. After that he lay down and slept till morning dawned, and the man came and unlocked the door and shook the sleeper.

'Here is the cap,' said Ian drowsily, drawing it from under his pillow. And he fell asleep again directly.

The sun was high in the heavens when he woke again, and this time he beheld a tall, brown-haired youth standing by him.

'I am the raven,' said the youth, 'and the spells are broken. But now get up and come with me.'

Then they two went together to the place where Ian had left the dead horse; but no horse was there now, only a beautiful maiden.

'I am the horse,' she said, 'and the spells are broken'; and she and the youth went away together.

In the meantime the smith had carried the cap to the castle, and bade a servant belonging to the knight's youngest daughter bear it to her mistress. But when the girl's eyes fell on it, she cried out:

'He speaks false; and if he does not bring me the man who really made the cap I will hang him on the tree beside my window.'

The servant was filled with fear at her words, and hastened and told the smith, who ran as fast as he could to seek for Ian. And when he found him and brought him into the castle, the girl was first struck dumb with joy; then she declared that she would marry nobody else. At this some one fetched to her the knight of Grianaig, and when Ian had told his tale, he vowed that the maiden was right, and that his elder daughters should never wed with men who had not only taken glory to themselves which did not belong to them, but had left the real doer of the deeds to his fate.

And the wedding guests said that the knight had spoken well; and the two elder brothers were fain to leave the country, for no one would converse with them.

The Fox and the Wolf

[From Tales of the West Highlands.]

At the foot of some high mountains there was, once upon a time, a small village, and a little way off two roads met, one of them going to the east and the other to the west. The villagers were quiet, hard-working folk, who toiled in the fields all day, and in the evening set out for home when the bell began to ring in the little church. In the summer mornings they led out their flocks to pasture, and were happy and contented from sunrise to sunset.

One summer night, when a round full moon shone down upon the white road, a great wolf came trotting round the corner.

'I positively must get a good meal before I go back to my den,' he said to himself; 'it is nearly a week since I have tasted anything but scraps, though perhaps no one would think it to look at my figure! Of course there are plenty of rabbits and hares in the mountains; but indeed one needs to be a greyhound to catch them, and I am not so young as I was! If I could only dine off that fox I saw a fortnight ago, curled up into a delicious hairy ball, I should ask nothing better; I would have eaten her then, but unluckily her husband was lying beside her, and one knows that foxes, great and small, run like the wind. Really it seems as if there was not a living creature left for me to prey upon but a wolf, and, as the proverb says: "One wolf does not bite another." However, let us see what this village can produce. I am as hungry as a schoolmaster.'

Now, while these thoughts were running through the mind of the wolf, the very fox he had been thinking of was galloping along the other road.

'The whole of this day I have listened to those village hens clucking till I could bear it no longer,' murmured she as she bounded along, hardly seeming to touch the ground. 'When you are fond of fowls and eggs it is the sweetest of all music. As sure as there is a sun in heaven I will have some of them this night, for I have grown so thin that my very bones rattle, and my poor babies are crying for food.' And as she spoke she reached a little plot of grass, where the two roads joined, and flung herself under a tree to take a little rest, and to settle her plans. At this moment the wolf came up.

At the sight of the fox lying within his grasp his mouth began to water, but his joy was somewhat checked when he noticed how thin she was. The fox's quick ears heard the sound of his paws, though they were soft as velvet, and turning her head she said politely:

'Is that you, neighbour? What a strange place to meet in! I hope you are quite well?'

'Quite well as regards my health,' answered the wolf, whose eye glistened greedily, 'at least, as well as one can be when one is very hungry. But what is the matter with you? A fortnight ago you were as plump as heart could wish!'

'I have been ill—very ill,' replied the fox, 'and what you say is quite true. A worm is fat in comparison with me.'

'He is. Still, you are good enough for me; for "to the hungry no bread is hard."'

'Oh, you are always joking! I'm sure you are not half as hungry as I!'

'That we shall soon see,' cried the wolf, opening his huge mouth and crouching for a spring.

'What are you doing?' exclaimed the fox, stepping backwards.

'What am I doing? What I am going to do is to make my supper off you, in less time than a cock takes to crow.'

'Well, I suppose you must have your joke,' answered the fox lightly, but never removing her eye from the wolf, who replied with a snarl which showed all his teeth:

'I don't want to joke, but to eat!'

'But surely a person of your talents must perceive that you might eat me to the very last morsel and never know that you had swallowed anything at all!'

'In this world the cleverest people are always the hungriest,' replied the wolf.

'Ah! how true that is; but—'

'I can't stop to listen to your "buts" and "yets,"' broke in the wolf rudely; 'let us get to the point, and the point is that I want to eat you and not talk to you.'

'Have you no pity for a poor mother?' asked the fox, putting her tail to her eyes, but peeping slily out of them all the same.

'I am dying of hunger,' answered the wolf, doggedly; 'and you know,' he added with a grin, 'that charity begins at home.'

'Quite so,' replied the fox; 'it would be unreasonable of me to object to your satisfying your appetite at my expense. But if the fox resigns herself to the sacrifice, the mother offers you one last request.'

'Then be quick and don't waste my time, for I can't wait much longer. What is it you want?'

'You must know,' said the fox, 'that in this village there is a rich man who makes in the summer enough cheeses to last him for the whole year, and keeps them in an old well, now dry, in his courtyard. By the well hang two buckets on a pole that were used, in former days, to draw up water. For many nights I have crept down to the palace, and have lowered myself in the bucket, bringing home with me enough cheese to feed the children. All I beg of you is to come with me, and, instead of hunting chickens and such things, I will make a good meal off cheese before I die.'

'But the cheeses may be all finished by now?'

'If you were only to see the quantities of them!' laughed the fox. 'And even if they were finished, there would always be ME to eat.'

'Well, I will come. Lead the way, but I warn you that if you try to escape or play any tricks you are reckoning without your host—that is to say, without my legs, which are as long as yours!'

All was silent in the village, and not a light was to be seen but that of the moon, which shone bright and clear in the sky. The wolf and the fox crept softly along, when suddenly they stopped and looked at each other; a savoury smell of frying bacon reached their noses, and reached the noses of the sleeping dogs, who began to bark greedily.

'Is it safe to go on, think you?' asked the wolf in a whisper. And the fox shook her head.

'Not while the dogs are barking,' said she; 'someone might come out to see if anything was the matter.' And she signed to the wolf to curl himself up in the shadow beside her.

In about half an hour the dogs grew tired of barking, or perhaps the bacon was eaten up and there was no smell to excite them. Then the wolf and the fox jumped up, and hastened to the foot of the wall.

'I am lighter than he is,' thought the fox to herself, 'and perhaps if I make haste I can get a start, and jump over the wall on the other side before he manages to spring over this one.' And she quickened her pace. But if the wolf could not run he could jump, and with one bound he was beside his companion.

'What were you going to do, comrade?'

'Oh, nothing,' replied the fox, much vexed at the failure of her plan.

'I think if I were to take a bit out of your haunch you would jump better,' said the wolf, giving a snap at her as he spoke. The fox drew back uneasily.

'Be careful, or I shall scream,' she snarled. And the wolf, understanding all that might happen if the fox carried out her threat, gave a signal to his companion to leap on the wall, where he immediately followed her.

Once on the top they crouched down and looked about them. Not a creature was to be seen in the courtyard, and in the furthest corner from the house stood the well, with its two buckets suspended from a pole, just as the fox had described it. The two thieves dragged themselves noiselessly along the wall till they were opposite the well, and by stretching out her neck as far as it would go the fox was able to make out that there was only very little water in the bottom, but just enough to reflect the moon, big, and round and yellow.

'How lucky!' cried she to the wolf. 'There is a huge cheese about the size of a mill wheel. Look! look! did you ever see anything so beautiful!'

'Never!' answered the wolf, peering over in his turn, his eyes glistening greedily, for he imagined that the moon's reflection in the water was really a cheese.

'And now, unbeliever, what have you to say?' and the fox laughed gently.

'That you are a woman—I mean a fox—of your word,' replied the wolf.

'Well, then, go down in that bucket and eat your fill,' said the fox.

'Oh, is that your game?' asked the wolf, with a grin. 'No! no! The person who goes down in the bucket will be you! And if you don't go down your head will go without you!'

'Of course I will go down, with the greatest pleasure,' answered the fox, who had expected the wolf's reply.

'And be sure you don't eat all the cheese, or it will be the worse for you,' continued the wolf. But the fox looked up at him with tears in her eyes.

'Farewell, suspicious one!' she said sadly. And climbed into the bucket.

In an instant she had reached the bottom of the well, and found that the water was not deep enough to cover her legs.

'Why, it is larger and richer than I thought,' cried she, turning towards the wolf, who was leaning over the wall of the well.

'Then be quick and bring it up,' commanded the wolf.

'How can I, when it weighs more than I do?' asked the fox.

'If it is so heavy bring it in two bits, of course,' said he.

'But I have no knife,' answered the fox. 'You will have to come down yourself, and we will carry it up between us.'

'And how am I to come down?' inquired the wolf.

'Oh, you are really very stupid! Get into the other bucket that is nearly over your head.'

The wolf looked up, and saw the bucket hanging there, and with some difficulty he climbed into it. As he weighed at least four times as much as the fox the bucket went down with a jerk, and the other bucket, in which the fox was seated, came to the surface.

As soon as he understood what was happening, the wolf began to speak like an angry wolf, but was a little comforted when he remembered that the cheese still remained to him.

'But where is the cheese?' he asked of the fox, who in her turn was leaning over the parapet watching his proceedings with a smile.

'The cheese?' answered the fox; 'why I am taking it home to my babies, who are too young to get food for themselves.'

'Ah, traitor!' cried the wolf, howling with rage. But the fox was not there to hear this insult, for she had gone off to a neighbouring fowl-house, where she had noticed some fat young chickens the day before.

'Perhaps I did treat him rather badly,' she said to herself. 'But it seems getting cloudy, and if there should be heavy rain the other bucket will fill and sink to the bottom, and his will go up—at least it may!'

How Ian Direach Got the Blue Falcon

[From Cuentos Populares, por Antonio de Trueba.]

Long ago a king and queen ruled over the islands of the west, and they had one son, whom they loved dearly. The boy grew up to be tall and strong and handsome, and he could run and shoot, and swim and dive better than any lad of his own age in the country. Besides, he knew how to sail about, and sing songs to the harp, and during the winter evenings, when everyone was gathered round the huge hall fire shaping bows or weaving cloth, Ian Direach would tell them tales of the deeds of his fathers.

So the time slipped by till Ian was almost a man, as they reckoned men in those days, and then his mother the queen died. There was great mourning throughout all the isles, and the boy and his father mourned her bitterly also; but before the new year came the king had married another wife, and seemed to have forgotten his old one. Only Ian remembered.

On a morning when the leaves were yellow in the trees of the glen, Ian slung his bow over his shoulder, and filling his quiver with arrows, went on to the hill in search of game. But not a bird was to be seen anywhere, till at length a blue falcon flew past him, and raising his bow he took aim at her. His eye was straight and his hand steady, but the falcon's flight was swift, and he only shot a feather from her wing. As the sun was now low over the sea he put the feather in his game bag, and set out homewards.

'Have you brought me much game to-day?' asked his stepmother as he entered the hall.

'Nought save this,' he answered, handing her the feather of the blue falcon, which she held by the tip and gazed at silently. Then she turned to Ian and said:

'I am setting it on you as crosses and as spells, and as the fall of the year! That you may always be cold, and wet and dirty, and that your shoes may ever have pools in them, till you bring me hither the blue falcon on which that feather grew.'

'If it is spells you are laying I can lay them too,' answered Ian Direach; 'and you shall stand with one foot on the great house and another on the castle, till I come back again, and your face shall be to the wind, from wheresoever it shall blow.' Then he went away to seek the bird, as his stepmother bade him; and, looking homewards from the hill, he saw the queen standing with one foot on the great house, and the other on the castle, and her face turned towards whatever tempest should blow.

On he journeyed, over hills, and through rivers till he reached a wide plain, and never a glimpse did he catch of the falcon. Darker and darker it grew, and the small birds were seeking their nests, and at length Ian Direach could see no more, and he lay down under some bushes and sleep came to him. And in his dream a soft nose touched him, and a warm body curled up beside him, and a low voice whispered to him:

'Fortune is against you, Ian Direach; I have but the cheek and the hoof of a sheep to give you, and with these you must be content.' With that Ian Direach awoke, and beheld Gille Mairtean the fox.

Between them they kindled a fire, and ate their supper. Then Gille Mairtean the fox bade Ian Direach lie down as before, and sleep till morning. And in the morning, when he awoke, Gille Mairtean said:

'The falcon that you seek is in the keeping of the Giant of the Five Heads, and the Five Necks, and the Five Humps. I will show you the way to his house, and I counsel you to do his bidding, nimbly and cheerfully, and, above all, to treat his birds kindly, for in this manner he may give you his falcon to feed and care for. And when this happens, wait till the giant is out of his house; then throw a cloth over the falcon and bear her away with you. Only see that not one of her feathers touches anything within the house, or evil will befall you.'

'I thank you for your counsel,' spake Ian Direach, 'and I will be careful to follow it.' Then he took the path to the giant's house.

'Who is there?' cried the giant, as someone knocked loudly on the door of his house.

'One who seeks work as a servant,' answered Ian Direach.

'And what can you do?' asked the giant again.

'I can feed birds and tend pigs; I can feed and milk a cow, and also goats and sheep, if you have any of these,' replied Ian Direach.

'Then enter, for I have great need of such a one,' said the giant.

So Ian Direach entered, and tended so well and carefully all the birds and beasts, that the giant was better satisfied than ever he had been, and at length he thought that he might even be trusted to feed the falcon. And the heart of Ian was glad, and he tended the blue falcon till his fathers shone like the sky, and the giant was well pleased; and one day he said to him:

'For long my brothers on the other side of the mountain have besought me to visit them, but never could I go for fear of my falcon. Now I think I can leave her with you for one day, and before nightfall I shall be back again.'

Scarcely was the giant out of sight next morning when Ian Direach seized the falcon, and throwing a cloth over her head hastened with her to the door. But the rays of the sun pierced through the thickness of the cloth, and as they passed the doorpost she gave a spring, and the tip of one of her feathers touched the post, which gave a scream, and brought the giant back in three strides. Ian Direach trembled as he saw him; but the giant only said:

'If you wish for my falcon you must first bring me the White Sword of Light that is in the house of the Big Women of Dhiurradh.'

'And where do they live?' asked Ian. But the giant answered:

'Ah, that is for you to discover.' And Ian dared say no more, and hastened down to the waste. There, as he hoped, he met his friend Gille Mairtean the fox, who bade him eat his supper and lie down to sleep. And when he had wakened next morning the fox said to him:

'Let us go down to the shore of the sea.' And to the shore of the sea they went. And after they had reached the shore, and beheld the sea stretching before them, and the isle of Dhiurradh in the midst of it, the soul of Ian sank, and he turned to Gille Mairtean and asked why he had brought him thither, for the giant, when he had sent him, had known full well that without a boat he could never find the Big Women.

'Do not be cast down,' answered the fox, 'it is quite easy! I will change myself into a boat, and you shall go on board me, and I will carry you over the sea to the Seven Big Women of Dhiurradh. Tell them that you are skilled in brightening silver and gold, and in the end they will take you as servant, and if you are careful to please them they will give you the White Sword of Light to make bright and shining. But when you seek to steal it, take heed that its sheath touches nothing inside the house, or ill will befall you.'

So Ian Direach did all things as the fox had told him, and the Seven Big Women of Dhiurradh took him for their servant, and for six weeks he worked so hard that his seven mistresses said to each other: 'Never has a servant had the skill to make all bright and shining like this one. Let us give him the White Sword of Light to polish like the rest.'

Then they brought forth the White Sword of Light from the iron closet where it hung, and bade him rub it till he could see his face in the shining blade; and he did so. But one day, when the Seven Big Women were out of the way, he bethought him that the moment had come for him to carry off the sword, and, replacing it in its sheath, he hoisted it on his shoulder. But just as he was passing through the door the tip of the sheath touched it, and the door gave a loud shriek. And the Big Women heard it, and came running back, and took the sword from him, and said:

'If it is our sword you want, you must first bring us the bay colt of the King of Erin.'

Humbled and ashamed, Ian Direach left the house, and sat by the side of the sea, and soon Gille Mairtean the fox came to him.

'Plainly I see that you have taken no heed to my words, Ian Direach,' spoke the fox. 'But eat first, and yet once more will I help you.'

At these words the heart returned again to Ian Direach, and he gathered sticks and made a fire and ate with Gille Mairtean the fox, and slept on the sand. At dawn next morning Gille Mairtean said to Ian Direach:

'I will change myself into a ship, and will bear you across the seas to Erin, to the land where dwells the king. And you shall offer yourself to serve in his stable, and to tend his horses, till at length so well content is he, that he gives you the bay colt to wash and brush. But when you run away with her see that nought except the soles of her hoofs touch anything within the palace gates, or it will go ill with you.'

After he had thus counselled Ian Direach, the fox changed himself into a ship, and set sail for Erin. And the king of that country gave into Ian Direach's hands the care of his horses, and never before did their skins shine so brightly or was their pace so swift. And the king was well pleased, and at the end of a month he sent for Ian and said to him:

'You have given me faithful service, and now I will entrust you with the most precious thing that my kingdom holds.' And when he had spoken, he led Ian Direach to the stable where stood the bay colt. And Ian rubbed her and fed her, and galloped with her all round the country, till he could leave one wind behind him and catch the other which was in front.

'I am going away to hunt,' said the king one morning while he was watching Ian tend the bay colt in her stable. 'The deer have come down from the hill, and it is time for me to give them chase.' Then he went away; and when he was no longer in sight, Ian Direach led the bay colt out of the stable, and sprang on her back. But as they rode through the gate, which stood between the palace and the outer world, the colt swished her tail against the post, which shrieked loudly. In a moment the king came running up, and he seized the colt's bridle.

'If you want my bay colt, you must first bring me the daughter of the king of the Franks.'

With slow steps went Ian Direach down to the shore where Gille Mairtean the fox awaited him.

'Plainly I see that you have not done as I bid you, nor will you ever do it,' spoke Gille Mairtean the fox; 'but I will help you yet again for a third time I will change myself into a ship, and we will sail to France.'

And to France they sailed, and, as he was the ship, the Gille Mairtean sailed where he would, and ran himself into the cleft of a rock, high on to the land. Then, he commanded Ian Direach to go up to the king's palace, saying that he had been wrecked, that his ship was made fast in a rock, and that none had been saved but himself only.

Ian Direach listened to the words of the fox, and he told a tale so pitiful, that the king and queen, and the princess their daughter, all came out to hear it. And when they had heard, nought would please them except to go down to the shore and visit the ship, which by now was floating, for the tide was up. Torn and battered was she, as if she had passed through many dangers, yet music of a wondrous sweetness poured forth from within.

'Bring hither a boat,' cried the princess, 'that I may go and see for myself the harp that gives forth such music.' And a boat was brought, and Ian Direach stepped in to row it to the side of the ship.

To the further side he rowed, so that none could see, and when he helped the princess on board he gave a push to the boat, so that she could not get back to it again. And the music sounded always sweeter, though they could never see whence it came, and sought it from one part of the vessel to another. When at last they reached the deck and looked around them, nought of land could they see, or anything save the rushing waters.

The princess stood silent, and her face grew grim. At last she said:

'An ill trick have you played me! What is this that you have done, and whither are we going?'

'It is a queen you will be,' answered Ian Direach, 'for the king of Erin has sent me for you, and in return he will give me his bay colt, that I may take him to the Seven Big Women of Dhiurradh, in exchange for the White Sword of Light. This I must carry to the giant of the Five Heads and Five Necks and Five Humps, and, in place of it, he will bestow on me the blue falcon, which I have promised my stepmother, so that she may free me from the spell which she has laid on me.'

'I would rather be wife to you,' answered the princess.

By-and-by the ship sailed into a harbour on the coast of Erin, and cast anchor there. And Gille Mairtean the fox bade Ian Direach tell the princess that she must bide yet a while in a cave amongst the rocks, for they had business on land, and after a while they would return to her. Then they took a boat and rowed up to some rocks, and as they touched the land Gille Mairtean changed himself into a fair woman, who laughed, and said to Ian Direach, 'I will give the king a fine wife.'

Now the king of Erin had been hunting on the hill, and when he saw a strange ship sailing towards the harbour, he guessed that it might be Ian Direach, and left his hunting, and ran down to the hill to the stable. Hastily he led the bay colt from his stall, and put the golden saddle on her back, and the silver bridle over his head, and with the colt's bridle in his hand, he hurried to meet the princess.

'I have brought you the king of France's daughter,' said Ian Direach. And the king of Erin looked at the maiden, and was well pleased, not knowing that it was Gille Mairtean the fox. And he bowed low, and besought her to do him the honour to enter the palace; and Gille Mairtean, as he went in, turned to look back at Ian Direach, and laughed.

In the great hall the king paused and pointed to an iron chest which stood in a corner.

'In that chest is the crown that has waited for you for many years,' he said, 'and at last you have come for it.' And he stooped down to unlock the box.

In an instant Gille Mairtean the fox had sprung on his back, and gave him such a bite that he fell down unconscious. Quickly the fox took his own shape again, and galloped away to the sea shore, where Ian Direach and the princess and the bay colt awaited him.

'I will become a ship,' cried Gille Mairtean, 'and you shall go on board me.' And so he did, and Ian Direach let the bay colt into the ship and the princess went after them, and they set sail for Dhiurradh. The wind was behind them, and very soon they saw the rocks of Dhiurradh in front. Then spoke Gille Mairtean the fox:

'Let the bay colt and the king's daughter hide in these rocks, and I will change myself into the colt, and go with you to the house of the Seven Big Women.'

Joy filed the hearts of the Big Women when they beheld the bay colt led up to their door by Ian Direach. And the youngest of them fetched the White Sword of Light, and gave it into the hands of Ian Direach, who took off the golden saddle and the silver bridle, and went down the hill with the sword to the place where the princess and the real colt awaited him.

'Now we shall have the ride that we have longed for!' cried the Seven Big Women; and they saddled and bridled the colt, and the eldest one got upon the saddle. Then the second sister sat on the back of the first, and the third on the back of the second, and so on for the whole seven. And when they were all seated, the eldest struck her side with a whip and the colt bounded forward. Over the moors she flew, and round and round the mountains, and still the Big Women clung to her and snorted with pleasure. At last she leapt high in the air, and came down on top of Monadh the high hill, where the crag is. And she rested her fore feet on the crag, and threw up her hind legs, and the Seven Big Women fell over the crag, and were dead when they reached the bottom. And the colt laughed, and became a fox again and galloped away to the sea shore, where Ian Direach, and the princess and the real colt and the White Sword of Light were awaiting him.

'I will make myself into a ship,' said Gille Mairtean the fox, 'and will carry you and the princess, and the bay colt and the White Sword of Light, back to the land.' And when the shore was reached, Gille Mairtean the fox took back his own shape, and spoke to Ian Direach in this wise:

'Let the princess and the White Sword of Light, and the bay colt, remain among the rocks, and I will change myself into the likeness of the White Sword of Light, and you shall bear me to the giant, and, instead, he will give you the blue falcon.' And Ian Direach did as the fox bade him, and set out for the giant's castle. From afar the giant beheld the blaze of the White Sword of Light, and his heart rejoiced; and he took the blue falcon and put it in a basket, and gave it to Ian Direach, who bore it swiftly away to the place where the princess, and the bay colt, and the real Sword of Light were awaiting him.

So well content was the giant to possess the sword he had coveted for many a year, that he began at once to whirl it through the air, and to cut and slash with it. For a little while Gille Mairtean let the giant play with him in this manner; then he turned in the giant's hand, and cut through the Five Necks, so that the Five Heads rolled on the ground. Afterwards he went back to Ian Direach and said to him:

'Saddle the colt with the golden saddle, and bridle her with the silver bridle, and sling the basket with the falcon over your shoulders, and hold the White Sword of Light with its back against your nose. Then mount the colt, and let the princess mount behind you, and ride thus to your father's palace. But see that the back of the sword is ever against your nose, else when your stepmother beholds you, she will change you into a dry faggot. If, however, you do as I bid you, she will become herself a bundle of sticks.'

Ian Direach hearkened to the words of Gille Mairtean, and his stepmother fell as a bundle of sticks before him; and he set fire to her, and was free from her spells for ever. After that he married the princess, who was the best wife in all the islands of the West. Henceforth he was safe from harm, for had he not the bay colt who could leave one wind behind her and catch the other wind, and the blue falcon to bring him game to eat, and the White Sword of Light to pierce through his foes?

And Ian Direach knew that all this he owed to Gille Mairtean the fox, and he made a compact with him that he might choose any beast out of his herds, whenever hunger seized him, and that henceforth no arrow should be let fly at him or at any of his race. But Gille Mairtean the fox would take no reward for the help he had given to Ian Direach, only his friendship. Thus all things prospered with Ian Direach till he died.

The Ugly Duckling

[From Tales of the West Highlands.]

It was summer in the land of Denmark, and though for most of the year the country looks flat and ugly, it was beautiful now. The wheat was yellow, the oats were green, the hay was dry and delicious to roll in, and from the old ruined house which nobody lived in, down to the edge of the canal, was a forest of great burdocks, so tall that a whole family of children might have dwelt in them and never have been found out.

It was under these burdocks that a duck had built herself a warm nest, and was not sitting all day on six pretty eggs. Five of them were white, but the sixth, which was larger than the others, was of an ugly grey colour. The duck was always puzzled about that egg, and how it came to be so different from the rest. Other birds might have thought that when the duck went down in the morning and evening to the water to stretch her legs in a good swim, some lazy mother might have been on the watch, and have popped her egg into the nest. But ducks are not clever at all, and are not quick at counting, so this duck did not worry herself about the matter, but just took care that the big egg should be as warm as the rest.

This was the first set of eggs that the duck had ever laid, and, to begin with, she was very pleased and proud, and laughed at the other mothers, who were always neglecting their duties to gossip with each other or to take little extra swims besides the two in the morning and evening that were necessary for health. But at length she grew tired of sitting there all day. 'Surely eggs take longer hatching than they did,' she said to herself; and she pined for a little amusement also. Still, she knew that if she left her eggs and the ducklings in them to die none of her friends would ever speak to her again; so there she stayed, only getting off the eggs several times a day to see if the shells were cracking—which may have been the very reason why they did not crack sooner.

She had looked at the eggs at least a hundred and fifty times, when, to her joy, she saw a tiny crack on two of them, and scrambling back to the nest she drew the eggs closer the one to the other, and never moved for the whole of that day. Next morning she was rewarded by noticing cracks in the whole five eggs, and by midday two little yellow heads were poking out from the shells. This encouraged her so much that, after breaking the shells with her bill, so that the little creatures could get free of them, she sat steadily for a whole night upon the nest, and before the sun arose the five white eggs were empty, and ten pairs of eyes were gazing out upon the green world.

Now the duck had been carefully brought up, and did not like dirt, and, besides, broken shells are not at all comfortable things to sit or walk upon; so she pushed the rest out over the side, and felt delighted to have some company to talk to till the big egg hatched. But day after day went on, and the big egg showed no signs of cracking, and the duck grew more and more impatient, and began to wish to consult her husband, who never came.

'I can't think what is the matter with it,' the duck grumbled to her neighbour who had called in to pay her a visit. 'Why I could have hatched two broods in the time that this one has taken!'

'Let me look at it,' said the old neighbour. 'Ah, I thought so; it is a turkey's egg. Once, when I was young, they tricked me to sitting on a brood of turkey's eggs myself, and when they were hatched the creatures were so stupid that nothing would make them learn to swim. I have no patience when I think of it.'

'Well, I will give it another chance,' sighed the duck, 'and if it does not come out of its shell in another twenty-four hours, I will just leave it alone and teach the rest of them to swim properly and to find their own food. I really can't be expected to do two things at once.' And with a fluff of her feathers she pushed the egg into the middle of the nest.

All through the next day she sat on, giving up even her morning bath for fear that a blast of cold might strike the big egg. In the evening, when she ventured to peep, she thought she saw a tiny crack in the upper part of the shell. Filled with hope, she went back to her duties, though she could hardly sleep all night for excitement. When she woke with the first steaks of light she felt something stirring under her. Yes, there it was at last; and as she moved, a big awkward bird tumbled head foremost on the ground.

There was no denying it was ugly, even the mother was forced to admit that to herself, though she only said it was 'large' and 'strong.' 'You won't need any teaching when you are once in the water,' she told him, with a glance of surprise at the dull brown which covered his back, and at his long naked neck. And indeed he did not, though he was not half so pretty to look at as the little yellow balls that followed her.

When they returned they found the old neighbour on the bank waiting for them to take them into the duckyard. 'No, it is not a young turkey, certainly,' whispered she in confidence to the mother, 'for though it is lean and skinny, and has no colour to speak of, yet there is something rather distinguished about it, and it holds its head up well.'

'It is very kind of you to say so,' answered the mother, who by this time had some secret doubts of its loveliness. 'Of course, when you see it by itself it is all right, though it is different, somehow, from the others. But one cannot expect all one's children to be beautiful!'

By this time they had reached the centre of the yard, where a very old duck was sitting, who was treated with great respect by all the fowls present.

'You must go up and bow low before her,' whispered the mother to her children, nodding her head in the direction of the old lady, 'and keep your legs well apart, as you see me do. No well-bred duckling turns in its toes. It is a sign of common parents.'

The little ducks tried hard to make their small fat bodies copy the movements of their mother, and the old lady was quite pleased with them; but the rest of the ducks looked on discontentedly, and said to each other:

'Oh, dear me, here are ever so many more! The yard is full already; and did you ever see anything quite as ugly as that great tall creature? He is a disgrace to any brood. I shall go and chase him out!' So saying she put up her feathers, and running to the big duckling bit his neck.

The duckling gave a loud quack; it was the first time he had felt any pain, and at the sound his mother turned quickly.

'Leave him alone,' she said fiercely, 'or I will send for his father. He was not troubling you.'

'No; but he is so ugly and awkward no one can put up with him,' answered the stranger. And though the duckling did not understand the meaning of the words, he felt he was being blamed, and became more uncomfortable still when the old Spanish duck who ruled the fowlyard struck in:

'It certainly is a great pity he is so different from these beautiful darlings. If he could only be hatched over again!'

The poor little fellow drooped his head, and did not know where to look, but was comforted when his mother answered:

'He may not be quite as handsome as the others, but he swims better, and is very strong; I am sure he will make his way in the world as well as anybody.'

'Well, you must feel quite at home here,' said the old duck waddling off. And so they did, all except the duckling, who was snapped at by everyone when they thought his mother was not looking. Even the turkey-cock, who was so big, never passed him without mocking words, and his brothers and sisters, who would not have noticed any difference unless it had been put into their heads, soon became as rude and unkind as the rest.

At last he could bear it no longer, and one day he fancied he saw signs of his mother turning against him too; so that night, when the ducks and hens were still asleep, he stole away through an open door, and under cover of the burdock leaves scrambled on by the bank of the canal, till he reached a wide grassy moor, full of soft marshy places where the reeds grew. Here he lay down, but he was too tired and too frightened to fall asleep, and with the earliest peep of the sun the reeds began to rustle, and he saw that he had blundered into a colony of wild ducks. But as he could not run away again he stood up and bowed politely.

'You are ugly,' said the wild ducks, when they had looked him well over; 'but, however, it is no business of ours, unless you wish to marry one of our daughters, and that we should not allow.' And the duckling answered that he had no idea of marrying anybody, and wanted nothing but to be left alone after his long journey.

So for two whole days he lay quietly among the reeds, eating such food as he could find, and drinking the water of the moorland pool, till he felt himself quite strong again. He wished he might stay were he was for ever, he was so comfortable and happy, away from everyone, with nobody to bite him and tell him how ugly he was.

He was thinking these thoughts, when two young ganders caught sight of him as they were having their evening splash among the reeds, looking for their supper.

'We are getting tired of this moor,' they said, 'and to-morrow we think of trying another, where the lakes are larger and the feeding better. Will you come with us?'

'Is it nicer than this?' asked the duckling doubtfully. And the words were hardly out of his mouth, when 'Pif! pah!' and the two new-comers were stretched dead beside him.

At the sound of the gun the wild ducks in the rushes flew into the air, and for a few minutes the firing continued.

Luckily for himself the duckling could not fly, and he floundered along through the water till he could hide himself amidst some tall ferns which grew in a hollow. But before he got there he met a huge creature on four legs, which he afterwards knew to be a dog, who stood and gazed at him with a long red tongue hanging out of his mouth. The duckling grew cold with terror, and tried to hide his head beneath his little wings; but the dog snuffed at him and passed on, and he was able to reach his place of shelter.

'I am too ugly even for a dog to eat,' said he to himself. 'Well, that is a great mercy.' And he curled himself up in the soft grass till the shots died away in the distance.

When all had been quiet for a long time, and there were only stars to see him, he crept out and looked about him.

He would never go near a pool again, never, thought he; and seeing that the moor stretched far away in the opposite direction from which he had come, he marched bravely on till he got to a small cottage, which seemed too tumbledown for the stones to hold together many hours longer. Even the door only hung upon one hinge, and as the only light in the room sprang from a tiny fire, the duckling edged himself cautiously in, and lay down under a chair close to the broken door, from which he could get out if necessary. But no one seemed to see him or smell him; so he spend the rest of the night in peace.

Now in the cottage dwelt an old woman, her cat, and a hen; and it was really they, and not she, who were masters of the house. The old woman, who passed all her days in spinning yarn, which she sold at the nearest town, loved both the cat and the hen as her own children, and never contradicted them in any way; so it was their grace, and not hers, that the duckling would have to gain.

It was only next morning, when it grew light, that they noticed their visitor, who stood trembling before them, with his eye on the door ready to escape at any moment. They did not, however, appear very fierce, and the duckling became less afraid as they approached him.

'Can you lay eggs?' asked the hen. And the duckling answered meekly:

'No; I don't know how.' Upon which the hen turned her back, and the cat came forward.

'Can you ruffle your fur when you are angry, or purr when you are pleased?' said she. And again the duckling had to admit that he could do nothing but swim, which did not seem of much use to anybody.

So the cat and the hen went straight off to the old woman, who was still in bed.

'Such a useless creature has taken refuge here,' they said. 'It calls itself a duckling; but it can neither lay eggs nor purr! What had we better do with it?'

'Keep it, to be sure!' replied the old woman briskly. 'It is all nonsense about it not laying eggs. Anyway, we will let it stay here for a bit, and see what happens.'

So the duckling remained for three weeks, and shared the food of the cat and the hen; but nothing in the way of eggs happened at all. Then the sun came out, and the air grew soft, and the duckling grew tired of being in a hut, and wanted with all his might to have a swim. And one morning he got so restless that even his friends noticed it.

'What is the matter?' asked the hen; and the duckling told her.

'I am so longing for the water again. You can't think how delicious it is to put your head under the water and dive straight to the bottom.'

'I don't think I should enjoy it,' replied the hen doubtfully. 'And I don't think the cat would like it either.' And the cat, when asked, agreed there was nothing she would hate so much.

'I can't stay here any longer, I Must get to the water,' repeated the duck. And the cat and the hen, who felt hurt and offended, answered shortly:

'Very well then, go.'

The duckling would have liked to say good-bye, and thank them for their kindness, as he was polite by nature; but they had both turned their backs on him, so he went out of the rickety door feeling rather sad. But, in spite of himself, he could not help a thrill of joy when he was out in the air and water once more, and cared little for the rude glances of the creatures he met. For a while he was quite happy and content; but soon the winter came on, and snow began to fall, and everything to grow very wet and uncomfortable. And the duckling soon found that it is one thing to enjoy being in the water, and quite another to like being damp on land.

The sun was setting one day, like a great scarlet globe, and the river, to the duckling's vast bewilderment, was getting hard and slippery, when he heard a sound of whirring wings, and high up in the air a flock of swans were flying. They were as white as snow which had fallen during the night, and their long necks with yellow bills were stretched southwards, for they were going—they did not quite know whither—but to a land where the sun shone all day. Oh, if he only could have gone with them! But that was not possible, of course; and besides, what sort of companion could an ugly thing like him be to those beautiful beings? So he walked sadly down to a sheltered pool and dived to the very bottom, and tried to think it was the greatest happiness he could dream of. But, all the same, he knew it wasn't!

And every morning it grew colder and colder, and the duckling had hard work to keep himself warm. Indeed, it would be truer to say that he never was warm at all; and at last, after one bitter night, his legs moved so slowly that the ice crept closer and closer, and when the morning light broke he was caught fast, as in a trap; and soon his senses went from him.

A few hours more and the poor duckling's life had been ended. But, by good fortune, a man was crossing the river on his way to his work, and saw in a moment what had happened. He had on thick wooden shoes, and he went and stamped so hard on the ice that it broke, and then he picked up the duckling and tucked him under his sheepskin coat, where his frozen bones began to thaw a little.

Instead of going on his work, the man turned back and took the bird to his children, who gave him a warm mess to eat and put him in a box by the fire, and when they came back from school he was much more comfortable than he had been since he had left the old woman's cottage. They were kind little children, and wanted to play with him; but, alas! the poor fellow had never played in his life, and thought they wanted to tease him, and flew straight into the milk-pan, and then into the butter-dish, and from that into the meal-barrel, and at last, terrified at the noise and confusion, right out of the door, and hid himself in the snow amongst the bushes at the back of the house.

He never could tell afterwards exactly how he had spent the rest of the winter. He only knew that he was very miserable and that he never had enough to eat. But by-and-by things grew better. The earth became softer, the sun hotter, the birds sang, and the flowers once more appeared in the grass. When he stood up, he felt different, somehow, from what he had done before he fell asleep among the reeds to which he had wandered after he had escaped from the peasant's hut. His body seemed larger, and his wings stronger. Something pink looked at him from the side of a hill. He thought he would fly towards it and see what it was.

Oh, how glorious it felt to be rushing through the air, wheeling first one way and then the other! He had never thought that flying could be like that! The duckling was almost sorry when he drew near the pink cloud and found it was made up of apple blossoms growing beside a cottage whose garden ran down to the banks of the canal. He fluttered slowly to the ground and paused for a few minutes under a thicket of syringas, and while he was gazing about him, there walked slowly past a flock of the same beautiful birds he had seen so many months ago. Fascinated, he watched them one by one step into the canal, and float quietly upon the waters as if they were part of them.

'I will follow them,' said the duckling to himself; 'ugly though I am, I would rather be killed by them than suffer all I have suffered from cold and hunger, and from the ducks and fowls who should have treated me kindly.' And flying quickly down to the water, he swam after them as fast as he could.

It did not take him long to reach them, for they had stopped to rest in a green pool shaded by a tree whose branches swept the water. And directly they saw him coming some of the younger ones swam out to meet him with cries of welcome, which again the duckling hardly understood. He approached them glad, yet trembling, and turning to one of the older birds, who by this time had left the shade of the tree, he said:

'If I am to die, I would rather you should kill me. I don't know why I was ever hatched, for I am too ugly to live.' And as he spoke, he bowed his head and looked down into the water.

Reflected in the still pool he saw many white shapes, with long necks and golden bills, and, without thinking, he looked for the dull grey body and the awkward skinny neck. But no such thing was there. Instead, he beheld beneath him a beautiful white swan!

'The new one is the best of all,' said the children when they came down to feed the swans with biscuit and cake before going to bed. 'His feathers are whiter and his beak more golden than the rest.' And when he heard that, the duckling thought that it was worth while having undergone all the persecution and loneliness that he had passed through, as otherwise he would never have known what it was to be really happy.

The Two Caskets

[Hans Andersen.]

Far, far away, in the midst of a pine forest, there lived a woman who had both a daughter and a stepdaughter. Ever since her own daughter was born the mother had given her all that she cried for, so she grew up to be as cross and disagreeable as she was ugly. Her stepsister, on the other hand, had spent her childhood in working hard to keep house for her father, who died soon after his second marriage; and she was as much beloved by the neighbours for her goodness and industry as she was for her beauty.

As the years went on, the difference between the two girls grew more marked, and the old woman treated her stepdaughter worse than ever, and was always on the watch for some pretext for beating her, or depriving her of her food. Anything, however foolish, was good enough for this, and one day, when she could think of nothing better, she set both the girls to spin while sitting on the low wall of the well.

'And you had better mind what you do,' said she, 'for the one whose thread breaks first shall be thrown to the bottom.'

But of course she took good care that her own daughter's flax was fine and strong, while the stepsister had only some coarse stuff, which no one would have thought of using. As might be expected, in a very little while the poor girl's thread snapped, and the old woman, who had been watching from behind a door, seized her stepdaughter by her shoulders, and threw her into the well.

'That is an end of you!' she said. But she was wrong, for it was only the beginning.

Down, down, down went the girl—it seemed as if the well must reach to the very middle of the earth; but at last her feet touched the ground, and she found herself in a field more beautiful than even the summer pastures of her native mountains. Trees waved in the soft breeze, and flowers of the brightest colours danced in the grass. And though she was quite alone, the girl's heart danced too, for she felt happier than she had since her father died. So she walked on through the meadow till she came to an old tumbledown fence—so old that it was a wonder it managed to stand up at all, and it looked as if it depended for support on the old man's beard that climbed all over it.

The girl paused for a moment as she came up, and gazed about for a place where she might safely cross. But before she could move a voice cried from the fence:

'Do not hurt me, little maiden; I am so old, so old, I have not much longer to live.'

And the maiden answered:

'No, I will not hurt you; fear nothing.' And then seeing a spot where the clematis grew less thickly than in other places, she jumped lightly over.

'May all go well with thee,' said the fence, as the girl walked on.

She soon left the meadow and turned into a path which ran between two flowery hedges. Right in front of her stood an oven, and through its open door she could see a pile of white loaves.

'Eat as many loaves as you like, but do me no harm, little maiden,' cried the oven. And the maiden told her to fear nothing, for she never hurt anything, and was very grateful for the oven's kindness in giving her such a beautiful white loaf. When she had finished it, down to the last crumb, she shut the oven door and said: 'Good-morning.'

'May all go well with thee,' said the oven, as the girl walked on.

By-and-by she became very thirsty, and seeing a cow with a milk-pail hanging on her horn, turned towards her.

'Milk me and drink as much as you will, little maiden,' cried the cow, 'but be sure you spill none on the ground; and do me no harm, for I have never harmed anyone.'

'Nor I,' answered the girl; 'fear nothing.' So she sat down and milked till the pail was nearly full. Then she drank it all up except a little drop at the bottom.

'Now throw any that is left over my hoofs, and hang the pail on my horns again,' said the cow. And the girl did as she was bid, and kissed the cow on her forehead and went her way.

Many hours had now passed since the girl had fallen down the well, and the sun was setting.

'Where shall I spend the night?' thought she. And suddenly she saw before her a gate which she had not noticed before, and a very old woman leaning against it.

'Good evening,' said the girl politely; and the old woman answered:

'Good evening, my child. Would that everyone was as polite as you. Are you in search of anything?'

'I am in search of a place,' replied the girl; and the woman smiled and said:

'Then stop a little while and comb my hair, and you shall tell me all the things you can do.'

'Willingly, mother,' answered the girl. And she began combing out the old woman's hair, which was long and white.

Half an hour passed in this way, and then the old woman said:

'As you did not think yourself too good to comb me, I will show you where you may take service. Be prudent and patient and all will go well.'

So the girl thanked her, and set out for a farm at a little distance, where she was engaged to milk the cows and sift the corn.

As soon as it was light next morning the girl got up and went into the cow-house. 'I'm sure you must be hungry,' said she, patting each in turn. And then she fetched hay from the barn, and while they were eating it, she swept out the cow-house, and strewed clean straw upon the floor. The cows were so pleased with the care she took of them that they stood quite still while she milked them, and did not play any of the tricks on her that they had played on other dairymaids who were rough and rude. And when she had done, and was going to get up from her stool, she found sitting round her a whole circle of cats, black and white, tabby and tortoise-shell, who all cried with one voice:

'We are very thirsty, please give us some milk!'

'My poor little pussies,' said she, 'of course you shall have some.' And she went into the dairy, followed by all the cats, and gave each one a little red saucerful. But before they drank they all rubbed themselves against her knees and purred by way of thanks.

The next thing the girl had to do was to go to the storehouse, and to sift the corn through a sieve. While she was busy rubbing the corn she heard a whirr of wings, and a flock of sparrows flew in at the window.

'We are hungry; give us some corn! give us some corn!' cried they; and the girl answered:

'You poor little birds, of course you shall have some!' and scattered a fine handful over the floor. When they had finished they flew on her shoulders and flapped their wings by way of thanks.

Time went by, and no cows in the whole country-side were so fat and well tended as hers, and no dairy had so much milk to show. The farmer's wife was so well satisfied that she gave her higher wages, and treated her like her own daughter. At length, one day, the girl was bidden by her mistress to come into the kitchen, and when there, the old woman said to her: 'I know you can tend cows and keep a diary; now let me see what you can do besides. Take this sieve to the well, and fill it with water, and bring it home to me without spilling one drop by the way.'

The girl's heart sank at this order; for how was it possible for her to do her mistress's bidding? However, she was silent, and taking the sieve went down to the well with it. Stopping over the side, she filled it to the brim, but as soon as she lifted it the water all ran out of the holes. Again and again she tried, but not a drop would remaining in the sieve, and she was just turning away in despair when a flock of sparrows flew down from the sky.

'Ashes! ashes!' they twittered; and the girl looked at them and said:

'Well, I can't be in a worse plight than I am already, so I will take your advice.' And she ran back to the kitchen and filled her sieve with ashes. Then once more she dipped the sieve into the well, and, behold, this time not a drop of water disappeared!

'Here is the sieve, mistress,' cried the girl, going to the room where the old woman was sitting.

'You are cleverer than I expected,' answered she; 'or else someone helped you who is skilled in magic.' But the girl kept silence, and the old woman asked her no more questions.

Many days passed during which the girl went about her work as usual, but at length one day the old woman called her and said:

'I have something more for you to do. There are here two yarns, the one white, the other black. What you must do is to wash them in the river till the black one becomes white and the white black.' And the girl took them to the river and washed hard for several hours, but wash as she would they never changed one whit.

'This is worse than the sieve,' thought she, and was about to give up in despair when there came a rush of wings through the air, and on every twig of the birch trees which grew by the bank was perched a sparrow.

'The black to the east, the white to the west!' they sang, all at once; and the girl dried her tears and felt brave again. Picking up the black yarn, she stood facing the east and dipped it in the river, and in an instant it grew white as snow, then turning to the west, she held the white yarn in the water, and it became as black as a crow's wing. She looked back at the sparrows and smiled and nodded to them, and flapping their wings in reply they flew swiftly away.

At the sight of the yarn the old woman was struck dumb; but when at length she found her voice she asked the girl what magician had helped her to do what no one had done before. But she got no answer, for the maiden was afraid of bringing trouble on her little friends.

For many weeks the mistress shut herself up in her room, and the girl went about her work as usual. She hoped that there was an end to the difficult tasks which had been set her; but in this she was mistaken, for one day the old woman appeared suddenly in the kitchen, and said to her:

'There is one more trial to which I must put you, and if you do not fail in that you will be left in peace for evermore. Here are the yarns which you washed. Take them and weave them into a web that is as smooth as a king's robe, and see that it is spun by the time that the sun sets.'

'This is the easiest thing I have been set to do,' thought the girl, who was a good spinner. But when she began she found that the skein tangled and broke every moment.

'Oh, I can never do it!' she cried at last, and leaned her head against the loom and wept; but at that instant the door opened, and there entered, one behind another, a procession of cats.

'What is the matter, fair maiden?' asked they. And the girl answered:

'My mistress has given me this yarn to weave into a piece of cloth, which must be finished by sunset, and I have not even begun yet, for the yarn breaks whenever I touch it.'

'If that is all, dry your eyes,' said the cats; 'we will manage it for you.' And they jumped on the loom, and wove so fast and so skilfully that in a very short time the cloth was ready and was as fine as any king ever wore. The girl was so delighted at the sight of it that she gave each cat a kiss on his forehead as they left the room behind one the other as they had come.

'Who has taught you this wisdom?' asked the old woman, after she had passed her hands twice or thrice over the cloth and could find no roughness anywhere. But the girl only smiled and did not answer. She had learned early the value of silence.

After a few weeks the old woman sent for her maid and told her that as her year of service was now up, she was free to return home, but that, for her part, the girl had served her so well that she hoped she might stay with her. But at these words the maid shook her head, and answered gently:

'I have been happy here, Madam, and I thank you for your goodness to me; but I have left behind me a stepsister and a stepmother, and I am fain to be with them once more.' The old woman looked at her for a moment, and then she said:

'Well, that must be as you like; but as you have worked faithfully for me I will give you a reward. Go now into the loft above the store house and there you will find many caskets. Choose the one which pleases you best, but be careful not to open it till you have set it in the place where you wish it to remain.'

The girl left the room to go to the loft, and as soon as she got outside, she found all the cats waiting for her. Walking in procession, as was their custom, they followed her into the loft, which was filled with caskets big and little, plain and splendid. She lifted up one and looked at it, and then put it down to examine another yet more beautiful. Which should she choose, the yellow or the blue, the red or the green, the gold or the silver? She hesitated long, and went first to one and then to another, when she heard the cats' voices calling: 'Take the black! take the black!'

The words make her look round—she had seen no black casket, but as the cats continued their cry she peered into several corners that had remained unnoticed, and at length discovered a little black box, so small and so black, that it might easily have been passed over.

'This is the casket that pleases me best, mistress,' said the girl, carrying it into the house. And the old woman smiled and nodded, and bade her go her way. So the girl set forth, after bidding farewell to the cows and the cats and the sparrows, who all wept as they said good-bye.

She walked on and on and on, till she reached the flowery meadow, and there, suddenly, something happened, she never knew what, but she was sitting on the wall of the well in her stepmother's yard. Then she got up and entered the house.

The woman and her daughter stared as if they had been turned into stone; but at length the stepmother gasped out:

'So you are alive after all! Well, luck was ever against me! And where have you been this year past?' Then the girl told how she had taken service in the under-world, and, beside her wages, had brought home with her a little casket, which she would like to set up in her room.

'Give me the money, and take the ugly little box off to the outhouse,' cried the woman, beside herself with rage, and the girl, quite frightened at her violence, hastened away, with her precious box clasped to her bosom.

The outhouse was in a very dirty state, as no one had been near it since the girl had fallen down the well; but she scrubbed and swept till everything was clean again, and then she placed the little casket on a small shelf in the corner.

'Now I may open it,' she said to herself; and unlocking it with the key which hung to its handle, she raised the lid, but started back as she did so, almost blinded by the light that burst upon her. No one would ever have guessed that that little black box could have held such a quantity of beautiful things! Rings, crowns, girdles, necklaces—all made of wonderful stones; and they shone with such brilliance that not only the stepmother and her daughter but all the people round came running to see if the house was on fire. Of course the woman felt quite ill with greed and envy, and she would have certainly taken all the jewels for herself had she not feared the wrath of the neighbours, who loved her stepdaughter as much as they hated her.

But if she could not steal the casket and its contents for herself, at least she could get another like it, and perhaps a still richer one. So she bade her own daughter sit on the edge of the well, and threw her into the water, exactly as she had done to the other girl; and, exactly as before, the flowery meadow lay at the bottom.

Every inch of the way she trod the path which her stepsister had trodden, and saw the things which she had seen; but there the likeness ended. When the fence prayed her to do it no harm, she laughed rudely, and tore up some of the stakes so that she might get over the more easily; when the oven offered her bread, she scattered the loaves onto the ground and stamped on them; and after she had milked the cow, and drunk as much as she wanted, she threw the rest on the grass, and kicked the pail to bits, and never heard them say, as they looked after her: 'You shall not have done this to me for nothing!'

Towards evening she reached the spot where the old woman was leaning against the gate-post, but she passed her by without a word.

'Have you no manners in your country?' asked the crone.

'I can't stop and talk; I am in a hurry,' answered the girl. 'It is getting late, and I have to find a place.'

'Stop and comb my hair for a little,' said the old woman, 'and I will help you to get a place.'

'Comb your hair, indeed! I have something better to do than that!' And slamming the gate in the crone's face she went her way. And she never heard the words that followed her: 'You shall not have done this to me for nothing!'

By-and-by the girl arrived at the farm, and she was engaged to look after the cows and sift the corn as her stepsister had been. But it was only when someone was watching her that she did her work; at other times the cow-house was dirty, and the cows ill-fed and beaten, so that they kicked over the pail, and tried to butt her; and everyone said they had never seen such thin cows or such poor milk. As for the cats, she chased them away, and ill-treated them, so that they had not even the spirit to chase the rats and mice, which nowadays ran about everywhere. And when the sparrows came to beg for some corn, they fared no better than the cows and the cats, for the girl threw her shoes at them, till they flew in a fright to the woods, and took shelter amongst the trees.

Months passed in this manner, when, one day, the mistress called the girl to her.

'All that I have given you to do you have done ill,' said she, 'yet will I give you another chance. For though you cannot tend cows, or divide the grain from the chaff, there may be other things that you can do better. Therefore take this sieve to the well, and fill it with water, and see that you bring it back without spilling a drop.'

The girl took the sieve and carried it to the well as her sister had done; but no little birds came to help her, and after dipping it in the well two or three times she brought it back empty.

'I thought as much,' said the old woman angrily; 'she that is useless in one thing is useless in another.'

Perhaps the mistress may have thought that the girl had learnt a lesson, but, if she did, she was quite mistaken, as the work was no better done than before. By-and-by she sent for her again, and gave her maid the black and white yarn to wash in the river; but there was no one to tell her the secret by which the black would turn white, and the white black; so she brought them back as they were. This time the old woman only looked at her grimly but the girl was too well pleased with herself to care what anyone thought about her.

After some weeks her third trial came, and the yarn was given her to spin, as it had been given to her stepsister before her.

But no procession of cats entered the room to weave a web of fine cloth, and at sunset she only brought back to her mistress an armful of dirty, tangled wool.

'There seems nothing in the world you can do,' said the old woman, and left her to herself.

Soon after this the year was up, and the girl went to her mistress to tell her that she wished to go home.

'Little desire have I to keep you,' answered the old woman, 'for no one thing have you done as you ought. Still, I will give you some payment, therefore go up into the loft, and choose for yourself one of the caskets that lies there. But see that you do not open it till you place it where you wish it to stay.'

This was what the girl had been hoping for, and so rejoiced was she, that, without even stopping to thank the old woman, she ran as fast as she could to the loft. There were the caskets, blue and red, green and yellow, silver and gold; and there in the corner stood a little black casket just like the one her stepsister had brought home.

'If there are so many jewels in that little black thing, this big red one will hold twice the number,' she said to herself; and snatching it up she set off on her road home without even going to bid farewell to her mistress.

'See, mother, see what I have brought!' cried she, as she entered the cottage holding the casket in both hands.

'Ah! you have got something very different from that little black box,' answered the old woman with delight. But the girl was so busy finding a place for it to stand that she took little notice of her mother.

'It will look best here—no, here,' she said, setting it first on one piece of furniture and then on another. 'No, after all it is to fine to live in a kitchen, let us place it in the guest chamber.'

So mother and daughter carried it proudly upstairs and put it on a shelf over the fireplace; then, untying the key from the handle, they opened the box. As before, a bright light leapt out directly the lid was raised, but it did not spring from the lustre of jewels, but from hot flames, which darted along the walls and burnt up the cottage and all that was in it and the mother and daughter as well.

As they had done when the stepdaughter came home, the neighbours all hurried to see what was the matter; but they were too late. Only the hen-house was left standing; and, in spite of her riches, there the stepdaughter lived happily to the end of her days.

The Goldsmith's Fortune

[From Thorpe's Yule-Tide Stories.]

Once upon a time there was a goldsmith who lived in a certain village where the people were as bad and greedy, and covetous, as they could possibly be; however, in spite of his surroundings, he was fat and prosperous. He had only one friend whom he liked, and that was a cowherd, who looked after cattle for one of the farmers in the village. Every evening the goldsmith would walk across to the cowherd's house and say: 'Come, let's go out for a walk!'

Now the cowherd didn't like walking in the evening, because, he said, he had been out grazing the cattle all day, and was glad to sit down when night came; but the goldsmith always worried him so that the poor man had to go against his will. This at last so annoyed him that he tried to think how he could pick a quarrel with the goldsmith, so that he should not beg him to walk with him any more. He asked another cowherd for advice, and he said the best thing he could do was to go across and kill the goldsmith's wife, for then the goldsmith would be sure to regard him as an enemy; so, being a foolish person, and there being no laws in that country by which a man would be certainly punished for such a crime, the cowherd one evening took a big stick and went across to the goldsmith's house when only Mrs. Goldsmith was at home, and banged her on the head so hard that she died then and there.

When the goldsmith came back and found his wife dead he said nothing, but just took her outside into the dark lane and propped her up against the wall of his house, and then went into the courtyard and waited. Presently a rich stranger came along the lane, and seeing someone there, as he supposed, he said:

'Good-evening, friend! a fine night to-night!' But the goldsmith's wife said nothing. The man then repeated his words louder; but still there was no reply. A third time he shouted:

'Good-evening, friend! are you deaf?' but the figure never replied. Then the stranger, being angry at what he thought very rude behaviour, picked up a big stone and threw it at Mrs. Goldsmith, crying:

'Let that teach you manners!'

Instantly poor Mrs. Goldsmith tumbled over; and the stranger, horrified at seeing what he had done, was immediately seized by the goldsmith, who ran out screaming:

'Wretch! you have killed my wife! Oh, miserable one; we will have justice done to thee!'

With many protestations and reproaches they wrangled together, the stranger entreating the goldsmith to say nothing and he would pay him handsomely to atone for the sad accident. At last the goldsmith quieted down, and agreed to accept one thousand gold pieces from the stranger, who immediately helped him to bury his poor wife, and then rushed off to the guest house, packed up his things and was off by daylight, lest the goldsmith should repent and accuse him as the murderer of his wife. Now it very soon appeared that the goldsmith had a lot of extra money, so that people began to ask questions, and finally demanded of him the reason for his sudden wealth.

'Oh,' said he, 'my wife died, and I sold her.'

'You sold your dead wife?' cried the people.

'Yes,' said the goldsmith.

'For how much?'

'A thousand gold pieces,' replied the goldsmith.

Instantly the villagers went away and each caught hold of his own wife and throttled her, and the next day they all went off to sell their dead wives. Many a weary mile did they tramp, but got nothing but hard words or laughter, or directions to the nearest cemetery, from people to whom they offered dead wives for sale. At last they perceived that they had been cheated somehow by that goldsmith. So off they rushed home, seized the unhappy man, and, without listening to his cries and entreaties, hurried him down to the river bank and flung him—plop!—into the deepest, weediest, and nastiest place they could find.

'That will teach him to play tricks on us,' said they. 'For as he can't swim he'll drown, and we sha'n't have any more trouble with him!'

Now the goldsmith really could not swim, and as soon as he was thrown into the deep river he sank below the surface; so his enemies went away believing that they had seen the last of him. But, in reality, he was carried down, half drowned, below the next bend in the river, where he fortunately came across a 'snag' floating in the water (a snag is, you know, a part of a tree or bush which floats very nearly under the surface of the water); and he held on to this snag, and by great good luck eventually came ashore some two or three miles down the river. At the place where he landed he came across a fine fat cow buffalo, and immediately he jumped on her back and rode home. When the village people saw him, they ran out in surprise, and said:

'Where on earth do you come from, and where did you get that buffalo?'

'Ah!' said the goldsmith, 'you little know what delightful adventures I have had! Why, down in that place in the river where you threw me in I found meadows, and trees, and fine pastures, and buffaloes, and all kinds of cattle. In fact, I could hardly tear myself away; but I thought that I must really let you all know about it.'

'Oh, oh!' thought the greedy village people; 'if there are buffaloes to be had for the taking we'll go after some too.' Encouraged by the goldsmith they nearly all ran off the very next morning to the river; and, in order that they might get down quickly to the beautiful place the goldsmith told them of, they tied great stones on to their feet and their necks, and one after another they jumped into the water as fast as the could, and were drowned. And whenever any one of them waved his hands about and struggled the goldsmith would cry out:

'Look! he's beckoning the rest of you to come; he's got a fine buffalo!' And others who were doubtful would jump in, until not one was left. Then the cunning goldsmith went back and took all the village for himself, and became very rich indeed. But do you think he was happy? Not a bit. Lies never made a man happy yet. Truly, he got the better of a set of wicked and greedy people, but only by being wicked and greedy himself; and, as it turned out, when he got so rich he got very fat; and at last was so fat that he couldn't move, and one day he got the apoplexy and died, and no one in the world cared the least bit.

The Enchanted Wreath

[Told by a Pathan to Major Campbell.]

Once upon a time there lived near a forest a man and his wife and two girls; one girl was the daughter of the man, and the other the daughter of his wife; and the man's daughter was good and beautiful, but the woman's daughter was cross and ugly. However, her mother did not know that, but thought her the most bewitching maiden that ever was seen.

One day the man called to his daughter and bade her come with him into the forest to cut wood. They worked hard all day, but in spite of the chopping they were very cold, for it rained heavily, and when they returned home, they were wet through. Then, to his vexation, the man found that he had left his axe behind him, and he knew that if it lay all night in the mud it would become rusty and useless. So he said to his wife:

'I have dropped my axe in the forest, bid your daughter go and fetch it, for mine has worked hard all day and is both wet and weary.'

But the wife answered:

'If your daughter is wet already, it is all the more reason that she should go and get the axe. Besides, she is a great strong girl, and a little rain will not hurt her, while my daughter would be sure to catch a bad cold.'

By long experience the man knew there was no good saying any more, and with a sigh he told the poor girl she must return to the forest for the axe.

The walk took some time, for it was very dark, and her shoes often stuck in the mud, but she was brave as well as beautiful and never thought of turning back merely because the path was both difficult and unpleasant. At last, with her dress torn by brambles that she could not see, and her fact scratched by the twigs on the trees, she reached the spot where she and her father had been cutting in the morning, and found the axe in the place he had left it. To her surprise, three little doves were sitting on the handle, all of them looking very sad.

'You poor little things,' said the girl, stroking them. 'Why do you sit there and get wet? Go and fly home to your nest, it will be much warmer than this; but first eat this bread, which I saved from my dinner, and perhaps you will feel happier. It is my father's axe you are sitting on, and I must take it back as fast as

I can, or I shall get a terrible scolding from my stepmother.' She then crumbled the bread on the ground, and was pleased to see the doves flutter quite cheerfully towards it.

'Good-bye,' she said, picking up the axe, and went her way homewards.

By the time they had finished all the crumbs the doves felt must better, and were able to fly back to their nest in the top of a tree.

'That is a good girl,' said one; 'I really was too weak to stretch out a wing before she came. I should like to do something to show how grateful I am.'

'Well, let us give her a wreath of flowers that will never fade as long as she wears it,' cried another.

'And let the tiniest singing birds in the world sit amongst the flowers,' rejoined the third.

'Yes, that will do beautifully,' said the first. And when the girl stepped into her cottage a wreath of rosebuds was on her head, and a crowd of little birds were singing unseen.

The father, who was sitting by the fire, thought that, in spite of her muddy clothes, he had never seen his daughter looking so lovely; but the stepmother and the other girl grew wild with envy.

'How absurd to walk about on such a pouring night, dressed up like that,' she remarked crossly, and roughly pulled off the wreath as she spoke, to place it on her own daughter. As she did so the roses became withered and brown, and the birds flew out of the window.

'See what a trumpery thing it is!' cried the stepmother; 'and now take your supper and go to bed, for it is near upon midnight.'

But though she pretended to despise the wreath, she longed none the less for her daughter to have one like it.

Now it happened that the next evening the father, who had been alone in the forest, came back a second time without his axe. The stepmother's heart was glad when she saw this, and she said quite mildly:

'Why, you have forgotten your axe again, you careless man! But now your daughter shall stay at home, and mine shall go and bring it back'; and throwing a cloak over the girl's shoulders, she bade her hasten to the forest.

With a very ill grace the damsel set forth, grumbling to herself as she went; for though she wished for the wreath, she did not at all want the trouble of getting it.

By the time she reached the spot where her stepfather had been cutting the wood the girl was in a very bad temper indeed, and when she caught sight of the axe, there were the three little doves, with drooping heads and soiled, bedraggled feathers, sitting on the handle.

'You dirty creatures,' cried she, 'get away at once, or I will throw stones at you! And the doves spread their wings in a fright and flew up to the very top of a tree, their bodies shaking with anger.

'What shall we do to revenge ourselves on her?' asked the smallest of the doves, 'we were never treated like that before.'

'Never,' said the biggest dove. 'We must find some way of paying her back in her own coin!'

'I know,' answered the middle dove; 'she shall never be able to say anything but "dirty creatures" to the end of her life.'

'Oh, how clever of you! That will do beautifully,' exclaimed the other two. And they flapped their wings and clucked so loud with delight, and made such a noise, that they woke up all the birds in the trees close by.

'What in the world is the matter?' asked the birds sleepily.

'That is our secret,' said the doves.

Meanwhile the girl had reached home crosser than ever; but as soon as her mother heard her lift the latch of the door she ran out to hear her adventures. 'Well, did you get the wreath?' cried she.

'Dirty creatures!' answered her daughter.

'Don't speak to me like that! What do you mean?' asked the mother again.

'Dirty creatures!' repeated the daughter, and nothing else could she say.

Then the woman saw that something evil had befallen her, and turned in her rage to her stepdaughter.

'You are at the bottom of this, I know,' she cried; and as the father was out of the way she took a stick and beat the girl till she screamed with pain and went to bed sobbing.

If the poor girl's life had been miserable before, it was ten times worse now, for the moment her father's back was turned the others teased and tormented her from morning till night; and their fury was increased by the sight of her wreath, which the doves had placed again on her head.

Things went on like this for some weeks, when, one day, as the king's son was riding through the forest, he heard some strange birds singing more sweetly than birds had ever sung before. He tied his horse to a tree, and followed where the sound led him, and, to his surprise, he saw before him a beautiful girl chopping wood, with a wreath of pink rose-buds, out of which the singing came. Standing in the shelter of a tree, he watched her a long while, and then, hat in hand, he went up and spoke to her.

'Fair maiden, who are you, and who gave you that wreath of singing roses?' asked he, for the birds were so tiny that till you looked closely you never saw them.

'I live in a hut on the edge of the forest,' she answered, blushing, for she had never spoken to a prince before. 'As to the wreath, I know not how it came there, unless it may be the gift of some doves whom I fed when they were starving! The prince was delighted with this answer, which showed the goodness of the girl's heart, and besides he had fallen in love with her beauty, and would not be content till she promised to return with him to the palace, and become his bride. The old king was naturally disappointed at his son's choice of a wife, as he wished him to marry a neighbouring princess; but as from his birth the prince had always done exactly as he like, nothing was said and a splendid wedding feast was got ready.

The day after her marriage the bride sent a messenger, bearing handsome presents to her father, and telling him of the good fortune which had befallen her. As may be imagined, the stepmother and her daughter were so filled with envy that they grew quite ill, and had to take to their beds, and nobody would have been sorry it they had never got up again; but that did not happen. At length, however, they began to feel better, for the mother invented a plan by which she could be revenged on the girl who had never done her any harm.

Her plan was this. In the town where she had lived before she was married there was an old witch, who had more skill in magic that any other witch she knew. To this witch she would go and beg her to make her a mask with the face of her stepdaughter, and when she had the mask the rest would be easy. She told her daughter what she meant to do, and although the daughter could only say 'dirty creatures,' in answer, she nodded and smiled and looked well pleased.

Everything fell out exactly as the woman had hoped. By the aid of her magic mirror the witch beheld the new princess walking in her gardens in a dress of green silk, and in a few minutes had produced a mask so like her, that very few people could have told the difference. However, she counselled the woman that when her daughter first wore it—for that, of course, was what she intended her to do—she had better pretend that she had a toothache, and cover her head with a lace veil. The woman thanked her and paid her well, and returned to her hut, carrying the mask under her cloak.

In a few days she heard that a great hunt was planned, and the prince would leave the palace very early in the morning, so that his wife would be alone all day. This was a chance not to be missed, and taking her daughter with her she went up to the palace, where she had never been before. The princess was too happy in her new home to remember all that she had suffered in the old one, and she welcomed them both gladly, and gave them quantities of beautiful things to take back with them. At last she took them down to the shore to see a pleasure boat which her husband had had made for her; and here, the woman seizing her opportunity, stole softly behind the girl and pushed her off the rock on which she was standing, into the deep water, where she instantly sank to the bottom. Then she fastened the mask on her daughter, flung over her shoulders a velvet cloak, which the princess had let fall, and finally arranged a lace veil over her head.

'Rest your cheek on your hand, as if you were in pain, when the prince returns,' said the mother; 'and be careful not to speak, whatever you do. I will go back to the witch and see if she cannot take off the spell laid on you by those horrible birds. Ah! why did I not think of it before!'

No sooner had the prince entered the palace than he hastened to the princess's apartments, where he found her lying on the sofa apparently in great pain.

'My dearest wife, what is the matter with you?' he cried, kneeling down beside her, and trying to take her hand; but she snatched it away, and pointing to her cheek murmured something he could not catch.

'What is it? tell me! Is the pain bad? When did it begin? Shall I send for your ladies to bath the place?' asked the prince, pouring out these and a dozen other questions, to which the girl only shook her head.

'But I can't leave you like this,' he continued, starting up, 'I must summon all the court physicians to apply soothing balsams to the sore place! And as he spoke he sprang to his feet to go in search of them once came near her the trick would at once be discovered, that she forgot her mother's counsel not to speak, and forgot even the spell that had been laid upon her, and catching hold of the prince's tunic, she cried in tones of entreaty: 'Dirty creatures!'

The young man stopped, not able to believe his ears, but supposed that pain had made the princess cross, as it sometimes does. However, he guessed somehow that she wised to be left alone, so he only said:

'Well, I dare say a little sleep will do you good, if you can manage to get it, and that you will wake up better to-morrow.'

Now, that night happened to be very hot and airless, and the prince, after vainly trying to rest, at length got up and went to the window. Suddenly he beheld in the moonlight a form with a wreath of roses on her head rise out of the sea below him and step on to the sands, holding out her arms as she did so towards the palace.

'That maiden is strangely like my wife,' thought he; 'I must see her closer! And he hastened down to the water. But when he got there, the princess, for she indeed it was, had disappeared completely, and he began to wonder if his eyes had deceived him.

The next morning he went to the false bride's room, but her ladies told him she would neither speak nor get up, though she ate everything they set before her. The prince was sorely perplexed as to what could be the matter with her, for naturally he could not guess that she was expecting her mother to return every moment, and to remove the spell the doves had laid upon her, and meanwhile was afraid to speak lest she should betray herself. At length he made up his mind to summon all the court physicians; he did not tell her what he was going to do, lest it should make her worse, but he went himself and begged the four learned leeches attached to the king's person to follow him to the princess's apartments. Unfortunately, as they entered, the princess was so enraged at the sight of them that she forgot all about the doves, and shrieked out: 'Dirty creatures! dirty creatures!' which so offended the physicians that they left the room at once, and nothing that the prince could say would prevail on them to remain. He then tried to persuade his wife to send them a message that she was sorry for her rudeness, but not a word would she say.

Late that evening, when he had performed all the tiresome duties which fall to the lot of every prince, the young man was leaning out of his window, refreshing himself with the cool breezes that blew off the sea. His thoughts went back to the scene of the morning, and he wondered if, after all, he had not made a great mistake in marrying a low-born wife, however beautiful she might be. How could he have imagined that the quiet, gentle girl who had been so charming a companion to him during the first days of their marriage, could have become in a day the rude, sulky woman, who could not control her temper even to benefit herself. One thing was clear, if she did not change her conduct very shortly he would have to send her away from court.

He was thinking these thoughts, when his eyes fell on the sea beneath him, and there, as before, was the figure that so closely resembled his wife, standing with her feet in the water, holding out her arms to him.

'Wait for me! Wait for me! Wait for me!' he cried; not even knowing he was speaking. But when he reached the shore there was nothing to be seen but the shadows cast by the moonlight.

A state ceremonial in a city some distance off caused the prince to ride away at daybreak, and he left without seeing his wife again.

'Perhaps she may have come to her senses by to-morrow,' said he to himself; 'and, anyhow, if I am going to send her back to her father, it might be better if we did not meet in the meantime! Then he put the matter from his mind, and kept his thoughts on the duty that lay before him.

It was nearly midnight before he returned to the palace, but, instead of entering, he went down to the shore and hid behind a rock. He had scarcely done so when the girl came out of the sea, and stretched out her arms towards his window. In an instant the prince had seized her hand, and though she made a frightened struggle to reach the water—for she in her turn had had a spell laid upon her—he held her fast.

'You are my own wife, and I shall never let you go,' he said. But the words were hardly out of his mouth when he found that it was a hare that he was holding by the paw. Then the hare changed into a fish, and the fish into a bird, and the bird into a slimy wriggling snake. This time the prince's hand nearly opened of itself, but with a strong effort he kept his fingers shut, and drawing his sword cut off its head, when the spell was broken, and the girl stood before him as he had seen her first, the wreath upon her head and the birds singing for joy.

The very next morning the stepmother arrived at the palace with an ointment that the old witch had given her to place upon her daughter's tongue, which would break the dove's spell, if the rightful bride had really been drowned in the sea; if not, then it would be useless. The mother assured her that she had seen her stepdaughter sink, and that there was no fear that she would ever come up again; but, to make all quite safe, the old woman might bewitch the girl; and so she did. After that the wicked stepmother travelled all through the night to get to the palace as soon as possible, and made her way straight into her daughter's room.

'I have got it! I have got it!' she cried triumphantly, and laid the ointment on her daughter's tongue.

'Now what do you say?' she asked proudly.

'Dirty creatures! dirty creatures!' answered the daughter; and the mother wrung her hands and wept, as she knew that all her plans had failed.

At this moment the prince entered with his real wife. 'You both deserved death,' he said, 'and if it were left to me, you should have it. But the princess has begged me to spare your lives, so you will be put into a ship and carried off to a desert island, where you will stay till you die.'

Then the ship was made ready and the wicked woman and her daughter were placed in it, and it sailed away, and no more was heard of them. But the prince and his wife lived together long and happily, and ruled their people well.

The Foolish Weaver

[Adapted from Thorpe's Yule-Tide Stories.]

Once a weaver, who was in want of work, took service with a certain farmer as a shepherd.

The farmer, knowing that the man was very slow-witted, gave him most careful instructions as to everything that he was to do.

Finally he said: 'If a wolf or any wild animal attempts to hurt the flock you should pick up a big stone like this' (suiting the action to the word) 'and throw a few such at him, and he will be afraid and go away.' The weaver said that he understood, and started with the flocks to the hillsides where they grazed all day.

By chance in the afternoon a leopard appeared, and the weaver instantly ran home as fast as he could to get the stones which the farmer had shown him, to throw at the creature. When he came back all the flock were scattered or killed, and when the farmer heard the tale he beat him soundly. 'Were there no stones on the hillside that you should run back to get them, you senseless one?' he cried; 'you are not fit to herd sheep. To-day you shall stay at home and mind my old mother who is sick, perhaps you will be able to drive flies off her face, if you can't drive beasts away from sheep!'

So, the next day, the weaver was left at home to take care of the farmer's old sick mother. Now as she lay outside on a bed, it turned out that the flies became very troublesome, and the weaver looked round for something to drive them away with; and as he had been told to pick up the nearest stone to drive the beasts away from the flock, he thought he would this time show how cleverly he could obey orders. Accordingly he seized the nearest stone, which was a big, heavy one, and dashed it at the flies; but, unhappily, he slew the poor old woman also; and then, being afraid of the wrath of the farmer, he fled and was not seen again in that neighbourhood.

All that day and all the next night he walked, and at length he came to a village where a great many weavers lived together.

'You are welcome,' said they. 'Eat and sleep, for to-morrow six of us start in search of fresh wool to weave, and we pray you to give us your company.'

'Willingly,' answered the weaver. So the next morning the seven weavers set out to go to the village where they could buy what they wanted. On the way they had to cross a ravine which lately had been full of water, but now was quite dry. The weavers, however, were accustomed to swim over this ravine; therefore, regardless of the fact that this time it was dry, they stripped, and, tying their clothes on their heads, they proceeded to swim across the dry sand and rocks that formed the bed of the ravine. Thus they got to the other side without further damage than bruised knees and elbows, and as soon as they were over, one of them began to count the party to make sure that all were safe there. He counted all except himself, and then cried out that somebody was missing! This set each of them counting; but each made the same mistake of counting all except himself, so that they became certain that one of their party was missing! They ran up and down the bank of the ravine wringing their hands in great distress and looking for signs of their lost comrade. There a farmer found them and asked what was the matter. 'Alas!' said one, 'seven of us started from the other bank and one must have been drowned on the crossing, as we can only find six remaining!' The farmer eyed them a minute, and then, picking up his stick, he dealt each a sounding blow, counting, as he did so, 'One! two! three!' and so on up to the seven. When the weavers found that there were seven of them they were overcome with gratitude to one whom they took for a magician as he could thus make seven out of an obvious six.

The Clever Cat

[From the Pushto.]

Once upon a time there lived an old man who dwelt with his son in a small hut on the edge of the plain. He was very old, and had worked very hard, and when at last he was struck down by illness he felt that he should never rise from his bed again.

So, one day, he bade his wife summon their son, when he came back from his journey to the nearest town, where he had been to buy bread.

'Come hither, my son,' said he; 'I know myself well to be dying, and I have nothing to leave you but my falcon, my cat and my greyhound; but if you make good use of them you will never lack food. Be good to your mother, as you have been to me. And now farewell!'

Then he turned his face to the wall and died.

There was great mourning in the hut for many days, but at length the son rose up, and calling to his greyhound, his cat and his falcon, he left the house saying that he would bring back something for dinner. Wandering over the plain, he noticed a troop of gazelles, and pointed to his greyhound to give chase. The dog soon brought down a fine fat beast, and slinging it over his shoulders, the young man turned homewards. On the way, however, he passed a pond, and as he approached a cloud of birds flew into the air. Shaking his wrist, the falcon seated on it darted into the air, and swooped down upon the quarry he had marked, which fell dead to the ground. The young man picked it up, and put it in his pouch and then went towards home again.

Near the hut was a small barn in which he kept the produce of the little patch of corn, which grew close to the garden. Here a rat ran out almost under his feet, followed by another and another; but quick as thought the cat was upon them and not one escaped her.

When all the rats were killed, the young man left the barn. He took the path leading to the door of the hut, but stopped on feeling a hand laid on his shoulder.

'Young man,' said the ogre (for such was the stranger), 'you have been a good son, and you deserve the piece of luck which has befallen you this day. Come with me to that shining lake yonder, and fear nothing.'

Wondering a little at what might be going to happen to him, the youth did as the ogre bade him, and when they reached the shore of the lake, the ogre turned and said to him:

'Step into the water and shut your eyes! You will find yourself sinking slowly to the bottom; but take courage, all will go well. Only bring up as much silver as you can carry, and we will divide it between us.'

So the young man stepped bravely into the lake, and felt himself sinking, sinking, till he reached firm ground at last. In front of him lay four heaps of silver, and in the midst of them a curious white shining stone, marked over with strange characters, such as he had never seen before. He picked it up in order to examine it more closely, and as he held it the stone spoke.

'As long as you hold me, all your wishes will come true,' it said. 'But hide me in your turban, and then call to the ogre that you are ready to come up.'

In a few minutes the young man stood again by the shores of the lake.

'Well, where is the silver?' asked the ogre, who was awaiting him.

'Ah, my father, how can I tell you! So bewildered was I, and so dazzled with the splendours of everything I saw, that I stood like a statue, unable to move. Then hearing steps approaching I got frightened, and called to you, as you know.'

'You are no better than the rest,' cried the ogre, and turned away in a rage.

When he was out of sight the young man took the stone from his turban and looked at it. 'I want the finest camel that can be found, and the most splendid garments,' said he.

'Shut your eyes then,' replied the stone. And he shut them; and when he opened them again the camel that he had wished for was standing before him, while the festal robes of a desert prince hung from his shoulders. Mounting the camel, he whistled the falcon to his wrist, and, followed by his greyhound and his cat, he started homewards.

His mother was sewing at her door when this magnificent stranger rode up, and, filled with surprise, she bowed low before him.

'Don't you know me, mother?' he said with a laugh. And on hearing his voice the good woman nearly fell to the ground with astonishment.

'How have you got that camel and those clothes?' asked she. 'Can a son of mine have committed murder in order to possess them?'

'Do not be afraid; they are quite honestly come by,' answered the youth. 'I will explain all by-and-by; but now you must go to the palace and tell the king I wish to marry his daughter.'

At these words the mother thought her son had certainly gone mad, and stared blankly at him. The young man guessed what was in her heart, and replied with a smile:

'Fear nothing. Promise all that he asks; it will be fulfilled somehow.'

So she went to the palace, where she found the king sitting in the Hall of Justice listening to the petitions of his people. The woman waited until all had been heard and the hall was empty, and then went up and knelt before the throne.

'My son has sent me to ask for the hand of the princess,' said she.

The king looked at her and thought that she was mad; but, instead of ordering his guards to turn her out, he answered gravely:

'Before he can marry the princess he must build me a palace of ice, which can be warmed with fires, and wherein the rarest singing-birds can live!'

'It shall be done, your Majesty,' said she, and got up and left the hall.

Her son was anxiously awaiting her outside the palace gates, dressed in the clothes that he wore every day.

'Well, what have I got to do?' he asked impatiently, drawing his mother aside so that no one could overhear them.

'Oh, something quite impossible; and I hope you will put the princess out of your head,' she replied.

'Well, but what is it?' persisted he.

'Nothing but to build a palace of ice wherein fires can burn that shall keep it so warm that the most delicate singing-birds can live in it!'

'I thought it would be something much harder than that,' exclaimed the young man. 'I will see about it at once.' And leaving his mother, he went into the country and took the stone from his turban.

'I want a palace of ice that can be warmed with fires and filled with the rarest singing-birds!'

'Shut your eyes, then,' said the stone; and he shut them, and when he opened them again there was the palace, more beautiful than anything he could have imagined, the fires throwing a soft pink glow over the ice.

'It is fit even for the princess,' thought he to himself.

As soon as the king awoke next morning he ran to the window, and there across the plain he beheld the palace.

'That young man must be a great wizard; he may be useful to me.' And when the mother came again to tell him that his orders had been fulfilled he received her with great honour, and bade her tell her son that the wedding was fixed for the following day.

The princess was delighted with her new home, and with her husband also; and several days slipped happily by, spent in turning over all the beautiful things that the palace contained. But at length the young man grew tired of always staying inside walls, and he told his wife that the next day he must leave her for a few hours, and go out hunting. 'You will not mind?' he asked. And she answered as became a good wife:

'Yes, of course I shall mind; but I will spend the day in planning out some new dresses; and then it will be so delightful when you come back, you know!'

So the husband went off to hunt, with the falcon on his wrist, and the greyhound and the cat behind him—for the palace was so warm that even the cat did not mind living in it.

No sooner had he gone, than the ogre who had been watching his chance for many days, knocked at the door of the palace.

'I have just returned from a far country,' he said, 'and I have some of the largest and most brilliant stones in the world with me. The princess is known to love beautiful things, perhaps she might like to buy some?'

Now the princess had been wondering for many days what trimming she should put on her dresses, so that they should outshine the dresses of the other ladies at the court balls. Nothing that she thought of seemed good enough, so, when the message was brought that the ogre and his wares were below, she at once ordered that he should be brought to her chamber.

Oh! what beautiful stones he laid before her; what lovely rubies, and what rare pearls! No other lady would have jewels like those—of that the princess was quite sure; but she cast down her eyes so that the ogre might not see how much she longed for them.

'I fear they are too costly for me,' she said carelessly; 'and besides, I have hardly need of any more jewels just now.'

'I have no particular wish to sell them myself,' answered the ogre, with equal indifference. 'But I have a necklace of shining stones which was left me by father, and one, the largest engraven with weird characters, is missing. I have heard that it is in your husband's possession, and if you can get me that stone you shall have any of these jewels that you choose. But you will have to pretend that you want it for yourself; and, above all, do not mention me, for he sets great store by it, and would never part with it to a stranger! To-morrow I will return with some jewels yet finer than those I have with me to-day. So, madam, farewell!'

Left alone, the princess began to think of many things, but chiefly as to whether she would persuade her husband to give her the stone or not. At one moment she felt he had already bestowed so much upon her that it was a shame to ask for the only object he had kept back. No, it would be mean; she could not do it! But then, those diamonds, and those string of pearls! After all, they had only been married a week, and the pleasure of giving it to her ought to be far greater than the pleasure of keeping it for himself. And she was sure it would be!

Well, that evening, when the young man had supped off his favourite dishes which the princess took care to have specially prepared for him, she sat down close beside him, and began stroking his head. For some time she did not speak, but listened attentively to all the adventures that had befallen him that day.

'But I was thinking of you all the time,' said he at the end, 'and wishing that I could bring you back something you would like. But, alas! what is there that you do not possess already?'

'How good of you not to forget me when you are in the midst of such dangers and hardships,' answered she. 'Yes, it is true I have many beautiful things; but if you want to give me a present—and to-morrow is my birthday—there IS one thing that I wish for very much.'

'And what is that? Of course you shall have it directly!' he asked eagerly.

'It is that bright stone which fell out of the folds of your turban a few days ago,' she answered, playing with his finger; 'the little stone with all those funny marks upon it. I never saw any stone like it before.'

The young man did not answer at first; then he said, slowly:

'I have promised, and therefore I must perform. But will you swear never to part from it, and to keep it safely about you always? More I cannot tell you, but I beg you earnestly to take heed to this.'

The princess was a little startled by his manner, and began to be sorry that she had every listened to the ogre. But she did not like to draw back, and pretended to be immensely delighted at her new toy, and kissed and thanked her husband for it.

'After all I needn't give it to the ogre,' thought she as she dropped off to sleep.

Unluckily the next morning the young man went hunting again, and the ogre, who was watching, knew this, and did not come till much later than before. At the moment that he knocked at the door of the palace the princess had tired of all her employments, and her attendants were at their wits' end how to amuse her, when a tall negro dressed in scarlet came to announce that the ogre was below, and desired to know if the princess would speak to him.

'Bring him hither at once!' cried she, springing up from her cushions, and forgetting all her resolves of the previous night. In another moment she was bending with rapture over the glittering gems.

'Have you got it?' asked the ogre in a whisper, for the princess's ladies were standing as near as they dared to catch a glimpse of the beautiful jewels.

'Yes, here,' she answered, slipping the stone from her sash and placing it among the rest. Then she raised her voice, and began to talk quickly of the prices of the chains and necklaces, and after some bargaining, to deceive the attendants, she declared that she liked one string of pearls better than all the rest, and that the ogre might take away the other things, which were not half as valuable as he supposed.

'As you please, madam,' said he, bowing himself out of the palace.

Soon after he had gone a curious thing happened. The princess carelessly touched the wall of her room, which was wont to reflect the warm red light of the fire on the hearth, and found her hand quite wet. She turned round, and— was it her fancy? or did the fire burn more dimly than before? Hurriedly she passed into the picture gallery, where pools of water showed here and there on the floor, and a cold chill ran through her whole body. At that instant her frightened ladies came running down the stairs, crying:

'Madam! madam! what has happened? The palace is disappearing under our eyes!'

'My husband will be home very soon,' answered the princess—who, though nearly as much frightened as her ladies, felt that she must set them a good example. 'Wait till then, and he will tell us what to do.'

So they waited, seated on the highest chairs they could find, wrapped in their warmest garments, and with piles of cushions under their feet, while the poor birds flew with numbed wings hither and thither, till they were so lucky as to discover an open window in some forgotten corner. Through this they vanished, and were seen no more.

At last, when the princess and her ladies had been forced to leave the upper rooms, where the walls and floors had melted away, and to take refuge in the hall, the young man came home. He had ridden back along a winding road from which he did not see the palace till he was close upon it, and stood horrified at the spectacle before him. He knew in an instant that his wife must have betrayed his trust, but he would not reproach her, as she must be suffering enough already. Hurrying on he sprang over all that was left of the palace walls, and the princess gave a cry of relief at the sight of him.

'Come quickly,' he said, 'or you will be frozen to death!' And a dreary little procession set out for the king's palace, the greyhound and the cat bringing up the rear.

At the gates he left them, though his wife besought him to allow her to enter.

'You have betrayed me and ruined me,' he said sternly; 'I go to seek my fortune alone.' And without another word he turned and left her.

With his falcon on his wrist, and his greyhound and cat behind him, the young man walked a long way, inquiring of everyone he met whether they had seen his enemy the ogre. But nobody had. Then he bade his falcon fly up into the sky—up, up, and up—and try if his sharp eyes could discover the old thief. The bird had to go so high that he did not return for some hours; but he told his master that the ogre was lying asleep in a splendid palace in a far country on the shores of the sea. This was delightful news to the young man, who instantly bought some meat for the falcon, bidding him make a good meal.

'To-morrow,' said he, 'you will fly to the palace where the ogre lies, and while he is asleep you will search all about him for a stone on which is engraved strange signs; this you will bring to me. In three days I shall expect you back here.'

'Well, I must take the cat with me,' answered the bird.

The sun had not yet risen before the falcon soared high into the air, the cat seated on his back, with his paws tightly clasping the bird's neck.

'You had better shut your eyes or you may get giddy,' said the bird; and the cat, you had never before been off the ground except to climb a tree, did as she was bid.

All that day and all that night they flew, and in the morning they saw the ogre's palace lying beneath them.

'Dear me,' said the cat, opening her eyes for the first time, 'that looks to me very like a rat city down there, let us go down to it; they may be able to help us.' So they alighted in some bushes in the heart of the rat city. The falcon remained where he was, but the cat lay down outside the principal gate, causing terrible excitement among the rats.

At length, seeing she did not move, one bolder than the rest put its head out of an upper window of the castle, and said, in a trembling voice:

'Why have you come here? What do you want? If it is anything in our power, tell us, and we will do it.'

'If you would have let me speak to you before, I would have told you that I come as a friend,' replied the cat; 'and I shall be greatly obliged if you would send four of the strongest and cunningest among you, to do me a service.'

'Oh, we shall be delighted,' answered the rat, much relieved. 'But if you will inform me what it is you wish them to do I shall be better able to judge who is most fitted for the post.'

'I thank you,' said the cat. 'Well, what they have to do is this: To-night they must burrow under the walls of the castle and go up to the room were an ogre lies asleep. Somewhere about him he has hidden a stone, on which are engraved strange signs. When they have found it they must take it from him without his waking, and bring it to me.'

'Your orders shall be obeyed,' replied the rat. And he went out to give his instructions.

About midnight the cat, who was still sleeping before the gate, was awakened by some water flung at her by the head rat, who could not make up his mind to open the doors.

'Here is the stone you wanted,' said he, when the cat started up with a loud mew; 'if you will hold up your paws I will drop it down.' And so he did. 'And now farewell,' continued the rat; 'you have a long way to go, and will do well to start before daybreak.'

'Your counsel is good,' replied the cat, smiling to itself; and putting the stone in her mouth she went off to seek the falcon.

Now all this time neither the cat nor the falcon had had any food, and the falcon soon got tired carrying such a heavy burden. When night arrived he declared he could go no further, but would spend it on the banks of a river.

'And it is my turn to take care of the stone,' said he, 'or it will seem as if you had done everything and I nothing.'

'No, I got it, and I will keep it,' answered the cat, who was tired and cross; and they began a fine quarrel. But, unluckily, in the midst of it, the cat raised her voice, and the stone fell into the ear of a big fish which happened to be swimming by, and though both the cat and the falcon sprang into the water after it, they were too late.

Half drowned, and more than half choked, the two faithful servants scrambled back to land again. The falcon flew to a tree and spread his wings in the sun to dry, but the cat, after giving herself a good shake, began to scratch up the sandy banks and to throw the bits into the stream.

'What are you doing that for?' asked a little fish. 'Do you know that you are making the water quite muddy?'

'That doesn't matter at all to me,' answered the cat. 'I am going to fill up all the river, so that the fishes may die.'

'That is very unkind, as we have never done you any harm,' replied the fish. 'Why are you so angry with us?'

'Because one of you has got a stone of mine—a stone with strange signs upon it—which dropped into the water. If you will promise to get it back for me, why, perhaps I will leave your river alone.'

'I will certainly try,' answered the fish in a great hurry; 'but you must have a little patience, as it may not be an easy task.' And in an instant his scales might be seen flashing quickly along.

The fish swam as fast as he could to the sea, which was not far distant, and calling together all his relations who lived in the neighbourhood, he told them of the terrible danger which threatened the dwellers in the river.

'None of us has got it,' said the fishes, shaking their heads; 'but in the bay yonder there is a tunny who, although he is so old, always goes everywhere. He will be able to tell you about it, if anyone can.' So the little fish swam off to the tunny, and again related his story.

'Why I was up that river only a few hours ago!' cried the tunny; 'and as I was coming back something fell into my ear, and there it is still, for I went to sleep, when I got home and forgot all about it. Perhaps it may be what you want.' And stretching up his tail he whisked out the stone.

'Yes, I think that must be it,' said the fish with joy. And taking the stone in his mouth he carried it to the place where the cat was waiting for him.

'I am much obliged to you,' said the cat, as the fish laid the stone on the sand, 'and to reward you, I will let your river alone.' And she mounted the falcon's back, and they flew to their master.

Ah, how glad he was to see them again with the magic stone in their possession. In a moment he had wished for a palace, but this time it was of green marble; and then he wished for the princess and her ladies to occupy it. And there they lived for many years, and when the old king died the princess's husband reigned in his stead.

The Story of Manus

[Adapted from Contes Berberes.]

Far away over the sea of the West there reigned a king who had two sons; and the name of the one was Oireal, and the name of the other was Iarlaid. When the boys were still children, their father and mother died, and a great council was held, and a man was chosen from among them who would rule the kingdom till the boys were old enough to rule it themselves.

The years passed on, and by-and-by another council was held, and it was agreed that the king's sons were now of an age to take the power which rightly belonged to them. So the youths were bidden to appear before the council, and Oireal the elder was smaller and weaker than his brother.

'I like not to leave the deer on the hill and the fish in the rivers, and sit in judgment on my people,' said Oireal, when he had listened to the words of the chief of the council. And the chief waxed angry, and answered quickly:

'Not one clod of earth shall ever be yours if this day you do not take on yourself the vows that were taken by the king your father.'

Then spake Iarlaid, the younger, and he said: 'Let one half be yours, and the other give to me; then you will have fewer people to rule over.'

'Yes, I will do that,' answered Oireal.

After this, one half of the men of the land of Lochlann did homage to Oireal, and the other half to Iarlaid. And they governed their kingdoms as they would, and in a few years they became grown men with beards on their chins; and Iarlaid married the daughter of the king of Greece, and Oireal the daughter of the king of Orkney. The next year sons were born to Oireal and Iarlaid; and the son of Oireal was big and strong, but the son of Iarlaid was little and weak, and each had six foster brothers who went everywhere with the princes.

One day Manus, son of Oireal, and his cousin, the son of Iarlaid, called to their foster brothers, and bade them come and play a game at shinny in the great field near the school where they were taught all that princes and nobles should know. Long they played, and swiftly did the ball pass from one to another, when Manus drove the ball at his cousin, the son of Iarlaid. The boy, who was not used to be roughly handled, even in jest, cried out that he was sorely hurt, and went home with his foster brothers and told his tale to his mother. The wife of Iarlaid grew white and angry as she listened, and thrusting her son aside, sought the council hall where Iarlaid was sitting.

'Manus has driven a ball at my son, and fain would have slain him,' said she. 'Let an end be put to him and his ill deeds.'

But Iarlaid answered:

'Nay, I will not slay the son of my brother.'

'And he shall not slay my son,' said the queen. And calling to her chamberlain she ordered him to lead the prince to the four brown boundaries of the world, and to leave him there with a wise man, who would care for him, and let no harm befall him. And the wise man set the boy on the top of a hill where the sun always shone, and he could see every man, but no man could see him.

Then she summoned Manus to the castle, and for a whole year she kept him fast, and his own mother could not get speech of him. But in the end, when the wife of Oireal fell sick, Manus fled from the tower which was his prison, and stole back to his on home.

For a few years he stayed there in peace, and then the wife of Iarlaid his uncle sent for him.

'It is time that you were married,' she said, when she saw that Manus had grown tall and strong like unto Iarlaid. 'Tall and strong you are, and comely of face. I know a bride that will suit you well, and that is the daughter of the mighty earl of Finghaidh, that does homage for his lands to me. I myself will go with a great following to his house, and you shall go with me.'

Thus it was done; and though the earl's wife was eager to keep her daughter with her yet a while, she was fain to yield, as the wife of Iarlaid vowed that not a rood of land should the earl have, unless he did her bidding. But if he would give his daughter to Manus, she would bestow on him the third part of her own kingdom, with much treasure beside. This she did, not from love to Manus, but because she wished to destroy him. So they were married, and rode back with the wife of Iarlaid to her own palace. And that night, while he was sleeping, there came a wise man, who was his father's friend, and awoke him saying: 'Danger lies very close to you, Manus, son of Oireal. You hold yourself favoured because you have as a bride the daughter of a mighty earl; but do you know what bride the wife of Iarlaid sought for her own son? It was no worldly wife she found for him, but the swift March wind, and never can you prevail against her.'

'Is it thus?' answered Manu. And at the first streak of dawn he went to the chamber where the queen lay in the midst of her maidens.

'I have come,' he said, 'for the third part of the kingdom, and for the treasure which you promised me.' But the wife of Iarlaid laughed as she heard him.

'Not a clod shall you have here,' spake she. 'You must go to the Old Bergen for that. Mayhap under its stones and rough mountains you may find a treasure!'

'Then give me your son's six foster brothers as well as my own,' answered he. And the queen gave them to him, and they set out for Old Bergen.

A year passed by, and found them still in that wild land, hunting the reindeer, and digging pits for the mountain sheep to fall into. For a time Manus and his companions lived merrily, but at length Manus grew weary of the strange country, and they all took ship for the land of Lochlann. The wind was fierce and cold, and long was the voyage; but, one spring day, they sailed into the harbour that lay beneath the castle of Iarlaid. The queen looked from her window and beheld him mounting the hill, with the twelve foster brothers behind him. Then she said to her husband: 'Manus has returned with his twelve foster brothers. Would that I could put an end to him and his murdering and his slaying.'

'That were a great pity,' answered Iarlaid. 'And it is not I that will do it.'

'If you will not do it I will,' said she. And she called the twelve foster brothers and made them vow fealty to herself. So Manus was left with no man, and sorrowful was he when he returned alone to Old Bergen. It was late when his foot touched the shore, and took the path towards the forest. On his way there met him a man in a red tunic.

'Is it you, Manus, come back again?' asked he.

'It is I,' answered Manus; 'alone have I returned from the land of Lochlann.'

The man eyed him silently for a moment, and then he said:

'I dreamed that you were girt with a sword and became king of Lochlann.' But Manus answered:

'I have no sword and my bow is broken.'

'I will give you a new sword if you will make me a promise,' said the man once more.

'To be sure I will make it, if ever I am king,' answered Manus. 'But speak, and tell me what promise I am to make.'

'I was your grandfather's armourer,' replied the man, 'and I wish to be your armourer also.'

'That I will promise readily,' said Manus; and followed the man into his house, which was at a little distance. But the house was not like other houses, for the walls of every room were hung so thick with arms that you could not see the boards.

'Choose what you will,' said the man; and Manus unhooked a sword and tried it across his knee, and it broke, and so did the next, and the next.

'Leave off breaking the swords,' cried the man, 'and look at this old sword and helmet and tunic that I wore in the wars of your grandfather. Perhaps you may find them of stouter steel.' And Manus bent the sword thrice across his knee but he could not break it. So he girded it to his side, and put on the old helmet. As he fastened the strap his eye fell on a cloth flapping outside the window.

'What cloth is that?' asked he.

'It is a cloth that was woven by the Little People of the forest,' said the man; 'and when you are hungry it will give you food and drink, and if you meet a foe, he will not hurt you, but will stoop and kiss the back of your hand in token of submission. Take it, and use it well.' Manus gladly wrapped the shawl round his arm, and was leaving the house, when he heard the rattling of a chain blown by the wind.

'What chain is that?' asked he.

'The creature who has that chain round his neck, need not fear a hundred enemies,' answered the armourer. And Manus wound it round him and passed on into the forest.

Suddenly there sprang out from the bushes two lions, and a lion cub with them. The fierce beasts bounded towards him, roaring loudly, and would fain have eaten him, but quickly Manus stooped and spread the cloth upon the ground. At that the lions stopped, and bowing their great heads, kissed the back of his wrist and went their ways. But the cub rolled itself up in the cloth; so Manus picked them both up, and carried them with him to Old Bergen.

Another year went by, and then he took the lion cub and set forth to the land of Lochlann. And the wife of Iarlaid came to meet him, and a brown dog, small but full of courage, came with her. When the dog beheld the lion cub he rushed towards him, thinking to eat him; but the cub caught the dog by the neck, and shook him, and he was dead. And the wife of Iarlaid mourned him sore, and her wrath was kindled, and many times she tried to slay Manus and his cub, but she could not. And at last they two went back to Old Bergen, and the twelve foster brothers went also.

'Let them go,' said the wife of Iarlaid, when she heard of it. 'My brother the Red Gruagach will take the head off Manus as well in Old Bergen as elsewhere.'

Now these words were carried by a messenger to the wife of Oireal, and she made haste and sent a ship to Old Bergen to bear away her son before the Red Gruagach should take the head off him. And in the ship was a pilot. But the wife of Iarlaid made a thick fog to cover the face of the sea, and the rowers could not row, lest they should drive the ship on to a rock. And when night came, the lion cub, whose eyes were bright and keen, stole up to Manus, and Manus got on his back, and the lion cub sprang ashore and bade Manus rest on the rock and wait for him. So Manus slept, and by-and-by a voice sounded in his ears, saying: 'Arise!' And he saw a ship in the water beneath him, and in the ship sat the lion cup in the shape of the pilot.

Then they sailed away through the fog, and none saw them; and they reached the land of Lochlann, and the lion cub with the chain round his neck sprang from the ship and Manus followed after. And the lion cub killed all the men that guarded the castle, and Iarlaid and his wife also, so that, in the end, Manus son of Oireal was crowned king of Lochlann.

Pinkel the Thief

[Shortened from West Highland Tales.]

Long, long ago there lived a widow who had three sons. The two eldest were grown up, and though they were known to be idle fellows, some of the neighbours had given them work to do on account of the respect in which their mother was held. But at the time this story begins they had both been so careless and idle that their masters declared they would keep them no longer.

So home they went to their mother and youngest brother, of whom they thought little, because he made himself useful about the house, and looked after the hens, and milked the cow. 'Pinkel,' they called him in scorn, and by-and-by 'Pinkel' became his name throughout the village.

The two young men thought it was much nicer to live at home and be idle than to be obliged to do a quantity of disagreeable things they did not like, and they would have stayed by the fire till the end of their lives had not the widow lost patience with them and said that since they would not look for work at home they must seek it elsewhere, for she would not have them under her roof any longer. But she repented bitterly of her words when Pinkel told her that he too was old enough to go out into the world, and that when he had made a fortune he would send for his mother to keep house for him.

The widow wept many tears at parting from her youngest son, but as she saw that his heart was set upon going with his brothers, she did not try to keep him. So the young men started off one morning in high spirits, never doubting that work such as they might be willing to do would be had for the asking, as soon as their little store of money was spent.

But a very few days of wandering opened their eyes. Nobody seemed to want them, or, if they did, the young men declared that they were not able to undertake all that the farmers or millers or woodcutters required of them. The youngest brother, who was wiser, would gladly have done some of the work that the others refused, but he was small and slight, and no one thought of offering him any. Therefore they went from one place to another, living only on the fruit and nuts they could find in the woods, and getting hungrier every day.

One night, after they had been walking for many hours and were very tired, they came to a large lake with an island in the middle of it. From the island streamed a strong light, by which they could see everything almost as clearly as if the sun had been shining, and they perceived that, lying half hidden in the rushes, was a boat.

'Let us take it and row over to the island, where there must be a house,' said the eldest brother; 'and perhaps they will give us food and shelter.' And they all got in and rowed across in the direction of the light. As they drew near the island they saw that it came from a golden lantern hanging over the door of a hut, while sweet tinkling music proceeded from some bells attached to the golden horns of a goat which was feeding near the cottage. The young men's hearts rejoiced as they thought that at last they would be able to rest their weary limbs, and they entered the hut, but were amazed to see an ugly old woman inside, wrapped in a cloak of gold which lighted up the whole house. They looked at each other uneasily as she came forward with her daughter, as they knew by the cloak that this was a famous witch.

'What do you want?' asked she, at the same time signing to her daughter to stir the large pot on the fire.

'We are tired and hungry, and would fain have shelter for the night,' answered the eldest brother.

'You cannot get it here,' said the witch, 'but you will find both food and shelter in the palace on the other side of the lake. Take your boat and go; but leave this boy with me—I can find work for him, though something tells me he is quick and cunning, and will do me ill.'

'What harm can a poor boy like me do a great Troll like you?' answered Pinkel. 'Let me go, I pray you, with my brothers. I will promise never to hurt you.' And at last the witch let him go, and he followed his brothers to the boat.

The way was further than they thought, and it was morning before they reached the palace.

Now, at last, their luck seemed to have turned, for while the two eldest were given places in the king's stables, Pinkel was taken as page to the little prince. He was a clever and amusing boy, who saw everything that passed under his eyes, and the king noticed this, and often employed him in his own service, which made his brothers very jealous.

Things went on this way for some time, and Pinkel every day rose in the royal favour. At length the envy of his brothers became so great that they could bear it no longer, and consulted together how best they might ruin his credit with the king. They did not wish to kill him—though, perhaps, they would not have been sorry if they had heard he was dead—but merely wished to remind him that he was after all only a child, not half so old and wise as they.

Their opportunity soon came. It happened to be the king's custom to visit his stables once a week, so that he might see that his horses were being properly cared for. The next time he entered the stables the two brothers managed to be in the way, and when the king praised the beautiful satin skins of the horses under their charge, and remarked how different was their condition when his grooms had first come across the lake, the young men at once began to speak of the wonderful light which sprang from the lantern over the hut. The king, who had a passion for collection all the rarest things he could find, fell into the trap directly, and inquired where he could get this marvellous lantern.

'Send Pinkel for it, Sire,' said they. 'It belongs to an old witch, who no doubt came by it in some evil way. But Pinkel has a smooth tongue, and he can get the better of any woman, old or young.'

'Then bid him go this very night,' cried the king; 'and if he brings me the lantern I will make him one of the chief men about my person.'

Pinkel was much pleased at the thought of his adventure, and without more ado he borrowed a little boat which lay moored to the shore, and rowed over to the island at once. It was late by the time he arrived, and almost dark, but he knew by the savoury smell that reached him that the witch was cooking her supper. So he climbed softly on to the roof, and, peering, watched till the old woman's back was turned, when he quickly drew a handful of salt from his pocket and threw it into the pot. Scarcely had he done this when the witch called her daughter and bade her lift the pot off the fire and put the stew into a dish, as it had been cooking quite long enough and she was hungry. But no sooner had she tasted it than she put her spoon down, and declared that her daughter must have been meddling with it, for it was impossible to eat anything that was all made of salt.

'Go down to the spring in the valley, and get some fresh water, that I may prepare a fresh supper,' cried she, 'for I feel half-starved.'

'But, mother,' answered the girl, 'how can I find the well in this darkness? For you know that the lantern's rays shed no light down there.'

'Well, then, take the lantern with you,' answered the witch, 'for supper I must have, and there is no water that is nearer.'

So the girl took her pail in one hand and the golden lantern in the other, and hastened away to the well, followed by Pinkel, who took care to keep out of the way of the rays. When at last she stooped to fill her pail at the well Pinkel pushed her into it, and snatching up the lantern hurried back to his boat and rowed off from the shore.

He was already a long distance from the island when the witch, who wondered what had become of her daughter, went to the door to look for her. Close around the hut was thick darkness, but what was that bobbing light that streamed across the water? The witch's heart sank as all at once it flashed upon her what had happened.

'Is that you, Pinkel?' cried she; and the youth answered:

'Yes, dear mother, it is I!'

'And are you not a knave for robbing me?' said she.

'Truly, dear mother, I am,' replied Pinkel, rowing faster than ever, for he was half afraid that the witch might come after him. But she had no power on the water, and turned angrily into the hut, muttering to herself all the while:

'Take care! take care! A second time you will not escape so easily!'

The sun had not yet risen when Pinkel returned to the palace, and, entering the king's chamber, he held up the lantern so that its rays might fall upon the bed. In an instant the king awoke, and seeing the golden lantern shedding its light upon him, he sprang up, and embraced Pinkel with joy.

'O cunning one,' cried he, 'what treasure hast thou brought me!' And calling for his attendants he ordered that rooms next his own should be prepared for Pinkel, and that the youth might enter his presence at any hour. And besides this, he was to have a seat on the council.

It may easily be guessed that all this made the brothers more envious than they were before; and they cast about in their minds afresh how best they might destroy him. At length they remembered the goat with golden horns and the bells, and they rejoiced; 'For,' said they, 'THIS time the old woman will be on the watch, and let him be as clever as he likes, the bells on the horns are sure to warn her.' So when, as before, the king came down to the stables and praised the cleverness of their brother, the young men told him of that other marvel possessed by the witch, the goat with the golden horns.

From this moment the king never closed his eyes at night for longing after this wonderful creature. He understood something of the danger that there might be in trying to steal it, now that the witch's suspicions were aroused, and he spent hours in making plans for outwitting her. But somehow he never could think of anything that would do, and at last, as the brothers had foreseen, he sent for Pinkel.

'I hear,' he said, 'that the old witch on the island has a goat with golden horns from which hang bells that tinkle the sweetest music. That goat I must have! But, tell me, how am I to get it? I would give the third part of my kingdom to anyone who would bring it to me.'

'I will fetch it myself,' answered Pinkel.

This time it was easier for Pinkel to approach the island unseen, as there was no golden lantern to thrown its beams over the water. But, on the other hand, the goat slept inside the hut, and would therefore have to be taken from under the very eyes of the old woman. How was he to do it? All the way across the lake he thought and thought, till at length a plan came into his head which seemed as if it might do, though he knew it would be very difficult to carry out.

The first thing he did when he reached the shore was to look about for a piece of wood, and when he had found it he hid himself close to the hut, till it grew quite dark and near the hour when the witch and her daughter went to bed. Then he crept up and fixed the wood under the door, which opened outwards, in such a manner that the more you tried to shut it the more firmly it stuck. And this was what happened when the girl went as usual to bolt the door and make all fast for the night.

'What are you doing?' asked the witch, as her daughter kept tugging at the handle.

'There is something the matter with the door; it won't shut,' answered she.

'Well, leave it alone; there is nobody to hurt us,' said the witch, who was very sleepy; and the girl did as she was bid, and went to bed. Very soon they both might have been heard snoring, and Pinkel knew that his time was come. Slipping off his shoes he stole into the hut on tiptoe, and taking from his pocket some food of which the goat was particularly fond, he laid it under his nose. Then, while the animal was eating it, he stuffed each golden bell with wool which he had also brought with him, stopping every minute to listen, lest the witch should awaken, and he should find himself changed into some dreadful bird or beast. But the snoring still continued, and he went on with his work as quickly as he could. When the last bell was done he drew another handful of food out of his pocket, and held it out to the goat, which instantly rose to its feet and followed Pinkel, who backed slowly to the door, and directly he got outside he seized the goat in his arms and ran down to the place where he had moored his boat.

As soon as he had reached the middle of the lake, Pinkel took the wool out of the bells, which began to tinkle loudly. Their sound awoke the witch, who cried out as before:

'Is that you, Pinkel?'

'Yes, dear mother, it is I,' said Pinkel.

'Have you stolen my golden goat?' asked she.

'Yes, dear mother, I have,' answered Pinkel.

'Are you not a knave, Pinkel?'

'Yes, dear mother, I am,' he replied. And the old witch shouted in a rage:

'Ah! beware how you come hither again, for next time you shall not escape me!'

But Pinkel laughed and rowed on.

The king was so delighted with the goat that he always kept it by his side, night and day; and, as he had promised, Pinkel was made ruler over the third part of the kingdom. As may be supposed, the brothers were more furious than ever, and grew quite thin with rage.

'How can we get rid of him?' said one to the other. And at length they remembered the golden cloak.

'He will need to be clever if he is to steal that!' they cried, with a chuckle. And when next the king came to see his horses they began to speak of Pinkel and his marvellous cunning, and how he had contrived to steal the lantern and the goat, which nobody else would have been able to do.

'But as he was there, it is a pity he could not have brought away the golden cloak,' added they.

'The golden cloak! what is that?' asked the king. And the young men described its beauties in such glowing words that the king declared he should never know a day's happiness till he had wrapped the cloak round his own shoulders.

'And,' added he, 'the man who brings it to me shall wed my daughter, and shall inherit my throne.'

'None can get it save Pinkel,' said they; for they did not imagine that the witch, after two warnings, could allow their brother to escape a third time. So Pinkel was sent for, and with a glad heart he set out.

He passed many hours inventing first one plan and then another, till he had a scheme ready which he thought might prove successful.

Thrusting a large bag inside his coat, he pushed off from the shore, taking care this time to reach the island in daylight. Having made his boat fast to a tree, he walked up to the hut, hanging his head, and putting on a face that was both sorrowful and ashamed.

'Is that you, Pinkel?' asked the witch when she saw him, her eyes gleaming savagely.

'Yes, dear mother, it is I,' answered Pinkel.

'So you have dared, after all you have done, to put yourself in my power!' cried she. 'Well, you sha'n't escape me THIS time!' And she took down a large knife and began to sharpen it.'

'Oh! dear mother, spare me!' shrieked Pinkel, falling on his knees, and looking wildly about him.

'Spare you, indeed, you thief! Where are my lantern and my goat? No! not! there is only one fate for robbers!' And she brandished the knife in the air so that it glittered in the firelight.

'Then, if I must die,' said Pinkel, who, by this time, was getting really rather frightened, 'let me at least choose the manner of my death. I am very hungry, for I have had nothing to eat all day. Put some poison, if you like, into the porridge, but at least let me have a good meal before I die.'

'That is not a bad idea,' answered the woman; 'as long as you do die, it is all one to me.' And ladling out a large bowl of porridge, she stirred some poisonous herbs into it, and set about work that had to be done. Then Pinkel hastily poured all the contents of the bowl into his bag, and make a great noise with his spoon, as if he was scraping up the last morsel.

'Poisoned or not, the porridge is excellent. I have eaten it, every scrap; do give me some more,' said Pinkel, turning towards her.

'Well, you have a fine appetite, young man,' answered the witch; 'however, it is the last time you will ever eat it, so I will give you another bowlful.' And rubbing in the poisonous herbs, she poured him out half of what remained, and then went to the window to call her cat.

In an instant Pinkel again emptied the porridge into the bag, and the next minute he rolled on the floor, twisting himself about as if in agony, uttering loud groans the while. Suddenly he grew silent and lay still.

'Ah! I thought a second dose of that poison would be too much for you,' said the witch looking at him. 'I warned you what would happen if you came back. I wish that all thieves were as dead as you! But why does not my lazy girl bring the wood I sent her for, it will soon be too dark for her to find her way? I suppose I must go and search for her. What a trouble girls are!' And she went to the door to watch if there were any signs of her daughter. But nothing could be seen of her, and heavy rain was falling.

'It is no night for my cloak,' she muttered; 'it would be covered with mud by the time I got back.' So she took it off her shoulders and hung it carefully up in a cupboard in the room. After that she put on her clogs and started to seek her daughter. Directly the last sound of the clogs had ceased, Pinkel jumped up and took down the cloak, and rowed off as fast as he could.

He had not gone far when a puff of wind unfolded the cloak, and its brightness shed gleams across the water. The witch, who was just entering the forest, turned round at that moment and saw the golden rays. She forgot all about her daughter, and ran down to the shore, screaming with rage at being outwitted a third time.

'Is that you, Pinkel?' cried she.

'Yes, dear mother, it is I.'

'Have you taken my gold cloak?'

'Yes, dear mother, I have.'

'Are you not a great knave?'

'Yes, truly dear mother, I am.'

And so indeed he was!

But, all the same, he carried the cloak to the king's palace, and in return he received the hand of the king's daughter in marriage. People said that it was the bride who ought to have worn the cloak at her wedding feast; but the king was so pleased with it that he would not part from it; and to the end of his life was never seen without it. After his death, Pinkel became king; and let up hope that he gave up his bad and thievish ways, and ruled his subjects well. As for his brothers, he did not punish them, but left them in the stables, where they grumbled all day long.

The Adventures of a Jackal

[Thorpe's Yule-Tide Stories.]

In a country which is full of wild beasts of all sorts there once lived a jackal and a hedgehog, and, unlike though they were, the two animals made great friends, and were often seen in each other's company.

One afternoon they were walking along a road together, when the jackal, who was the taller of the two, exclaimed:

'Oh! there is a barn full of corn; let us go and eat some.'

'Yes, do let us!' answered the hedgehog. So they went to the barn, and ate till they could eat no more. Then the jackal put on his shoes, which he had taken off so as to make no noise, and they returned to the high road.

After they had gone some way they met a panther, who stopped, and bowing politely, said:

'Excuse my speaking to you, but I cannot help admiring those shoes of yours. Do you mind telling me who made them?'

'Yes, I think they are rather nice,' answered the jackal; 'I made them myself, though.'

'Could you make me a pair like them?' asked the panther eagerly.

'I would do my best, of course,' replied the jackal; 'but you must kill me a cow, and when we have eaten the flesh I will take the skin and make your shoes out of it.'

So the panther prowled about until he saw a fine cow grazing apart from the rest of the herd. He killed it instantly, and then gave a cry to the jackal and hedgehog to come to the place where he was. They soon skinned the dead beasts, and spread its skin out to dry, after which they had a grand feast before they curled themselves up for the night, and slept soundly.

Next morning the jackal got up early and set to work upon the shoes, while the panther sat by and looked on with delight. At last they were finished, and the jackal arose and stretched himself.

'Now go and lay them in the sun out there,' said he; 'in a couple of hours they will be ready to put on; but do not attempt to wear them before, or you will feel them most uncomfortable. But I see the sun is high in the heavens, and we must be continuing our journey.'

The panther, who always believed what everybody told him, did exactly as he was bid, and in two hours' time began to fasten on the shoes. They certainly set off his paws wonderfully, and he stretched out his forepaws and looked at them with pride. But when he tried to walk—ah! that was another story! They were so stiff and hard that he nearly shrieked every step he took, and at last he sank down where he was, and actually began to cry.

After some time some little partridges who were hopping about heard the poor panther's groans, and went up to see what was the matter. He had never tried to make his dinner off them, and they had always been quite friendly.

'You seem in pain,' said one of them, fluttering close to him, 'can we help you?'

'Oh, it is the jackal! He made me these shoes; they are so hard and tight that they hurt my feet, and I cannot manage to kick them off.'

'Lie still, and we will soften them,' answered the kind little partridge. And calling to his brothers, they all flew to the nearest spring, and carried water in their beaks, which they poured over the shoes. This they did till the hard leather grew soft, and the panther was able to slip his feet out of them.

'Oh, thank you, thank you,' he cried, skipping round with joy. 'I feel a different creature. Now I will go after the jackal and pay him my debts.' And he bounded away into the forest.

But the jackal had been very cunning, and had trotted backwards and forwards and in and out, so that it was very difficult to know which track he had really followed. At length, however, the panther caught sight of his enemy, at the same moment that the jackal had caught sight of him. The panther gave a loud roar, and sprang forward, but the jackal was too quick for him and plunged into a dense thicket, where the panther could not follow.

Disgusted with his failure, but more angry than ever, the panther lay down for a while to consider what he should do next, and as he was thinking, an old man came by.

'Oh! father, tell me how I can repay the jackal for the way he has served me!' And without more ado he told his story.

'If you take my advice,' answered the old man, 'you will kill a cow, and invite all the jackals in the forest to the feast. Watch them carefully while they are eating, and you will see that most of them keep their eyes on their food. But if one of them glances at you, you will know that is the traitor.'

The panther, whose manners were always good, thanked the old man, and followed his counsel. The cow was killed, and the partridges flew about with invitations to the jackals, who gathered in large numbers to the feast. The wicked jackal came amongst them; but as the panther had only seen him once he could not distinguish him from the rest. However, they all took their places on wooden seats placed round the dead cow, which was laid across the boughs of a fallen tree, and began their dinner, each jackal fixing his eyes greedily on the piece of meat before him. Only one of them seemed uneasy, and every now and then glanced in the direction of his host. This the panther noticed, and suddenly made a bound at the culprit and seized his tail; but again the jackal was too quick for him, and catching up a knife he cut off his tail and darted into the forest, followed by all the rest of the party. And before the panther had recovered from his surprise he found himself alone.

'What am I to do now?' he asked the old man, who soon came back to see how things had turned out.

'It is very unfortunate, certainly,' answered he; 'but I think I know where you can find him. There is a melon garden about two miles from here, and as jackals are very fond of melons they are nearly sure to have gone there to feed. If you see a tailless jackal you will know that he is the one you want.' So the panther thanked him and went his way.

Now the jackal had guessed what advice the old man would give his enemy, and so, while his friends were greedily eating the ripest melons in the sunniest corner of the garden, he stole behind them and tied their tails together. He had only just finished when his ears caught the sound of breaking branches; and he cried: 'Quick! quick! here comes the master of the garden!' And the jackals sprang up and ran away in all directions, leaving their tails behind them. And how was the panther to know which was his enemy?

'They none of them had any tails,' he said sadly to the old man, 'and I am tired of hunting them. I shall leave them alone and go and catch something for supper.'

Of course the hedgehog had not been able to take part in any of these adventures; but as soon as all danger was over, the jackal went to look for his friend, whom he was lucky enough to find at home.

'Ah, there you are,' he said gaily. 'I have lost my tail since I saw you last. And other people have lost theirs too; but that is no matter! I am hungry, so come with me to the shepherd who is sitting over there, and we will ask him to sell us one of his sheep.'

'Yes, that is a good plan,' answered the hedgehog. And he walked as fast as his little legs would go to keep up with the jackal. When they reached the shepherd the jackal pulled out his purse from under his foreleg, and made his bargain.

'Only wait till to-morrow,' said the shepherd, 'and I will give you the biggest sheep you ever saw. But he always feeds at some distance from the rest of the flock, and it would take me a long time to catch him.'

'Well, it is very tiresome, but I suppose I must wait,' replied the jackal. And he and the hedgehog looked about for a nice dry cave in which to make themselves comfortable for the night. But, after they had gone, the shepherd killed one of his sheep, and stripped off his skin, which he sewed tightly round a greyhound he had with him, and put a cord round its neck. Then he lay down and went to sleep.

Very, very early, before the sun was properly up, the jackal and the hedgehog were pulling at the shepherd's cloak.

'Wake up,' they said, 'and give us that sheep. We have had nothing to eat all night, and are very hungry.'

The shepherd yawned and rubbed his eyes. 'He is tied up to that tree; go and take him.' So they went to the tree and unfastened the cord, and turned to go back to the cave where they had slept, dragging the greyhound after them. When they reached the cave the jackal said to the hedgehog.

'Before I kill him let me see whether he is fat or thin.' And he stood a little way back, so that he might the better examine the animal. After looking at him, with his head on one side, for a minute or two, he nodded gravely.

'He is quite fat enough; he is a good sheep.'

But the hedgehog, who sometimes showed more cunning than anyone would have guessed, answered:

'My friend, you are talking nonsense. The wool is indeed a sheep's wool, but the paws of my uncle the greyhound peep out from underneath.'

'He is a sheep,' repeated the jackal, who did not like to think anyone cleverer than himself.

'Hold the cord while I look at him,' answered the hedgehog.

Very unwillingly the jackal held the rope, while the hedgehog walked slowly round the greyhound till he reached the jackal again. He knew quite well by the paws and tail that it was a greyhound and not a sheep, that the shepherd had sold them; and as he could not tell what turn affairs might take, he resolved to get out of the way.

'Oh! yes, you are right,' he said to the jackal; 'but I never can eat till I have first drunk. I will just go and quench my thirst from that spring at the edge of the wood, and then I shall be ready for breakfast.'

'Don't be long, then,' called the jackal, as the hedgehog hurried off at his best pace. And he lay down under a rock to wait for him.

More than an hour passed by and the hedgehog had had plenty of time to go to the spring and back, and still there was no sign of him. And this was very natural, as he had hidden himself in some long grass under a tree!

At length the jackal guessed that for some reason his friend had run away, and determined to wait for his breakfast no longer. So he went up to the place where the greyhound had been tethered and untied the rope. But just as he was about to spring on his back and give him a deadly bite, the jackal heard a low growl, which never proceeded from the throat of any sheep. Like a flash of lightning the jackal threw down the cord and was flying across the plain; but though his legs were long, the greyhound's legs were longer still, and he soon came up with his prey. The jackal turned to fight, but he was no match for the greyhound, and in a few minutes he was lying dead on the ground, while the greyhound was trotting peacefully back to the shepherd.

The Adventures of the Jackal's Eldest Son

[Nouveaux Contes Berberes, par Rene Basset.]

Now, though the jackal was dead, he had left two sons behind him, every whit as cunning and tricky as their father. The elder of the two was a fine handsome creature, who had a pleasant manner and made many friends. The animal he saw most of was a hyena; and one day, when they were taking a walk together, they picked up a beautiful green cloak, which had evidently been dropped by some one riding across the plain on a camel. Of course each wanted to have it, and they almost quarrelled over the matter; but at length it was settled that the hyena should wear the cloak by day and the jackal by night. After a little while, however, the jackal became discontented with this arrangement, declaring that none of his friends, who were quite different from those of the hyena, could see the splendour of the mantle, and that it was only fair that he should sometimes be allowed to wear it by day. To this the hyena would by no means consent, and they were on the eve of a quarrel when the hyena proposed that they should ask the lion to judge between them. The jackal agreed to this, and the hyena wrapped the cloak about him, and they both trotted off to the lion's den.

The jackal, who was fond of talking, at once told the story; and when it was finished the lion turned to the hyena and asked if it was true.

'Quite true, your majesty,' answered the hyena.

'Then lay the cloak on the ground at my feet,' said the lion, 'and I will give my judgment.' So the mantle was spread upon the red earth, the hyena and the jackal standing on each side of it.

There was silence for a few moments, and then the lion sat up, looking very great and wise.

'My judgment is that the garment shall belong wholly to whoever first rings the bell of the nearest mosque at dawn to-morrow. Now go; for much business awaits me!'

All that night the hyena sat up, fearing lest the jackal should reach the bell before him, for the mosque was close at hand. With the first streak of dawn he bounded away to the bell, just as the jackal, who had slept soundly all night, was rising to his feet.

'Good luck to you,' cried the jackal. And throwing the cloak over his back he darted away across the plain, and was seen no more by his friend the hyena.

After running several miles the jackal thought he was safe from pursuit, and seeing a lion and another hyena talking together, he strolled up to join them.

'Good morning,' he said; 'may I ask what is the matter? You seem very serious about something.'

'Pray sit down,' answered the lion. 'We were wondering in which direction we should go to find the best dinner. The hyena wishes to go to the forest, and I to the mountains. What do you say?'

'Well, as I was sauntering over the plain, just now, I noticed a flock of sheep grazing, and some of them had wandered into a little valley quite out of sight of the shepherd. If you keep among the rocks you will never be observed. But perhaps you will allow me to go with you and show you the way?'

'You are really very kind,' answered the lion. And they crept steadily along till at length they reached the mouth of the valley where a ram, a sheep and a lamb were feeding on the rich grass, unconscious of their danger.

'How shall we divide them?' asked the lion in a whisper to the hyena.

'Oh, it is easily done,' replied the hyena. 'The lamb for me, the sheep for the jackal, and the ram for the lion.'

'So I am to have that lean creature, which is nothing but horns, am I?' cried the lion in a rage. 'I will teach you to divide things in that manner!' And he gave the hyena two great blows, which stretched him dead in a moment. Then he turned to the jackal and said: 'How would you divide them?'

'Quite differently from the hyena,' replied the jackal. 'You will breakfast off the lamb, you will dine off the sheep, and you will sup off the ram.'

'Dear me, how clever you are! Who taught you such wisdom?' exclaimed the lion, looking at him admiringly.

'The fate of the hyena,' answered the jackal, laughing, and running off at his best speed; for he saw two men armed with spears coming close behind the lion!

The jackal continued to run till at last he could run no longer. He flung himself under a tree panting for breath, when he heard a rustle amongst the grass, and his father's old friend the hedgehog appeared before him.

'Oh, is it you?' asked the little creature; 'how strange that we should meet so far from home!'

'I have just had a narrow escape of my life,' gasped the jackal, 'and I need some sleep. After that we must think of something to do to amuse ourselves.' And he lay down again and slept soundly for a couple of hours.

'Now I am ready,' said he; 'have you anything to propose?'

'In a valley beyond those trees,' answered the hedgehog, 'there is a small farmhouse where the best butter in the world is made. I know their ways, and in an hour's time the farmer's wife will be off to milk the cows, which she keeps at some distance. We could easily get in at the window of the shed where she keeps the butter, and I will watch, lest some one should come unexpectedly, while you have a good meal. Then you shall watch, and I will eat.'

'That sounds a good plan,' replied the jackal; and they set off together.

But when they reached the farmhouse the jackal said to the hedgehog: 'Go in and fetch the pots of butter and I will hide them in a safe place.'

'Oh no,' cried the hedgehog, 'I really couldn't. They would find out directly! And, besides, it is so different just eating a little now and then.'

'Do as I bid you at once,' said the jackal, looking at the hedgehog so sternly that the little fellow dared say no more, and soon rolled the jars to the window where the jackal lifted them out one by one.

When they were all in a row before him he gave a sudden start.

'Run for your life,' he whispered to his companion; 'I see the woman coming over the hill!' And the hedgehog, his heart beating, set off as fast as he could. The jackal remained where he was, shaking with laughter, for the woman was not in sight at all, and he had only sent the hedgehog away because he did not want him to know where the jars of butter were buried. But every day he stole out to their hiding-place and had a delicious feast.

At length, one morning, the hedgehog suddenly said:

'You never told me what you did with those jars?'

'Oh, I hid them safely till the farm people should have forgotten all about them,' replied the jackal. 'But as they are still searching for them we must wait a little longer, and then I'll bring them home, and we will share them between us.'

So the hedgehog waited and waited; but every time he asked if there was no chance of getting jars of butter the jackal put him off with some excuse. After a while the hedgehog became suspicious, and said:

'I should like to know where you have hidden them. To-night, when it is quite dark, you shall show me the place.'

'I really can't tell you,' answered the jackal. 'You talk so much that you would be sure to confide the secret to somebody, and then we should have had our trouble for nothing, besides running the risk of our necks being broken by the farmer. I can see that he is getting disheartened, and very soon he will give up the search. Have patience just a little longer.'

The hedgehop said no more, and pretended to be satisfied; but when some days had gone by he woke the jackal, who was sleeping soundly after a hunt which had lasted several hours.

'I have just had notice,' remarked the hedgehog, shaking him, 'that my family wish to have a banquet to-morrow, and they have invited you to it. Will you come?'

'Certainly,' answered the jackal, 'with pleasure. But as I have to go out in the morning you can meet me on the road.'

'That will do very well,' replied the hedgehog. And the jackal went to sleep again, for he was obliged to be up early.

Punctual to the moment the hedgehog arrived at the place appointed for their meeting, and as the jackal was not there he sat down and waited for him.

'Ah, there you are!' he cried, when the dusky yellow form at last turned the corner. 'I had nearly given you up! Indeed, I almost wish you had not come, for I hardly know where I shall hide you.'

'Why should you hide me anywhere?' asked the jackal. 'What is the matter with you?'

'Well, so many of the guests have brought their dogs and mules with them, that I fear it may hardly be safe for you to go amongst them. No; don't run off that way,' he added quickly, 'because there is another troop that are coming over the hill. Lie down here, and I will throw these sacks over you; and keep still for your life, whatever happens.'

And what did happen was, that when the jackal was lying covered up, under a little hill, the hedgehog set a great stone rolling, which crushed him to death.

The Adventures of the Younger Son of the Jackal

[Contes Berberes.]

Now that the father and elder brother were both dead, all that was left of the jackal family was one son, who was no less cunning than the others had been. He did not like staying in the same place any better than they, and nobody ever knew in what part of the country he might be found next.

One day, when we was wandering about he beheld a nice fat sheep, which was cropping the grass and seemed quite contented with her lot.

'Good morning,' said the jackal, 'I am so glad to see you. I have been looking for you everywhere.'

'For ME?' answered the sheep, in an astonished voice; 'but we have never met before!'

'No; but I have heard of you. Oh! You don't know what fine things I have heard! Ah, well, some people have all the luck!'

'You are very kind, I am sure,' answered the sheep, not knowing which way to look. 'Is there any way in which I can help you?'

'There is something that I had set my heart on, though I hardly like to propose it on so short an acquaintance; but from what people have told me, I thought that you and I might keep house together comfortably, if you would only agree to try. I have several fields belonging to me, and if they are kept well watered they bear wonderful crops.'

'Perhaps I might come for a short time,' said the sheep, with a little hesitation; 'and if we do not get on, we can part company.'

'Oh, thank you, thank you,' cried the jackal; 'do not let us lose a moment.' And he held out his paw in such an inviting manner that the sheep got up and trotted beside him till they reached home.

'Now,' said the jackal, 'you go to the well and fetch the water, and I will pour it into the trenches that run between the patches of corn.' And as he did so he sang lustily. The work was very hard, but the sheep did not grumble, and by-and-by was rewarded at seeing the little green heads poking themselves through earth. After that the hot sun ripened them quickly, and soon harvest time was come. Then the grain was cut and ground and ready for sale.

When everything was complete, the jackal said to the sheep:

'Now let us divide it, so that we can each do what we like with his share.'

'You do it,' answered the sheep; 'here are the scales. You must weigh it carefully.'

So the jackal began to weigh it, and when he had finished, he counted out loud:

'One, two, three, four, five, six, seven parts for the jackal, and one part for the sheep. If she likes it she can take it, if not, she can leave it.'

The sheep looked at the two heaps in silence—one so large, the other so small; and then she answered:

'Wait for a minute, while I fetch some sacks to carry away my share.'

But it was not sacks that the sheep wanted; for as soon as the jackal could no longer see her she set forth at her best pace to the home of the greyhound, where she arrived panting with the haste she had made.

'Oh, good uncle, help me, I pray you!' she cried, as soon as she could speak.

'Why, what is the matter?' asked the greyhound, looking up with astonishment.

'I beg you to return with me, and frighten the jackal into paying me what he owes me,' answered the sheep. 'For months we have lived together, and I have twice every day drawn the water, while he only poured it into the trenches. Together we have reaped our harvest; and now, when the moment to divide our crop has come, he has taken seven parts for himself, and only left one for me.'

She finished, and giving herself a twist, passed her woolly tail across her eyes; while the greyhound watched her, but held his peace. Then he said:

'Bring me a sack.' And the sheep hastened away to fetch one. Very soon she returned, and laid the sack down before him.

'Open it wide, that I may get in,' cried he; and when he was comfortably rolled up inside he bade the sheep take him on her back, and hasten to the place where she had left the jackal.

She found him waiting for her, and pretending to be asleep, though she clearly saw him wink one of his eyes. However, she took no notice, but throwing the sack roughly on the ground, she exclaimed:

'Now measure!'

At this the jackal got up, and going to the heap of grain which lay close by, he divided it as before into eight portions—seven for himself and one for the sheep.

'What are you doing that for?' asked she indignantly. 'You know quite well that it was I who drew the water, and you who only poured it into the trenches.'

'You are mistaken,' answered the jackal. 'It was I who drew the water, and you who poured it into the trenches. Anybody will tell you that! If you like, I will ask those people who are digging there!'

'Very well,' replied the sheep. And the jackal called out:

'Ho! You diggers, tell me: Who was it you heard singing over the work?'

'Why, it was you, of course, jackal! You sang so loud that the whole world might have heard you!'

'And who it is that sings—he who draws the water, or he who empties it?'

'Why, certainly he who draws the water!'

'You hear?' said the jackal, turning to the sheep. 'Now come and carry away your own portion, or else I shall take it for myself.'

'You have got the better of me,' answered the sheep; 'and I suppose I must confess myself beaten! But as I bear no malice, go and eat some of the dates that I have brought in that sack.' And the jackal, who loved dates, ran instantly back, and tore open the mouth of the sack. But just as he was about to plunge his nose in he saw two brown eyes calmly looking at him. In an instant he had let fall the flap of the sack and bounded back to where the sheep was standing.

'I was only in fun; and you have brought my uncle the greyhound. Take away the sack, we will make the division over again.' And he began rearranging the heaps.

'One, two, three, four, five, six, seven, for my mother the sheep, and one for the jackal,' counted he; casting timid glances all the while at the sack.

'Now you can take your share and go,' said the sheep. And the jackal did not need twice telling! Whenever the sheep looked up, she still saw him flying, flying across the plain; and, for all I know, he may be flying across it still.

The Three Treasures of the Giants

[Contes Berberes, par Rene Basset.]

Long, long ago, there lived an old man and his wife who had three sons; the eldest was called Martin, the second Michael, while the third was named Jack.

One evening they were all seated round the table, eating their supper of bread and milk.

'Martin,' said the old man suddenly, 'I feel that I cannot live much longer. You, as the eldest, will inherit this hut; but, if you value my blessing, be good to your mother and brothers.'

'Certainly, father; how can you suppose I should do them wrong?' replied Martin indignantly, helping himself to all the best bits in the dish as he spoke. The old man saw nothing, but Michael looked on in surprise, and Jack was so astonished that he quite forgot to eat his own supper.

A little while after, the father fell ill, and sent for his sons, who were out hunting, to bid him farewell. After giving good advice to the two eldest, he turned to Jack.

'My boy,' he said, 'you have not got quite as much sense as other people, but if Heaven has deprived you of some of your wits, it was given you a kind heart. Always listen to what it says, and take heed to the words of your mother and brothers, as well as you are able!' So saying the old man sank back on his pillows and died.

The cries of grief uttered by Martin and Michael sounded through the house, but Jack remained by the bedside of his father, still and silent, as if he were dead also. At length he got up, and going into the garden, hid himself in some trees, and wept like a child, while his two brothers made ready for the funeral.

No sooner was the old man buried than Martin and Michael agreed that they would go into the world together to seek their fortunes, while Jack stayed at home with their mother. Jack would have liked nothing better than to sit and dream by the fire, but the mother, who was very old herself, declared that there was no work for him to do, and that he must seek it with his brothers.

So, one fine morning, all three set out; Martin and Michael carried two great bags full of food, but Jack carried nothing. This made his brothers very angry, for the day was hot and the bags were heavy, and about noon they sat down under a tree and began to eat. Jack was as hungry as they were, but he knew that it was no use asking for anything; and he threw himself under another tree, and wept bitterly.

'Another time perhaps you won't be so lazy, and will bring food for yourself,' said Martin, but to his surprise Jack answered:

'You are a nice pair! You talk of seeking your fortunes so as not to be a burden on our mother, and you begin by carrying off all the food she has in the house!'

This reply was so unexpected that for some moments neither of the brothers made any answer. Then they offered their brother some of their food, and when he had finished eating they went their way once more.

Towards evening they reached a small hut, and knocking at the door, asked if they might spend the night there. The man, who was a wood-cutter, invited them him, and begged them to sit down to supper. Martin thanked him, but being very proud, explained that it was only shelter they wanted, as they had plenty of food with them; and he and Michael at once opened their bags and began to eat, while Jack hid himself in a corner. The wife, on seeing this, took pity on him, and called him to come and share their supper, which he gladly did, and very good he found it. At this, Martin regretted deeply that he had been so foolish as to refuse, for his bits of bread and cheese seemed very hard when he smelt the savoury soup his brother was enjoying.

'He shan't have such a chance again,' thought he; and the next morning he insisted on plunging into a thick forest where they were likely to meet nobody.

For a long time they wandered hither and thither, for they had no path to guide them; but at last they came upon a wide clearing, in the midst of which stood a castle. Jack shouted with delight, but Martin, who was in a bad temper, said sharply:

'We must have taken a wrong turning! Let us go back.'

'Idiot!' replied Michael, who was hungry too, and, like many people when they are hungry, very cross also. 'We set out to travel through the world, and what does it matter if we go to the right or to the left?' And, without another word, took the path to the castle, closely followed by Jack, and after a moment by Martin likewise.

The door of the castle stood open, and they entered a great hall, and looked about them. Not a creature was to be seen, and suddenly Martin—he did not know why—felt a little frightened. He would have left the castle at once, but stopped when Jack boldly walked up to a door in the wall and opened it. He could not for very shame be outdone by his younger brother, and passed behind him into another splendid hall, which was filled from floor to ceiling with great pieces of copper money.

The sight quite dazzled Martin and Michael, who emptied all the provisions that remained out of their bags, and heaped them up instead with handfuls of copper.

Scarcely had they done this when Jack threw open another door, and this time it led to a hall filled with silver. In an instant his brothers had turned their bags upside down, so that the copper money tumbled out on to the floor, and were shovelling in handfuls of the silver instead. They had hardly finished, when Jack opened yet a third door, and all three fell back in amazement, for this room as a mass of gold, so bright that their eyes grew sore as they looked at it. However, they soon recovered from their surprise, and quickly emptied their bags of silver, and filled them with gold instead. When they would hold no more, Martin said:

'We had better hurry off now lest somebody else should come, and we might not know what to do'; and, followed by Michael, he hastily left the castle. Jack lingered behind for a few minutes to put pieces of gold, silver, and copper into his pocket, and to eat the food that his brothers had thrown down in the first room. Then he went after them, and found them lying down to rest in the midst of a forest. It was near sunset, and Martin began to feel hungry, so, when Jack arrived, he bade him return to the castle and bring the bread and cheese that they had left there.

'It is hardly worth doing that,' answered Jack; 'for I picked up the pieces and ate them myself.'

At this reply both brothers were beside themselves with anger, and fell upon the boy, beating him, and calling him names, till they were quite tired.

'Go where you like,' cried Martin with a final kick; 'but never come near us again.' And poor Jack ran weeping into the woods.

The next morning his brothers went home, and bought a beautiful house, where they lived with their mother like great lords.

Jack remained for some hours in hiding, thankful to be safe from his tormentors; but when no one came to trouble him, and his back did not ache so much, he began to think what he had better do. At length he made up his mind to go to the caste and take away as much money with him as would enable him to live in comfort for the rest of his life. This being decided, he sprang up, and set out along the path which led to the castle. As before, the door stood open, and he went on till he had reached the hall of gold, and there he took off his jacket and tied the sleeves together so that it might make a kind of bag. He then began to pour in the gold by handfuls, when, all at once, a noise like thunder shook the castle. This was followed by a voice, hoarse as that of a bull, which cried:

'I smell the smell of a man.' And two giants entered.

'So, little worm! it is you who steal our treasures!' exclaimed the biggest. 'Well, we have got you now, and we will cook you for supper!' But here the other giant drew him aside, and for a moment or two they whispered together. At length the first giant spoke:

'To please my friend I will spare your life on condition that, for the future, you shall guard our treasures. If you are hungry take this little table and rap on it, saying, as you do so: "The dinner of an emperor!" and you will get as much food as you want.'

With a light heart Jack promised all that was asked of him, and for some days enjoyed himself mightily. He had everything he could wish for, and did nothing from morning till night; but by-and-by he began to get very tired of it all.

'Let the giants guard their treasures themselves,' he said to himself at last; 'I am going away. But I will leave all the gold and silver behind me, and will take nought but you, my good little table.'

So, tucking the table under his arm, he started off for the forest, but he did not linger there long, and soon found himself in the fields on the other side. There he saw an old man, who begged Jack to give him something to eat.

'You could not have asked a better person,' answered Jack cheerfully. And signing to him to sit down with him under a tree, he set the table in front of them, and struck it three times, crying:

'The dinner of an emperor!' He had hardly uttered the words when fish and meat of all kinds appeared on it!

'That is a clever trick of yours,' said the old man, when he had eaten as much as he wanted. 'Give it to me in exchange for a treasure I have which is still better. Do you see this cornet? Well, you have only to tell it that you wish for an army, and you will have as many soldiers as you require.'

Now, since he had been left to himself, Jack had grown ambitious, so, after a moment's hesitation, he took the cornet and gave the table in exchange. The old man bade him farewell, and set off down one path, while Jack chose another, and for a long time he was quite pleased with his new possession. Then, as he felt hungry, he wished for his table back again, as no house was in sight, and he wanted some supper badly. All at once he remembered his cornet, and a wicked thought entered his mind.

'Two hundred hussars, forward!' cried he. And the neighing of horses and the clanking of swords were heard close at hand. The officer who rode at their head approached Jack, and politely inquired what he wished them to do.

'A mile or two along that road,' answered Jack, 'you will find an old man carrying a table. Take the table from him and bring it to me.'

The officer saluted and went back to his men, who started at a gallop to do Jack's bidding.

In ten minutes they had returned, bearing the table with them.

'That is all, thank you,' said Jack; and the soldiers disappeared inside the cornet.

Oh, what a good supper Jack had that night, quite forgetting that he owed it to a mean trick. The next day he breakfasted early, and then walked on towards the nearest town. On the way thither he met another old man, who begged for something to eat.

'Certainly, you shall have something to eat,' replied Jack. And, placing the table on the ground he cried:

'The dinner of an emperor!' when all sorts of food dishes appeared. At first the old man ate quite greedily, and said nothing; but, after his hunger was satisfied, he turned to Jack and said:

'That is a very clever trick of yours. Give the table to me and you shall have something still better.'

'I don't believe that there is anything better,' answered Jack.

'Yes, there is. Here is my bag; it will give you as many castles as you can possibly want.'

Jack thought for a moment; then he replied: 'Very well, I will exchange with you.' And passing the table to the old man, he hung the bag over his arm.

Five minutes later he summoned five hundred lancers out of the cornet and bade them go after the old man and fetch back the table.

Now that by his cunning he had obtained possession of the three magic objects, he resolved to return to his native place. Smearing his face with dirt, and tearing his clothes so as to look like a beggar, he stopped the passers by and, on pretence of seeking money or food, he questioned them about the village gossip. In this manner he learned that his brothers had become great men, much respected in all the country round. When he heard that, he lost no time in going to the door of their fine house and imploring them to give him food and shelter; but the only thing he got was hard words, and a command to beg elsewhere. At length, however, at their mother's entreaty, he was told that he might pass the night in the stable. Here he waited until everybody in the house was sound asleep, when he drew his bag from under his cloak, and desired that a castle might appear in that place; and the cornet gave him soldiers to guard the castle, while the table furnished him with a good supper. In the morning, he caused it all to vanish, and when his brothers entered the stable they found him lying on the straw.

Jack remained here for many days, doing nothing, and—as far as anybody knew—eating nothing. This conduct puzzled his brothers greatly, and they put such constant questions to him, that at length he told them the secret of the table, and even gave a dinner to them, which far outdid any they had ever seen or heard of. But though they had solemnly promised to reveal nothing, somehow or other the tale leaked out, and before long reached the ears of the king himself. That very evening his chamberlain arrived at Jack's dwelling, with a request from the king that he might borrow the table for three days.

'Very well,' answered Jack, 'you can take it back with you. But tell his majesty that if he does not return it at the end of the three days I will make war upon him.'

So the chamberlain carried away the table and took it straight to the king, telling him at the same time of Jack's threat, at which they both laughed till their sides ached.

Now the king was so delighted with the table, and the dinners it gave him, that when the three days were over he could not make up his mind to part with it. Instead, he sent for his carpenter, and bade him copy it exactly, and when it was done he told his chamberlain to return it to Jack with his best thanks. It happened to be dinner time, and Jack invited the chamberlain, who knew nothing of the trick, to stay and dine with him. The good man, who had eaten several excellent meals provided by the table in the last three days, accepted the invitation with pleasure, even though he was to dine in a stable, and sat down on the straw beside Jack.

'The dinner of an emperor!' cried Jack. But not even a morsel of cheese made its appearance.

'The dinner of an emperor!' shouted Jack in a voice of thunder. Then the truth dawned on him; and, crushing the table between his hands, he turned to the chamberlain, who, bewildered and half-frightened, was wondering how to get away.

'Tell your false king that to-morrow I will destroy his castle as easily as I have broken this table.'

The chamberlain hastened back to the palace, and gave the king Jack's message, at which he laughed more than before, and called all his courtiers to hear the story. But they were not quite so merry when they woke next morning and beheld ten thousand horsemen, and as many archers, surrounding the palace. The king saw it was useless to hold out, and he took the white flag of truce in one hand, and the real table in the other, and set out to look for Jack.

'I committed a crime,' said he; 'but I will do my best to make up for it. Here is your table, which I own with shame that I tried to steal, and you shall have besides, my daughter as your wife!'

There was no need to delay the marriage when the table was able to furnish the most splendid banquet that ever was seen, and after everyone had eaten and drunk as much as they wanted, Jack took his bag and commanded a castle filled with all sorts of treasures to arise in the park for himself and his bride.

At this proof of his power the king's heart died within him.

'Your magic is greater than mine,' he said; 'and you are young and strong, while I am old and tired. Take, therefore, the sceptre from my hand, and my crown from my head, and rule my people better than I have done.'

So at last Jack's ambition was satisfied. He could not hope to be more than king, and as long as he had his cornet to provide him with soldiers he was secure against his enemies. He never forgave his brothers for the way they had treated him, though he presented his mother with a beautiful castle, and everything she could possibly wish for. In the centre of his own palace was a treasure chamber, and in this chamber the table, the cornet, and the bag were kept as the most prized of all his possessions, and not a week passed without a visit from king John to make sure they were safe. He reigned long and well, and died a very old man, beloved by his people. But his good example was not followed by his sons and his grandsons. They grew so proud that they were ashamed to think that the founder of their race had once been a poor boy; and as they and all the world could not fail to remember it, as long as the table, the cornet, and the bag were shown in the treasure chamber, one king, more foolish than the rest, thrust them into a dark and damp cellar.

For some time the kingdom remained, though it became weaker and weaker every year that passed. Then, one day, a rumour reached the king that a large army was marching against him. Vaguely he recollected some tales he had heard about a magic cornet which could provide as many soldiers as would serve to conquer the earth, and which had been removed by his grandfather to a cellar. Thither he hastened that he might renew his power once more, and in that black and slimy spot he found the treasures indeed. But the table fell to pieces as he touched it, in the cornet there remained only a few fragments of leathern belts which the rats had gnawed, and in the bag nothing but broken bits of stone.

And the king bowed his head to the doom that awaited him, and in his heart cursed the ruin wrought by the pride and foolishness of himself and his forefathers.

The Rover of the Plain

[From Contes Populaires Slaves, par Louis Leger.]

A long way off, near the sea coast of the east of Africa, there dwelt, once upon a time, a man and his wife. They had two children, a son and a daughter, whom they loved very much, and, like parents in other countries, they often talked of the fine marriages the young people would make some day. Out there both boys and girls marry early, and very soon, it seemed to the mother, a message was sent by a rich man on the other side of the great hills offering a fat herd of oxen in exchange for the girl. Everyone in the house and in the village rejoiced, and the maiden was despatched to her new home. When all was quiet again the father said to his son:

'Now that we own such a splendid troop of oxen you had better hasten and get yourself a wife, lest some illness should overtake them. Already we have seen in the villages round about one or two damsels whose parents would gladly part with them for less than half the herd. Therefore tell us which you like best, and we will buy her for you.'

But the son answered:

'Not so; the maidens I have seen do not please me. If, indeed, I must marry, let me travel and find a wife for myself.'

'It shall be as you wish,' said the parents; 'but if by-and-by trouble should come of it, it will be your fault and not ours.'

The youth, however, would not listen; and bidding his father and mother farewell, set out on his search. Far, far away he wandered, over mountains and across rivers, till he reached a village where the people were quite different from those of his own race. He glanced about him and noticed that the girls were fair to look upon, as they pounded maize or stewed something that smelt very nice in earthen pots—especially if you were hot and tired; and when one of the maidens turned round and offered the stranger some dinner, he made up his mind that he would wed her and nobody else.

So he sent a message to her parents asking their leave to take her for his wife, and they came next day to bring their answer.

'We will give you our daughter,' said they, 'if you can pay a good price for her. Never was there so hardworking a girl; and how we shall do without her we cannot tell! Still—no doubt your father and mother will come themselves and bring the price?'

'No; I have the price with me,' replied the young man; laying down a handful of gold pieces. 'Here it is—take it.'

The old couple's eyes glittered greedily; but custom forbade them to touch the price before all was arranged.

'At least,' said they, after a moment's pause, 'we may expect them to fetch your wife to her new home?'

'No; they are not used to travelling,' answered the bridegroom. 'Let the ceremony be performed without delay, and we will set forth at once. It is a long journey.'

Then the parents called in the girl, who was lying in the sun outside the hut, and, in the presence of all the village, a goat was killed, the sacred dance took place, and a blessing was said over the heads of the young people. After that the bride was led aside by her father, whose duty it was to bestow on her some parting advice as to her conduct in her married life.

'Be good to your husband's parents,' added he, 'and always do the will of your husband.' And the girl nodded her head obediently. Next it was the mother's turn; and, as was the custom of the tribe, she spoke to her daughter:

'Will you choose which of your sisters shall go with you to cut your wood and carry your water?'

'I do not want any of them,' answered she; 'they are no use. They will drop the wood and spill the water.'

'Then will you have any of the other children? There are enough to spare,' asked the mother again. But the bride said quickly:

'I will have none of them! You must give me our buffalo, the Rover of the Plain; he alone shall serve me.'

'What folly you talk!' cried the parents. 'Give you our buffalo, the Rover of the Plain? Why, you know that our life depends on him. Here he is well fed and lies on soft grass; but how can you tell what will befall him in another country? The food may be bad, he will die of hunger; and, if he dies we die also.'

'No, no,' said the bride; 'I can look after him as well as you. Get him ready, for the sun is sinking and it is time we set forth.'

So she went away and put together a small pot filled with healing herms, a horn that she used in tending sick people, a little knife, and a calabash containing deer fat; and, hiding these about her, she took leave of her father and mother and started across the mountains by the side of her husband.

But the young man did not see the buffalo that followed them, which had left his home to be the servant of his wife.

No one ever knew how the news spread to the kraal that the young man was coming back, bringing a wife with him; but, somehow or other, when the two entered the village, every man and woman was standing in the road uttering shouts of welcome.

'Ah, you are not dead after all,' cried they; 'and have found a wife to your liking, though you would have none of our girls. Well, well, you have chosen your own path; and if ill comes of it beware lest you grumble.'

Next day the husband took his wife to the fields and showed her which were his, and which belonged to his mother. The girl listened carefully to all he told her, and walked with him back to the hut; but close to the door she stopped, and said:

'I have dropped my necklace of beads in the field, and I must go and look for it.' But in truth she had done nothing of the sort, and it was only an excuse to go and seek the buffalo.

The beast was crouching under a tree when she came up, and snorted with pleasure at the sight of her.

'You can roam about this field, and this, and this,' she said, 'for they belong to my husband; and that is his wood, where you may hide yourself. But the other fields are his mother's, so beware lest you touch them.'

'I will beware,' answered the buffalo; and, patting his head, the girl left him.

Oh, how much better a servant he was than any of the little girls the bride had refused to bring with her! If she wanted water, she had only to cross the patch of maize behind the hut and seek out the place where the buffalo lay hidden, and put down her pail beside him. Then she would sit at her ease while he went to the lake and brought the bucket back brimming over. If she wanted wood, he would break the branches off the trees and lay them at her feet. And the villagers watched her return laden, and said to each other:

'Surely the girls of her country are stronger than our girls, for none of them could cut so quickly or carry so much!' But then, nobody knew that she had a buffalo for a servant.

Only, all this time she never gave the poor buffalo anything to eat, because she had just one dish, out of which she and her husband ate; while in her old home there was a dish put aside expressly for the Rover of the Plain. The buffalo bore it as long as he could; but, one day, when his mistress bade him go to the lake and fetch water, his knees almost gave way from hunger. He kept silence, however, till the evening, when he said to his mistress:

'I am nearly starved; I have not touched food since I came here. I can work no more.'

'Alas!' answered she, 'what can I do? I have only one dish in the house. You will have to steal some beans from the fields. Take a few here and a few there; but be sure not to take too many from one place, or the owner may notice it.'

Now the buffalo had always lived an honest life, but if his mistress did not feed him, he must get food for himself. So that night, when all the village was asleep, he came out from the wood and ate a few beans here and a few there, as his mistress had bidden him. And when at last his hunger was satisfied, he crept back to his lair. But a buffalo is not a fairy, and the next morning, when the women arrived to work in the fields, they stood still with astonishment, and said to each other:

'Just look at this; a savage beast has been destroying our crops, and we can see the traces of his feet!' And they hurried to their homes to tell their tale.

In the evening the girl crept out to the buffalo's hiding-place, and said to him:

'They perceived what happened, of course; so to-night you had better seek your supper further off.' And the buffalo nodded his head and followed her counsel; but in the morning, when these women also went out to work, the races of hoofs were plainly to be seen, and they hastened to tell their husbands, and begged them to bring their guns, and to watch for the robber.

It happened that the stranger girl's husband was the best marksman in all the village, and he hid himself behind the trunk of a tree and waited.

The buffalo, thinking that they would probably make a search for him in the fields he had laid waste the evening before, returned to the bean patch belonging to his mistress.

The young man saw him coming with amazement.

'Why, it is a buffalo!' cried he; 'I never have beheld one in this country before!' And raising his gun, he aimed just behind the ear.

The buffalo gave a leap into the air, and then fell dead.

'It was a good shot,' said the young man. And he ran to the village to tell them that the thief was punished.

When he entered his hut he found his wife, who had somehow heard the news, twisting herself to and fro and shedding tears.

'Are you ill?' asked he. And she answered: 'Yes; I have pains all over my body.' But she was not ill at all, only very unhappy at the death of the buffalo which had served her so well. Her husband felt anxious, and sent for the medicine man; but though she pretended to listen to him, she threw all his medicine out of the door directly he had gone away.

With the first rays of light the whole village was awake, and the women set forth armed with baskets and the men with knives in order to cut up the buffalo. Only the girl remained in her hut; and after a while she too went to join them, groaning and weeping as she walked along.

'What are you doing here?' asked her husband when he saw her. 'If you are ill you are better at home.'

'Oh! I could not stay alone in the village,' said she. And her mother-in-law left off her work to come and scold her, and to tell her that she would kill herself if she did such foolish things. But the girl would not listen and sat down and looked on.

When they had divided the buffalo's flesh, and each woman had the family portion in her basket, the stranger wife got up and said:

'Let me have the head.'

'You could never carry anything so heavy,' answered the men, 'and now you are ill besides.'

'You do not know how strong I am,' answered she. And at last they gave it her.

She did not walk to the village with the others, but lingered behind, and, instead of entering her hut, she slipped into the little shed where the pots for cooking and storing maize were kept. Then she laid down the buffalo's head and sat beside it. Her husband came to seek her, and begged her to leave the shed and go to bed, as she must be tired out; but the girl would not stir, neither would she attend to the words of her mother-in-law.

'I wish you would leave me alone!' she answered crossly. 'It is impossible to sleep if somebody is always coming in.' And she turned her back on them, and would not even eat the food they had brought. So they went away, and the young man soon stretched himself out on his mat; but his wife's odd conduct made him anxious, and he lay wake all night, listening.

When all was still the girl made a fire and boiled some water in a pot. As soon as it was quite hot she shook in the medicine that she had brought from home, and then, taking the buffalo's head, she made incisions with her little knife behind the ear, and close to the temple where the shot had struck him. Next she applied the horn to the spot and blew with all her force till, at length, the blood began to move. After that she spread some of the deer fat out of the calabash over the wound, which she held in the steam of the hot water. Last of all, she sang in a low voice a dirge over the Rover of the Plain.

As she chanted the final words the head moved, and the limbs came back. The buffalo began to feel alive again and shook his horns, and stood up and stretched himself. Unluckily it was just at this moment that the husband said to himself:

'I wonder if she is crying still, and what is the matter with her! Perhaps I had better go and see.' And he got up and, calling her by name, went out to the shed.

'Go away! I don't want you!' she cried angrily. But it was too late. The buffalo had fallen to the ground, dead, and with the wound in his head as before.

The young man who, unlike most of his tribe, was afraid of his wife, returned to his bed without having seen anything, but wondering very much what she could be doing all this time. After waiting a few minutes, she began her task over again, and at the end the buffalo stood on his feet as before. But just as the girl was rejoicing that her work was completed, in came the husband once more to see what his wife was doing; and this time he sat himself down in the hut, and said that he wished to watch whatever was going on. Then the girl took up the pitcher and all her other things and left the shed, trying for the third time to bring the buffalo back to life.

She was too late; the dawn was already breaking, and the head fell to the ground, dead and corrupt as it was before.

The girl entered the hut, where her husband and his mother were getting ready to go out.

'I want to go down to the lake, and bathe,' said she.

'But you could never walk so far,' answered they. 'You are so tired, as it is, that you can hardly stand!'

However, in spite of their warnings, the girl left the hut in the direction of the lake. Very soon she came back weeping, and sobbed out:

'I met some one in the village who lives in my country, and he told me that my mother is very, very ill, and if I do not go to her at once she will be dead before I arrive. I will return as soon as I can, and now farewell.' And she set forth in the direction of the mountains. But this story was not true; she knew nothing about her mother, only she wanted an excuse to go home and tell her family that their prophecies had come true, and that the buffalo was dead.

Balancing her basket on her head, she walked along, and directly she had left the village behind her she broke out into the song of the Rover of the Plain, and at last, at the end of the day, she came to the group of huts where her parents lived. Her friends all ran to meet her, and, weeping, she told them that the buffalo was dead.

This sad news spread like lightning through the country, and the people flocked from far and near to bewail the loss of the beast who had been their pride.

'If you had only listened to us,' they cried, 'he would be alive now. But you refused all the little girls we offered you, and would have nothing but the buffalo. And remember what the medicine-man said: "If the buffalo dies you die also!"'

So they bewailed their fate, one to the other, and for a while they did not perceive that the girl's husband was sitting in their midst, leaning his gun against a tree. Then one man, turning, beheld him, and bowed mockingly.

'Hail, murderer! hail! you have slain us all!'

The young man stared, not knowing what he meant, and answered, wonderingly:

'I shot a buffalo; is that why you call me a murderer?'

'A buffalo—yes; but the servant of your wife! It was he who carried the wood and drew the water. Did you not know it?'

'No; I did not know it,' replied the husband in surprise. 'Why did no one tell me? Of course I should not have shot him!'

'Well, he is dead,' answered they, 'and we must die too.'

At this the girl took a cup in which some poisonous herbs had been crushed, and holding it in her hands, she wailed: 'O my father, Rover of the Plain!' Then drinking a deep draught from it, fell back dead. One by one her parents, her brothers and her sisters, drank also and died, singing a dirge to the memory of the buffalo.

The girl's husband looked on with horror; and returned sadly home across the mountains, and, entering his hut, threw himself on the ground. At first he was too tired to speak; but at length he raised his head and told all the story to his father and mother, who sat watching him. When he had finished they shook their heads and said:

'Now you see that we spoke no idle words when we told you that ill would come of your marriage! We offered you a good and hard-working wife, and you would have none of her. And it is not only your wife you have lost, but your fortune also. For who will give you back your money if they are all dead?'

'It is true, O my father,' answered the young man. But in his heart he thought more of the loss of his wife than of the money he had given for her.

The White Doe

[From L'Etude Ethnographique sur les Baronga, par Henri Junod.]

Once upon a time there lived a king and queen who loved each other dearly, and would have been perfectly happy if they had only had a little son or daughter to play with. They never talked about it, and always pretended that there was nothing in the world to wish for; but, sometimes when they looked at other people's children, their faces grew sad, and their courtiers and attendants knew the reason why.

One day the queen was sitting alone by the side of a waterfall which sprung from some rocks in the large park adjoining the castle. She was feeling more than usually miserable, and had sent away her ladies so that no one might witness her grief. Suddenly she heard a rustling movement in the pool below the waterfall, and, on glancing up, she saw a large crab climbing on to a stone beside her.

'Great queen,' said the crab, 'I am here to tell you that the desire of your heart will soon be granted. But first you must permit me to lead you to the palace of the fairies, which, though hard by, has never been seen by mortal eyes because of the thick clouds that surround it. When there you will know more; that is, if you will trust yourself to me.'

The queen had never before heard an animal speak, and was struck dumb with surprise. However, she was so enchanted at the words of the crab that she smiled sweetly and held out her hand; it was taken, not by the crab, which had stood there only a moment before, but by a little old woman smartly dressed in white and crimson with green ribbons in her grey hair. And, wonderful to say, not a drop of water fell from her clothes.

The old woman ran lightly down a path along which the queen had been a hundred times before, but it seemed so different she could hardly believe it was the same. Instead of having to push her way through nettles and brambles, roses and jasmine hung about her head, while under her feet the ground was sweet with violets. The orange trees were so tall and thick that, even at mid-day, the sun was never too hot, and at the end of the path was a glimmer of something so dazzling that the queen had to shade her eyes, and peep at it only between her fingers.

'What can it be?' she asked, turning to her guide; who answered:

'Oh, that is the fairies' palace, and here are some of them coming to meet us.'

As she spoke the gates swung back and six fairies approached, each bearing in her hand a flower made of precious stones, but so like a real one that it was only by touching you could tell the difference.

'Madam,' they said, 'we know not how to thank you for this mark of your confidence, but have the happiness to tell you that in a short time you will have a little daughter.'

The queen was so enchanted at this news that she nearly fainted with joy; but when she was able to speak, she poured out all her gratitude to the fairies for their promised gift.

'And now,' she said, 'I ought not to stay any longer, for my husband will think that I have run away, or that some evil beast has devoured me.'

In a little while it happened just as the fairies had foretold, and a baby girl was born in the palace. Of course both the king and queen were delighted, and the child was called Desiree, which means 'desired,' for she had been 'desired' for five years before her birth.

At first the queen could think of nothing but her new plaything, but then she remembered the fairies who had sent it to her. Bidding her ladies bring her the posy of jewelled flowers which had been given her at the palace, she took each flower in her hand and called it by name, and, in turn, each fairy appeared before her. But, as unluckily often happens, the one to whom she owed the most, the crab-fairy, was forgotten, and by this, as in the case of other babies you have read about, much mischief was wrought.

However, for the moment all was gaiety in the palace, and everybody inside ran to the windows to watch the fairies' carriages, for no two were alike. One had a car of ebony, drawn by white pigeons, another was lying back in her ivory chariot, driving ten black crows, while the rest had chosen rare woods or many-coloured sea-shells, with scarlet and blue macaws, long-tailed peacocks, or green love-birds for horses. These carriages were only used on occasions of state, for when they went to war flying dragons, fiery serpents, lions or leopards, took the place of the beautiful birds.

The fairies entered the queen's chamber followed by little dwarfs who carried their presents and looked much prouder than their mistresses. One by one their burdens were spread upon the ground, and no one had ever seen such lovely things. Everything that a baby could possibly wear or play with was there, and besides, they had other and more precious gifts to give her, which only children who have fairies for godmothers can ever hope to possess.

They were all gathered round the heap of pink cushions on which the baby lay asleep, when a shadow seemed to fall between them and the sun, while a cold wind blew through the room. Everybody looked up, and there was the crab-fairy, who had grown as tall as the ceiling in her anger.

'So I am forgotten!' cried she, in a voice so loud that the queen trembled as she heard it. 'Who was it soothed you in your trouble? Who was it led you to the fairies? Who was it brought you back in safety to your home again? Yet I—I—am overlooked, while these who have done nothing in comparison, are petted and thanked.'

The queen, almost dumb with terror, in vain tried to think of some explanation or apology; but there was none, and she could only confess her fault and implore forgiveness. The fairies also did their best to soften the wrath of their sister, and knowing that, like many plain people who are not fairies, she was very vain, they entreated her to drop her crab's disguise, and to become once more the charming person they were accustomed to see.

For some time the enraged fairy would listen to nothing; but at length the flatteries began to take effect. The crab's shell fell from her, she shrank into her usual size, and lost some of her fierce expression.

'Well,' she said, 'I will not cause the princess's death, as I had meant to do, but at the same time she will have to bear the punishment of her mother's fault, as many other children have done before her. The sentence I pass upon her is, that if she is allowed to see one ray of daylight before her fifteenth birthday she will rue it bitterly, and it may perhaps cost her her life.' And with these words she vanished by the window through which she came, while the fairies comforted the weeping queen and took counsel how best the princess might be kept safe during her childhood.

At the end of half an hour they had made up their minds what to do, and at the command of the fairies, a beautiful palace sprang up, close to that of the king and queen, but different from every palace in the world in having no windows, and only a door right under the earth. However, once within, daylight was hardly missed, so brilliant were the multitudes of tapers that were burning on the walls.

Now up to this time the princess's history has been like the history of many a princess that you have read about; but, when the period of her imprisonment was nearly over, her fortunes took another turn. For almost fifteen years the fairies had taken care of her, and amused her and taught her, so that when she came into the world she might be no whit behind the daughters of other kings in all that makes a princess charming and accomplished. They all loved her dearly, but the fairy Tulip loved her most of all; and as the princess's fifteenth birthday drew near, the fairy began to tremble lest something terrible should happen—some accident which had not been foreseen. 'Do not let her out of your sight,' said Tulip to the queen, 'and meanwhile, let her portrait be painted and carried to the neighbouring Courts, as is the custom in order that the kings may see how far her beauty exceeds that of every other princess, and that they may demand her in marriage for their sons.'

And so it was done; and as the fairy had prophesied, all the young princes fell in love with the picture; but the last one to whom it was shown could think of nothing else, and refused to let it be removed from his chamber, where he spent whole days gazing at it.

The king his father was much surprised at the change which had come over his son, who generally passed all his time in hunting or hawking, and his anxiety was increased by a conversation he overheard between two of his courtiers that they feared the prince must be going out of his mind, so moody had he become. Without losing a moment the king went to visit his son, and no sooner had he entered the room than the young man flung himself at his father's feet.

'You have betrothed me already to a bride I can never love!' cried he; 'but if you will not consent to break off the match, and ask for the hand of the princess Desiree, I shall die of misery, thankful to be alive no longer.'

These words much displeased the king, who felt that, in breaking off the marriage already arranged he would almost certainly be bringing on his subjects a long and bloody war; so, without answering, he turned away, hoping that a few days might bring his son to reason. But the prince's condition grew rapidly so much worse that the king, in despair, promised to send an embassy at once to Desiree's father.

This news cured the young man in an instant of all his ills; and he began to plan out every detail of dress and of horses and carriages which were necessary to make the train of the envoy, whose name was Becasigue, as splendid as possible. He longed to form part of the embassy himself, if only in the disguise of a page; but this the king would not allow, and so the prince had to content himself with searching the kingdom for everything that was rare and beautiful to send to the princess. Indeed, he arrived, just as the embassy was starting, with his portrait, which had been painted in secret by the court painter.

The king and queen wished for nothing better than that their daughter marry into such a great and powerful family, and received the ambassador with every sign of welcome. They even wished him to see the princess Desiree, but this was prevented by the fairy Tulip, who feared some ill might come of it.

'And be sure you tell him,' added she, 'that the marriage cannot be celebrated till she is fifteen years old, or else some terrible misfortune will happen to the child.'

So when Becasigue, surround by his train, made a formal request that the princess Desiree might be given in marriage to his master's son, the king replied that he was much honoured, and would gladly give his consent; but that no one could even see the princess till her fifteenth birthday, as the spell laid upon her in her cradle by a spiteful fairy, would not cease to work till that was past. The ambassador was greatly surprised and disappointed, but he knew too much about fairies to venture to disobey them, therefore he had to content himself with presenting the prince's portrait to the queen, who lost no time in carrying it to the princess. As the girl took it in her hands it suddenly spoke, as it had been taught to do, and uttered a compliment of the most delicate and charming sort, which made the princess flush with pleasure.

'How would you like to have a husband like that?' asked the queen, laughing.

'As if I knew anything about husbands!' replied Desiree, who had long ago guessed the business of the ambassador.

'Well, he will be your husband in three months,' answered the queen, ordering the prince's presents to be brought in. The princess was very pleased with them, and admired them greatly, but the queen noticed that all the while her eyes constantly strayed from the softest silks and most brilliant jewels to the portrait of the prince.

The ambassador, finding that there was no hope of his being allowed to see the princess, took his leave, and returned to his own court; but here a new difficulty appeared. The prince, though transported with joy at the thought that Desiree was indeed to be his bride, was bitterly disappointed that she had not been allowed to return with Becasigue, as he had foolishly expected; and never having been taught to deny himself anything or to control his feelings, he fell as ill as he had done before. He would eat nothing nor take pleasure in anything, but lay all day on a heap of cushions, gazing at the picture of the princess.

'If I have to wait three months before I can marry the princess I shall die!' was all this spoilt boy would say; and at length the king, in despair, resolved to send a fresh embassy to Desiree's father to implore him to permit the marriage to be celebrated at once. 'I would have presented my prayer in person, he added in his letter, 'but my great age and infirmities do not suffer me to travel; however my envoy has orders to agree to any arrangement that you may propose.'

On his arrival at the palace Becasigue pleaded his young master's cause as fervently as the king his father could have done, and entreated that the princess might be consulted in the matter. The queen hastened to the marble tower, and told her daughter of the sad state of the prince. Des the prince without risking the doom pronounced over her by the wicked fairy.

'I see!' she exclaimed joyfully at last. 'Let a carriage be built through which no light can come, and let it be brought into my room. I will then get into it, and we can travel swiftly during the night and arrive before dawn at the palace of the prince. Once there, I can remain in some underground chamber, where no light can come.'

'Ah, how clever you are,' cried the queen, clasping her in her arms. And she hurried away to tell the king.

'What a wife our prince will have!' said Becasigue bowing low; 'but I must hasten back with the tidings, and to prepare the underground chamber for the princess.' And so he took his leave.

In a few days the carriage commanded by the princess was ready. It was of green velvet, scattered over with large golden thistles, and lined inside with silver brocade embroidered with pink roses. It had no windows, of course; but the fairy Tulip, whose counsel had been asked, had managed to light it up with a soft glow that came no one knew whither.

It was carried straight up into the great hall of the tower, and the princess stepped into it, followed by her faithful maid of honour, Eglantine, and by her lady in waiting Cerisette, who also had fallen in love with the prince's portrait and was bitterly jealous of her mistress. The fourth place in the carriage was filled by Cerisette's mother, who had been sent by the queen to look after the three young people.

Now the Fairy of the Fountain was the godmother of the princess Nera, to whom the prince had been betrothed before the picture of Desiree had made him faithless. She was very angry at the slight put upon her godchild, and from that moment kept careful watch on the princess. In this journey she saw her chance, and it was she who, invisible, sat by Cerisette, and put bad thoughts into the minds of both her and her mother.

The way to the city where the prince lived ran for the most part through a thick forest, and every night when there was no moon, and not a single star could be seen through the trees, the guards who travelled with the princess opened the carriage to give it an airing. This went on for several days, till only twelve hours journey lay between them and the palace. The Cerisette persuaded her mother to cut a great hole in the side of the carriage with a sharp knife which she herself had brought for the purpose. In the forest the darkness was so intense that no one perceived what she had done, but when they left the last trees behind them, and emerged into the open country, the sun was up, and for the first time since her babyhood, Desiree found herself in the light of day.

She looked up in surprise at the dazzling brilliance that streamed through the hole; then gave a sigh which seemed to come from her heart. The carriage door swung back, as if by magic, and a white doe sprang out, and in a moment was lost to sight in the forest. But, quick as she was, Eglantine, her maid of honour, had time to see where she went, and jumped from the carriage in pursuit of her, followed at a distance by the guards.

Cerisette and her mother looked at each other in surprise and joy. They could hardly believe in their good fortune, for everything had happened exactly as they wished. The first thing to be done was to conceal the hole which had been cut, and when this was managed (with the help of the angry fairy, though they did not know it), Cerisette hastened to take off her own clothes, and put on those of the princess, placing the crown of diamonds on her head. She found this heavier than she expected; but then, she had never been accustomed to wear crowns, which makes all the difference.

At the gates of the city the carriage was stopped by a guard of honour sent by the king as an escort to his son's bride. Though Cerisette and her mother could of course see nothing of what was going on outside, they heard plainly the shouts of welcome from the crowds along the streets.

The carriage stopped at length in the vast hall which Becasigue had prepared for the reception of the princess. The grand chamberlain and the lord high steward were awaiting her, and when the false bride stepped into the brilliantly lighted room, they bowed low, and said they had orders to inform his highness the moment she arrived. The prince, whom the strict etiquette of the court had prevented from being present in the underground hall, was burning with impatience in his own apartments.

'So she had come!' cried he, throwing down the bow he had been pretending to mend. 'Well, was I not right? Is she not a miracle of beauty and grace? And has she her equal in the whole world?' The ministers looked at each other, and made no reply; till at length the chamberlain, who was the bolder of the two, observed:

'My lord, as to her beauty, you can judge of that for yourself. No doubt it is as great as you say; but at present it seems to have suffered, as is natural, from the fatigues of the journey.'

This was certainly not what the prince had expected to hear. Could the portrait have flattered her? He had known of such things before, and a cold shiver ran through him; but with an effort he kept silent from further questioning, and only said:

'Has the king been told that the princess is in the palace?'

'Yes, highness; and he has probably already joined her.'

'Then I will go too,' said the prince.

Weak as he was from his long illness, the prince descended the staircase, supported by the ministers, and entered the room just in time to hear his father's loud cry of astonishment and disgust at the sight of Cerisette.

'There was been treachery at work,' he exclaimed, while the prince leant, dumb with horror, against the doorpost. But the lady in waiting, who had been prepared for something of the sort, advanced, holding in her hand the letters which the king and queen had entrusted to her.

'This is the princess Desiree,' said she, pretending to have heard nothing, 'and I have the honour to present to you these letters from my liege lord and lady, together with the casket containing the princess' jewels.'

The king did not move or answer her; so the prince, leaning on the arm of Becasigue, approached a little closer to the false princess, hoping against hope that his eyes had deceived him. But the longer he looked the more he agreed with his father that there was treason somewhere, for in no single respect did the portrait resemble the woman before him. Cerisette was so tall that the dress of the princess did not reach her ankles, and so thin that her bones showed through the stuff. Besides that her nose was hooked, and her teeth black and ugly.

In his turn, the prince stood rooted to the spot. At last he spoke, and his words were addressed to his father, and not to the bride who had come so far to marry him.

'We have been deceived,' he said, 'and it will cost me my life.' And he leaned so heavily on the envoy that Becasigue feared he was going to faint, and hastily laid him on the floor. For some minutes no one could attend to anybody but the prince; but as soon as he revived the lady in waiting made herself heard.

'Oh, my lovely princess, why did we ever leave home?' cried she. 'But the king your father will avenge the insults that have been heaped on you when we tell him how you have been treated.'

'I will tell him myself,' replied the king in wrath; 'he promised me a wonder of beauty, he has sent me a skeleton! I am not surprised that he has kept her for fifteen years hidden away from the eyes of the world. Take them both away,' he continued, turning to his guards, 'and lodge them in the state prison. There is something more I have to learn of this matter.'

His orders were obeyed, and the prince, loudly bewailing his sad fate, was led back to bed, where for many days he lay in a high fever. At length he slowly began to gain strength, but his sorrow was still so great that he could not bear the sight of a strange face, and shuddered at the notion of taking his proper part in the court ceremonies. Unknown to the king, or to anybody but Becasigue, he planned that, as soon as he was able, he would make his escape and pass the rest of his life alone in some solitary place. It was some weeks before he had regained his health sufficiently to carry out his design; but finally, one beautiful starlight night, the two friends stole away, and when the king woke next morning he found a letter lying by his bed, saying that his son had gone, he knew not whither. He wept bitter tears at the news, for he loved the prince dearly; but he felt that perhaps the young man had done wisely, and he trusted to time and Becasigue's influence to bring the wanderer home.

And while these things were happening, what had become of the white doe? Though when she sprang from the carriage she was aware that some unkind fate had changed her into an animal, yet, till she saw herself in a stream, she had no idea what it was.

'Is it really, I, Desiree?' she said to herself, weeping. 'What wicked fairy can have treated me so; and shall I never, never take my own shape again? My only comfort that, in this great forest, full of lions and serpents, my life will be a short one.'

Now the fairy Tulip was as much grieved at the sad fate of the princess as Desiree's own mother could have been if she had known of it. Still, she could not help feeling that if the king and queen had listened to her advice the girl would by this time be safely in the walls of her new home. However, she loved Desiree too much to let her suffer more than could be helped, and it was she who guided Eglantine to the place where the white doe was standing, cropping the grass which was her dinner.

At the sound of footsteps the pretty creature lifted her head, and when she saw her faithful companion approaching she bounded towards her, and rubbed her head on Eglantine's shoulder. The maid of honour was surprised; but she was fond of animals, and stroked the white doe tenderly, speaking gently to her all the while. Suddenly the beautiful creature lifted her head, and looked up into Eglantine's face, with tears streaming from her eyes. A thought flashed through her mind, and quick as lightning the girl flung herself on her knees, and lifting the animal's feet kissed them one by one. 'My princess! O my dear princess!' cried she; and again the white doe rubbed her head against her, for thought the spiteful fairy had taken away her power of speech, she had not deprived her of her reason!

All day long the two remained together, and when Eglantine grew hungry she was led by the white doe to a part of the forest where pears and peaches grew in abundance; but, as night came on, the maid of honour was filled with the terrors of wild beasts which had beset the princess during her first night in the forest.

'Is there no hut or cave we could go into?' asked she. But the doe only shook her head; and the two sat down and wept with fright.

The fairy Tulip, who, in spite of her anger, was very soft-hearted, was touched at their distress, and flew quickly to their help.

'I cannot take away the spell altogether,' she said, 'for the Fairy of the Fountain is stronger than I; but I can shorten the time of your punishment, and am able to make it less hard, for as soon as darkness fall you shall resume your own shape.'

To think that by-and-by she would cease to be a white doe—indeed, that she would at once cease to be one during the night—was for the present joy enough for Desiree, and she skipped about on the grass in the prettiest manner.

'Go straight down the path in front of you,' continued the fairy, smiling as she watched her; 'go straight down the path and you will soon reach a little hut where you will find shelter.' And with these words she vanished, leaving her hearers happier than they ever thought they could be again.

An old woman was standing at the door of the hut when Eglantine drew near, with the white doe trotting by her side.

'Good evening!' she said; 'could you give me a night's lodging for myself and my doe?'

'Certainly I can,' replied the old woman. And she led them into a room with two little white beds, so clean and comfortable that it made you sleepy even to look at them.

The door had hardly closed behind the old woman when the sun sank below the horizon, and Desiree became a girl again.

'Oh, Eglantine! what should I have done if you had not followed me,' she cried. And she flung herself into her friend's arms in a transport of delight.

Early in the morning Eglantine was awakened by the sound of someone scratching at the door, and on opening her eyes she saw the white doe struggling to get out. The little creature looked up and into her face, and nodded her head as the maid of honour unfastened the latch, but bounded away into the woods, and was lost to sight in a moment.

Meanwhile, the prince and Becasigue were wandering through the wood, till at last the prince grew so tired, that he lay down under a tree, and told Becasigue that he had better go in search of food, and of some place where they could sleep. Becasigue had not gone very far, when a turn of the path brought him face to face with the old woman who was feeding her doves before her cottage.

'Could you give me some milk and fruit?' asked he. 'I am very hungry myself, and, besides, I have left a friend behind me who is still weak from illness.'

'Certainly I can,' answered the old woman. 'But come and sit down in my kitchen while I catch the goat and milk it.'

Becasigue was glad enough to do as he was bid, and in a few minutes the old woman returned with a basket brimming over with oranges and grapes.

'If your friend has been ill he should not pass the night in the forest,' said she. 'I have room in my hut—tiny enough, it is true; but better than nothing, and to that you are both heartily welcome.'

Becasigue thanked her warmly, and as by this time it was almost sunset, he set out to fetch the prince. It was while he was absent that Eglantine and the white doe entered the hut, and having, of course, no idea that in the very next room was the man whose childish impatience had been the cause of all their troubles.

In spite of his fatigue, the prince slept badly, and directly it was light he rose, and bidding Becasigue remain where he was, as he wished to be alone, he strolled out into the forest. He walked on slowly, just as his fancy led him, till, suddenly, he came to a wide open space, and in the middle was the white doe quietly eating her breakfast. She bounded off at the sight of a man, but not before the prince, who had fastened on his bow without thinking, had let fly several arrows, which the fairy Tulip took care should do her no harm. But, quickly as she ran, she soon felt her strength failing her, for fifteen years of life in a tower had not taught her how to exercise her limbs.

Luckily, the prince was too weak to follow her far, and a turn of a path brought her close to the hut, where Eglantine was awaiting her. Panting for breath, she entered their room, and flung herself down on the floor.

When it was dark again, and she was once more the princess Desiree, she told Eglantine what had befallen her.

'I feared the Fairy of the Fountain, and the cruel beasts,' said she; 'but somehow I never thought of the dangers that I ran from men. I do not know now what saved me.'

'You must stay quietly here till the time of your punishment is over,' answered Eglantine. But when the morning dawned, and the girl turned into a doe, the longing for the forest came over her, and she sprang away as before.

As soon as the prince was awake he hastened to the place where, only the day before, he had found the white doe feeding; but of course she had taken care to go in the opposite direction. Much disappointed, he tried first one green path and then another, and at last, wearied with walking, he threw himself down and went fast asleep.

Just at this moment the white doe sprang out of a thicket near by, and started back trembling when she beheld her enemy lying there. Yet, instead of turning to fly, something bade her go and look at him unseen. As she gazed a thrill ran through her, for she felt that, worn and wasted though he was by illness, it was the face of her destined husband. Gently stooping over him she kissed his forehead, and at her touch he awoke.

For a minute they looked at each other, and to his amazement he recognized the white doe which had escaped him the previous day. But in an instant the animal was aroused to a sense of her danger, and she fled with all her strength into the thickest part of the forest. Quick as lightning the prince was on her track, but this time it was with no wish to kill or even wound the beautiful creature.

'Pretty doe! pretty doe! stop! I won't hurt you,' cried he, but his words were carried away by the wind.

At length the doe could run no more, and when the prince reached her, she was lying stretched out on the grass, waiting for her death blow. But instead the prince knelt at her side, and stroked her, and bade her fear nothing, as he would take care of her. So he fetched a little water from the stream in his horn hunting cup, then, cutting some branches from the trees, he twisted them into a litter which he covered with moss, and laid the white doe gently on it.

For a long time they remained thus, but when Desiree saw by the way that the light struck the trees, that he sun must be near its setting, she was filled with alarm lest the darkness should fall, and the prince should behold her in her human shape.

'No, he must not see me for the first time here,' she thought, and instantly began to plan how to get rid of him. Then she opened her mouth and let her tongue hang out, as if she were dying of thirst, and the prince, as she expected, hastened to the stream to get her some more water.

When he returned, the white doe was gone.

That night Desiree confessed to Eglantine that her pursuer was no other than the prince, and that far from flattering him, the portrait had never done him justice.

'Is it not hard to meet him in this shape,' wept she, 'when we both love each other so much?' But Eglantine comforted her, and reminded her that in a short time all would be well.

The prince was very angry at the flight of the white doe, for whom he had taken so much trouble, and returning to the cottage he poured out his adventures and his wrath to Becasigue, who could not help smiling.

'She shall not escape me again,' cried the prince. 'If I hunt her every day for a year, I will have her at last.' And in this frame of mind he went to bed.

When the white doe entered the forest next morning, she had not made up her mind whether she would go and meet the prince, or whether she would shun him, and hide in thickets of which he knew nothing. She decided that the last plan was the best; and so it would have been if the prince had not taken the very same direction in search of her.

Quite by accident he caught sight of her white skin shining through the bushes, and at the same instant she heard a twig snap under his feet. In a moment she was up and away, but the prince, not knowing how else to capture her, aimed an arrow at her leg, which brought her to the ground.

The young man felt like a murderer as he ran hastily up to where the white doe lay, and did his best to soothe the pain she felt, which, in reality, was the last part of the punishment sent by the Fairy of the Fountain. First he brought her some water, and then he fetched some healing herbs, and having crushed them in his hand, laid them on the wound.

'Ah! what a wretch I was to have hurt you,' cried he, resting her head upon his knees; 'and now you will hate me and fly from me for ever!'

For some time the doe lay quietly where she was, but, as before, she remembered that the hour of her transformation was near. She struggled to her feet, but the prince would not hear of her walking, and thinking the old woman might be able to dress her wound better than he could, he took her in his arms to carry her back to the hut. But, small as she was, she made herself so heavy that, after staggering a few steps under her weight, he laid her down, and tied her fast to a tree with some of the ribbons of his hat. This done he went away to get help.

Meanwhile Eglantine had grown very uneasy at the long absence of her mistress, and had come out to look for her. Just as the prince passed out of sight the fluttering ribbons dance before her eyes, and she descried her beautiful princess bound to a tree. With all her might she worked at the knots, but not a single one could she undo, though all appeared so easy. She was still busy with them when a voice behind her said:

'Pardon me, fair lady, but it is MY doe you are trying to steal!'

'Excuse me, good knight' answered Eglantine, hardly glancing at him, 'but it is MY doe that is tied up here! And if you wish for a proof of it, you can see if she knows me or not. Touch my heart, my little one,' she continued, dropping on her knees. And the doe lifted up its fore-foot and laid it on her side. 'Now put your arms round my neck, and sigh.' And again the doe did as she was bid.

'You are right,' said the prince; 'but it is with sorrow I give her up to you, for though I have wounded her yet I love her deeply.'

To this Eglantine answered nothing; but carefully raising up the doe, she led her slowly to the hut.

Now both the prince and Becasigue were quite unaware that the old woman had any guests besides themselves, and, following afar, were much surprised to behold Eglantine and her charge enter the cottage. They lost no time in questioning the old woman, who replied that she knew nothing about the lady and her white doe, who slept next the chamber occupied by the prince and his friend, but that they were very quiet, and paid her well. Then she went back to her kitchen.

'Do you know,' said Becasigue, when they were alone, 'I am certain that the lady we saw is the maid of honour to the Princess Desiree, whom I met at the palace. And, as her room is next to this, it will be easy to make a small hole through which I can satisfy myself whether I am right or not.'

So, taking a knife out of his pocket, he began to saw away the woodwork. The girls heard the grating noise, but fancying it was a mouse, paid no attention, and Becasigue was left in peace to pursue his work. At length the hole was large enough for him to peep through, and the sight was one to strike him dumb with amazement. He had guessed truly: the tall lady was Eglantine herself; but the other—where had he seen her? Ah! now he knew—it was the lady of the portrait!

Desiree, in a flowing dress of green silk, was lying stretched out upon cushions, and as Eglantine bent over her to bathe the wounded leg, she began to talk:

'Oh! let me die,' cried she, 'rather than go on leading this life. You cannot tell the misery of being a beast all the day, and unable to speak to the man I love, to whose impatience I owe my cruel fate. Yet, even so, I cannot bring myself to hate him.'

These words, low though they were spoken, reached Becasigue, who could hardly believe his ears. He stood silent for a moment; then, crossing to the window out of which the prince was gazing, he took his arm and led him across the room. A single glance was sufficient to show the prince that it was indeed Desiree; and how another had come to the palace bearing her name, at that instant he neither knew nor cared. Stealing on tip-toe from the room, he knocked at the next door, which was opened by Eglantine, who thought it was the old woman bearing their supper.

She started back at the sight of the prince, whom this time she also recognised. But he thrust her aside, and flung himself at the feet of Desiree, to whom he poured out all his heart!

Dawn found them still conversing; and the sun was high in the heavens before the princess perceived that she retained her human form. Ah! how happy she was when she knew that the days of her punishment were over; and with a glad voice she told the prince the tale of her enchantment.

So the story ended well after all; and the fairy Tulip, who turned out to be the old woman of the hut, made the young couple such a wedding feast as had never been seen since the world began. And everybody was delighted, except Cerisette and her mother, who were put in a boat and carried to a small island, where they had to work hard for their living.

The Girl-Fish

[Contes des Fees, par Madame d'Aulnoy.]

Once upon a time there lived, on the bank of a stream, a man and a woman who had a daughter. As she was an only child, and very pretty besides, they never could make up their minds to punish her for her faults or to teach her nice manners; and as for work—she laughed in her mother's face if she asked her to help cook the dinner or to wash the plates. All the girl would do was to spend her days in dancing and playing with her friends; and for any use she was to her parents they might as well have no daughter at all.

However, one morning her mother looked so tired that even the selfish girl could not help seeing it, and asked if there was anything she was able to do, so that her mother might rest a little.

The good woman looked so surprised and grateful for this offer that the girl felt rather ashamed, and at that moment would have scrubbed down the house if she had been requested; but her mother only begged her to take the fishing-net out to the bank of the river and mend some holes in it, as her father intended to go fishing that night.

The girl took the net and worked so hard that soon there was not a hole to be found. She felt quite pleased with herself, though she had had plenty to amuse her, as everybody who passed by had stopped and had a chat with her. But by this time the sun was high overhead, and she was just folding her net to carry it home again, when she heard a splash behind her, and looking round she saw a big fish jump into the air. Seizing the net with both hands, she flung it into the water where the circles were spreading one behind the other, and, more by luck than skill, drew out the fish.

'Well, you are a beauty!' she cried to herself; but the fish looked up to her and said:

'You had better not kill me, for, if you do, I will turn you into a fish yourself!'

The girl laughed contemptuously, and ran straight in to her mother.

'Look what I have caught,' she said gaily; 'but it is almost a pity to eat it, for it can talk, and it declares that, if I kill it, it will turn me into a fish too.'

'Oh, put it back, put it back!' implored the mother. 'Perhaps it is skilled in magic. And I should die, and so would your father, if anything should happen to you.'

'Oh, nonsense, mother; what power could a creature like that have over me? Besides, I am hungry, and if I don't have my dinner soon, I shall be cross.' And off she went to gather some flowers to stick in her hair.

About an hour later the blowing of a horn told her that dinner was ready.

'Didn't I say that fish would be delicious?' she cried; and plunging her spoon into the dish the girl helped herself to a large piece. But the instant it touched her mouth a cold shiver ran through her. Her head seemed to flatten, and her eyes to look oddly round the corners; her legs and her arms were stuck to her sides, and she gasped wildly for breath. With a mighty bound she sprang through the window and fell into the river, where she soon felt better, and was able to swim to the sea, which was close by.

No sooner had she arrived there than the sight of her sad face attracted the notice of some of the other fishes, and they pressed round her, begging her to tell them her story.

'I am not a fish at all,' said the new-comer, swallowing a great deal of salt water as she spoke; for you cannot learn how to be a proper fish all in a moment. 'I am not a fish at all, but a girl; at least I was a girl a few minutes ago, only—' And she ducked her head under the waves so that they should not see her crying.

'Only you did not believe that the fish you caught had power to carry out its threat,' said an old tunny. 'Well, never mind, that has happened to all of us, and it really is not a bad life. Cheer up and come with us and see our queen, who lives in a palace that is much more beautiful than any your queens can boast of.'

The new fish felt a little afraid of taking such a journey; but as she was still more afraid of being left alone, she waved her tail in token of consent, and off they all set, hundreds of them together. The people on the rocks and in the ships that saw them pass said to each other:

'Look what a splendid shoal!' and had no idea that they were hastening to the queen's palace; but, then, dwellers on land have so little notion of what goes on in the bottom of the sea! Certainly the little new fish had none. She had watched jelly-fish and nautilus swimming a little way below the surface, and beautiful coloured sea-weeds floating about; but that was all. Now, when she plunged deeper her eyes fell upon strange things.

Wedges of gold, great anchors, heaps of pearl, inestimable stones, unvalued jewels—all scattered in the bottom of the sea! Dead men's bones were there also, and long white creatures who had never seen the light, for they mostly dwelt in the clefts of rocks where the sun's rays could not come. At first our little fish felt as if she were blind also, but by-and-by she began to make out one object after another in the green dimness, and by the time she had swum for a few hours all became clear.

'Here we are at last,' cried a big fish, going down into a deep valley, for the sea has its mountains and valleys just as much as the land. 'That is the palace of the queen of the fishes, and I think you must confess that the emperor himself has nothing so fine.'

'It is beautiful indeed,' gasped the little fish, who was very tired with trying to swim as fast as the rest, and beautiful beyond words the palace was. The walls were made of pale pink coral, worn smooth by the waters, and round the windows were rows of pearls; the great doors were standing open, and the whole troop floated into the chamber of audience, where the queen, who was half a woman after all, was seated on a throne made of a green and blue shell.

'Who are you, and where do you come from?' said she to the little fish, whom the others had pushed in front. And in a low, trembling voice, the visitor told her story.

'I was once a girl too,' answered the queen, when the fish had ended; 'and my father was the king of a great country. A husband was found for me, and on my wedding-day my mother placed her crown on my head and told me that as long as I wore it I should likewise be queen. For many months I was as happy as a girl could be, especially when I had a little son to play with. But, one morning, when I was walking in my gardens, there came a giant and snatched the crown from my head. Holding me fast, he told me that he intended to give the crown to his daughter, and to enchant my husband the prince, so that he should not know the difference between us. Since then she has filled my place and been queen in my stead. As for me, I was so miserable that I threw myself into the sea, and my ladies, who loved me, declared that they would die too; but, instead of dying, some wizard, who pitied my fate, turned us all into fishes, though he allowed me to keep the face and body of a woman. And fished we must remain till someone brings me back my crown again!'

'I will bring it back if you tell me what to do!' cried the little fish, who would have promised anything that was likely to carry her up to earth again. And the queen answered:

'Yes, I will tell you what to do.'

She sat silent for a moment, and then went on:

'There is no danger if you will only follow my counsel; and first you must return to earth, and go up to the top of a high mountain, where the giant has built his castle. You will find him sitting on the steps weeping for his daughter, who has just died while the prince was away hunting. At the last she sent her father my crown by a faithful servant. But I warn you to be careful, for if he sees you he may kill you. Therefore I will give you the power to change yourself into any creature that may help you best. You have only to strike your forehead, and call out its name.'

This time the journey to land seemed much shorter than before, and when once the fish reached the shore she struck her forehead sharply with her tail, and cried:

'Deer, come to me!'

In a moment the small, slimy body disappeared, and in its place stood a beautiful beast with branching horns and slender legs, quivering with longing to be gone. Throwing back her head and snuffing the air, she broke into a run, leaping easily over the rivers and walls that stood in her way.

It happened that the king's son had been hunting since daybreak, but had killed nothing, and when the deer crossed his path as he was resting under a tree he determined to have her. He flung himself on his horse, which went like the wind, and as the prince had often hunted the forest before, and knew all the short cuts, he at last came up with the panting beast.

'By your favour let me go, and do not kill me,' said the deer, turning to the prince with tears in her eyes, 'for I have far to run and much to do.' And as the prince, struck dumb with surprise, only looked at her, the deer cleared the next wall and was soon out of sight.

'That can't really be a deer,' thought the prince to himself, reining in his horse and not attempting to follow her. 'No deer ever had eyes like that. It must be an enchanted maiden, and I will marry her and no other.' So, turning his horse's head, he rode slowly back to his palace.

The deer reached the giant's castle quite out of breath, and her heart sank as she gazed at the tall, smooth walls which surrounded it. Then she plucked up courage and cried:

'Ant, come to me!' And in a moment the branching horns and beautiful shape had vanished, and a tiny brown ant, invisible to all who did not look closely, was climbing up the walls.

It was wonderful how fast she went, that little creature! The wall must have appeared miles high in comparison with her own body; yet, in less time than would have seemed possible, she was over the top and down in the courtyard on the other side. Here she paused to consider what had best be done next, and looking about her she saw that one of the walls had a tall tree growing by it, and in the corner was a window very nearly on a level with the highest branches of the tree.

'Monkey, come to me!' cried the ant; and before you could turn round a monkey was swinging herself from the topmost branches into the room where the giant lay snoring.

'Perhaps he will be so frightened at the sight of me that he may die of fear, and I shall never get the crown,' thought the monkey. 'I had better become something else.' And she called softly: 'Parrot, come to me!'

Then a pink and grey parrot hopped up to the giant, who by this time was stretching himself and giving yawns which shook the castle. The parrot waited a little, until he was really awake, and then she said boldly that she had been sent to take away the crown, which was not his any longer, now his daughter the queen was dead.

On hearing these words the giant leapt out of bed with an angry roar, and sprang at the parrot in order to wring her neck with his great hands. But the bird was too quick for him, and, flying behind his back, begged the giant to have patience, as her death would be of no use to him.

'That is true,' answered the giant; 'but I am not so foolish as to give you that crown for nothing. Let me think what I will have in exchange!' And he scratched his huge head for several minutes, for giants' minds always move slowly.

'Ah, yes, that will do!' exclaimed the giant at last, his face brightening. 'You shall have the crown if you will bring me a collar of blue stones from the Arch of St. Martin, in the Great City.'

Now when the parrot had been a girl she had often heard of this wonderful arch and the precious stones and marbles that had been let into it. It sounded as if it would be a very hard thing to get them away from the building of which they formed a part, but all had gone well with her so far, and at any rate she could but try. So she bowed to the giant, and made her way back to the window where the giant could not see her. Then she called quickly:

'Eagle, come to me!'

Before she had even reached the tree she felt herself borne up on strong wings ready to carry her to the clouds if she wished to go there, and seeming a mere speck in the sky, she was swept along till she beheld the Arch of St. Martin far below, with the rays of the sun shining on it. Then she swooped down, and, hiding herself behind a buttress so that she could not be detected from below, she set herself to dig out the nearest blue stones with her beak. It was even harder work than she had expected; but at last it was done, and hope arose in her heart. She next drew out a piece of string that she had found hanging from a tree, and sitting down to rest strung the stones together. When the necklace was finished she hung it round her neck, and called: 'Parrot, come to me!' And a little later the pink and grey parrot stood before the giant.

'Here is the necklace you asked for,' said the parrot. And the eyes of the giant glistened as he took the heap of blue stones in his hand. But for all that he was not minded to give up the crown.

'They are hardly as blue as I expected,' he grumbled, though the parrot knew as well as he did that he was not speaking the truth; 'so you must bring me something else in exchange for the crown you covet so much. If you fail it will cost you not only the crown but you life also.'

'What is it you want now?' asked the parrot; and the giant answered:

'If I give you my crown I must have another still more beautiful; and this time you shall bring me a crown of stars.'

The parrot turned away, and as soon as she was outside she murmured:

'Toad, come to me!' And sure enough a toad she was, and off she set in search of the starry crown.

She had not gone far before she came to a clear pool, in which the stars were reflected so brightly that they looked quite real to touch and handle. Stooping down she filled a bag she was carrying with the shining water and, returning to the castle, wove a crown out of the reflected stars. Then she cried as before:

'Parrot, come to me!' And in the shape of a parrot she entered the presence of the giant.

'Here is the crown you asked for,' she said; and this time the giant could not help crying out with admiration. He knew he was beaten, and still holding the chaplet of stars, he turned to the girl.

'Your power is greater than mine: take the crown; you have won it fairly!'

The parrot did not need to be told twice. Seizing the crown, she sprang on to the window, crying: 'Monkey, come to me!' And to a monkey, the climb down the tree into the courtyard did not take half a minute. When she had reached the ground she said again: 'Ant, come to me!' And a little ant at once began to crawl over the high wall. How glad the ant was to be out of the giant's castle, holding fast the crown which had shrunk into almost nothing, as she herself had done, but grew quite big again when the ant exclaimed:

'Deer, come to me!'

Surely no deer ever ran so swiftly as that one! On and on she went, bounding over rivers and crashing through tangles till she reached the sea. Here she cried for the last time:

'Fish, come to me!' And, plunging in, she swam along the bottom as far as the palace, where the queen and all the fishes gathered together awaiting her.

The hours since she had left had gone very slowly—as they always do to people that are waiting—and many of them had quite given up hope.

'I am tired of staying here,' grumbled a beautiful little creature, whose colours changed with every movement of her body, 'I want to see what is going on in the upper world. It must be months since that fish went away.'

'It was a very difficult task, and the giant must certainly have killed her or she would have been back long ago,' remarked another.

'The young flies will be coming out now,' murmured a third, 'and they will all be eaten up by the river fish! It is really too bad!' When, suddenly, a voice was heard from behind: 'Look! look! what is that bright thing that is moving so swiftly towards us?' And the queen started up, and stood on her tail, so excited was she.

A silence fell on all the crowd, and even the grumblers held their peace and gazed like the rest. On and on came the fish, holding the crown tightly in her mouth, and the others moved back to let her pass. On she went right up to the queen, who bent and, taking the crown, placed it on her own head. Then a wonderful thing happened. Her tail dropped away or, rather, it divided and grew into two legs and a pair of the prettiest feet in the world, while her maidens, who were grouped around her, shed their scales and became girls again. They all turned and looked at each other first, and next at the little fish who had regained her own shape and was more beautiful than any of them.

'It is you who have given us back our life; you, you!' they cried; and fell to weeping from very joy.

So they all went back to earth and the queen's palace, and quite forgot the one that lay under the sea. But they had been so long away that they found many changes. The prince, the queen's husband, had died some years since, and in his place was her son, who had grown up and was king! Even in his joy at seeing his mother again an air of sadness clung to him, and at last the queen could bear it no longer, and begged him to walk with her in the garden. Seated together in a bower of jessamine—where she had passed long hours as a bride—she took her son's hand and entreated him to tell her the cause of his sorrow. 'For,' said she, 'if I can give you happiness you shall have it.'

'It is no use,' answered the prince; 'nobody can help me. I must bear it alone.'

'But at least let me share your grief,' urged the queen.

'No one can do that,' said he. 'I have fallen in love with what I can never marry, and I must get on as best I can.'

'It may not be as impossible as you think,' answered the queen. 'At any rate, tell me.'

There was silence between them for a moment, then, turning away his head, the prince answered gently:

'I have fallen in love with a beautiful deer!'

'Ah, if that is all,' exclaimed the queen joyfully. And she told him in broken words that, as he had guessed, it was no deer but an enchanted maiden who had won back the crown and brought her home to her own people.

'She is here, in my palace,' added the queen. 'I will take you to her.'

But when the prince stood before the girl, who was so much more beautiful than anything he had ever dreamed of, he lost all his courage, and stood with bent head before her.

Then the maiden drew near, and her eyes, as she looked at him, were the eyes of the deer that day in the forest. She whispered softly:

'By your favour let me go, and do not kill me.'

And the prince remembered her words, and his heart was filled with happiness. And the queen, his mother, watched them and smiled.

The Owl and the Eagle

[From Cuentos Populars Catalans, por lo Dr. D. Francisco de S. Maspons y Labros.]

Once upon a time, in a savage country where the snow lies deep for many months in the year, there lived an owl and an eagle. Though they were so different in many ways they became great friends, and at length set up house together, one passing the day in hunting and the other the night. In this manner they did not see very much of each other—and perhaps agreed all the better for that; but at any rate they were perfectly happy, and only wanted one thing, or, rather, two things, and that was a wife for each.

'I really am too tired when I come home in the evening to clean up the house,' said the eagle.

'And I am much too sleepy at dawn after a long night's hunting to begin to sweep and dust,' answered the owl. And they both made up their minds that wives they must have.

They flew about in their spare moments to the young ladies of their acquaintance, but the girls all declared they preferred one husband to two. The poor birds began to despair, when, one evening, after they had been for a wonder hunting together, they found two sisters fast asleep on their two beds. The eagle looked at the owl and the owl looked at the eagle.

'They will make capital wives if they will only stay with us,' said they. And they flew off to give themselves a wash, and to make themselves smart before the girls awoke.

For many hours the sisters slept on, for they had come a long way, from a town where there was scarcely anything to eat, and felt weak and tired. But by-and-by they opened their eyes and saw the two birds watching them.

'I hope you are rested?' asked the owl politely.

'Oh, yes, thank you,' answered the girls. 'Only we are so very hungry. Do you think we could have something to eat?'

'Certainly!' replied the eagle. And he flew away to a farmhouse a mile or two off, and brought back a nest of eggs in his strong beak; while the owl, catching up a tin pot, went to a cottage where lived an old woman and her cow, and entering the shed by the window dipped the pot into the pail of new milk that stood there.

The girls were so much delighted with the kindness and cleverness of their hosts that, when the birds inquired if they would marry them and stay there for ever, they accepted without so much as giving it a second thought. So the eagle took the younger sister to wife, and the owl the elder, and never was a home more peaceful than theirs!

All went well for several months, and then the eagle's wife had a son, while, on the same day, the owl's wife gave birth to a frog, which she placed directly on the banks of a stream near by, as he did not seem to like the house. The children both grew quickly, and were never tired of playing together, or wanted any other companions.

One night in the spring, when the ice had melted, and the snow was gone, the sisters sat spinning in the house, awaiting their husbands' return. But long though they watched, neither the owl nor the eagle ever came; neither that day nor the next, nor the next, nor the next. At last the wives gave up all hope of their return; but, being sensible women, they did not sit down and cry, but called their children, and set out, determined to seek the whole world over till the missing husbands were found.

Now the women had no idea in which direction the lost birds had gone, but they knew that some distance off was a thick forest, where good hunting was to be found. It seemed a likely place to find them, or, at any rate, they might hear something of them, and they walked quickly on, cheered by the thought that they were doing something. Suddenly the younger sister, who was a little in front, gave a cry of surprise.

'Oh! look at that lake!' she said, 'we shall never get across it.'

'Yes we shall,' answered the elder; 'I know what to do.' And taking a long piece of string from her pocket, fastened it into the frog's mouth, like a bit.

'You must swim across the lake,' she said, stooping to put him in, 'and we will walk across on the line behind you.' And so they did, till they got to about the middle of the lake, when the frog boy stopped.

'I don't like it, and I won't go any further,' cried he sulkily. And his mother had to promise him all sorts of nice things before he would go on again.

When at last they reached the other side, the owl's wife untied the line from the frog's mouth and told him he might rest and play by the lake till they got back from the forest. Then she and her sister and the boy walked on, with the great forest looming before them. But they had by this time come far and were very tired, and felt glad enough to see some smoke curling up from a little hut in front of them.

'Let us go in and ask for some water,' said the eagle's wife; and in they went.

The inside of the hut was so dark that at first they could see nothing at all; but presently they heard a feeble croak from one corner. But sisters turned to look, and there, tied by wings and feet, and their eyes sunken, were the husbands that they sought. Quick as lightning the wives cut the deer-thongs which bound them; but the poor birds were too weak from pain and starvation to do more than utter soft sounds of joy. Hardly, however, were they set free, than a voice of thunder made the two sisters jump, while the little boy clung tightly round his mother's neck.

'What are you doing in my house?' cried she. And the wives answered boldly that now they had found their husbands they meant to save them from such a wicked witch.

'Well, I will give you your chance,' answered the ogress, with a hideous grin; 'we will see if you can slide down this mountain. If you can reach the bottom of the cavern, you shall have your husbands back again.' And as she spoke she pushed them before her out of the door to the edge of a precipice, which went straight down several hundreds of feet. Unseen by the witch, the frog's mother fastened one end of the magic line about her, and whispered to the little boy to hold fast the other. She had scarcely done so when the witch turned round.

'You don't seem to like your bargain,' said she; but the girl answered:

'Oh, yes, I am quite ready. I was only waiting for you!' And sitting down she began her slide. On, on, she went, down to such a depth that even the witch's eyes could not follow her; but she took for granted that the woman was dead, and told the sister to take her place. At that instant, however, the head of the elder appeared above the rock, brought upwards by the magic line. The witch gave a howl of disgust, and hid her face in her hands; thus giving the younger sister time to fasten the cord to her waist before the ogress looked up.

'You can't expect such luck twice,' she said; and the girl sat down and slid over the edge. But in a few minutes she too was back again, and the witch saw that she had failed, and feared lest her power was going. Trembling with rage though she was, she dared not show it, and only laughed hideously.

'I sha'n't let my prisoners go as easily as all that!' she said. 'Make my hair grow as thick and as black as yours, or else your husbands shall never see daylight again.'

'That is quite simple,' replied the elder sister; 'only you must do as we did—and perhaps you won't like the treatment.'

'If you can bear it, of course I can,' answered the witch. And so the girls told her they had first smeared their heads with pitch and then laid hot stones upon them.

'It is very painful,' said they, 'but there is no other way that we know of. And in order to make sure that all will go right, one of us will hold you down while the other pours on the pitch.'

And so they did; and the elder sister let down her hair till it hung over the witch's eyes, so that she might believe it was her own hair growing. Then the other brought a huge stone, and, in short, there was an end of the witch. The sisters were savages who had never seen a missionary.

So when the sisters saw that she was dead they went to the hut, and nursed their husbands till they grew strong. Then they picked up the frog, and all went to make another home on the other side of the great lake.

The Frog and the Lion Fairy

[From the Journal of the Anthropological Institute.]

Once upon a time there lived a king who was always at war with his neighbours, which was very strange, as he was a good and kind man, quite content with his own country, and not wanting to seize land belonging to other people. Perhaps he may have tried too much to please everybody, and that often ends in pleasing nobody; but, at any rate, he found himself, at the end of a hard struggle, defeated in battle, and obliged to fall back behind the walls of his capital city. Once there, he began to make preparations for a long siege, and the first thing he did was to plan how best to send his wife to a place of security.

The queen, who loved her husband dearly, would gladly have remained with him to share his dangers, but he would not allow it. So they parted, with many tears, and the queen set out with a strong guard to a fortified castle on the outskirts of a great forest, some two hundred miles distant. She cried nearly all the way, and when she arrived she cried still more, for everything in the castle was dusty and old, and outside there was only a gravelled courtyard, and the king had forbidden her to go beyond the walls without at least two soldiers to take care of her.

Now the queen had only been married a few months, and in her own home she had been used to walk and ride all over the hills without any attendants at all; so she felt very dull at her being shut up in this way. However, she bore it for a long while because it was the king's wish, but when time passed and there were no signs of the war drifting in the direction of the castle, she grew bolder, and sometimes strayed outside the walls, in the direction of the forest.

Then came a dreadful period, when news from the king ceased entirely.

'He must surely be ill or dead,' thought the poor girl, who even now was only sixteen. 'I can bear it no longer, and if I do not get a letter from him soon I shall leave this horrible place and go back to see what is the matter. Oh! I do wish I had never come away!'

So, without telling anyone what she intended to do, she ordered a little low carriage to be built, something like a sledge, only it was on two wheels—just big enough to hold one person.

'I am tired of being always in the castle,' she said to her attendants; 'and I mean to hunt a little. Quite close by, of course,' she added, seeing the anxious look on their faces. 'And there is no reason that you should not hunt too.'

All the faces brightened at that, for, to tell the truth, they were nearly as dull as their mistress; so the queen had her way, and two beautiful horses were brought from the stable to draw the little chariot. At first the queen took care to keep near the rest of the hunt, but gradually she stayed away longer and longer, and at last, one morning, she took advantage of the appearance of a wild boar, after which her whole court instantly galloped, to turn into a path in the opposite direction.

Unluckily, it did not happen to lead towards the king's palace, where she intended to go, but she was so afraid her flight would be noticed that she whipped up her horses till they ran away.

When she understood what was happening the poor young queen was terribly frightened, and, dropping the reins, clung to the side of the chariot. The horses, thus left without any control, dashed blindly against a tree, and the queen was flung out on the ground, where she lay for some minutes unconscious.

A rustling sound near her at length caused her to open her eyes; before her stood a huge woman, almost a giantess, without any clothes save a lion's skin, which was thrown over her shoulders, while a dried snake's skin was plaited into her hair. In one hand she held a club on which she leaned, and in the other a quiver full of arrows.

At the sight of this strange figure the queen thought she must be dead, and gazing on an inhabitant of another world. So she murmured softly to herself:

'I am not surprised that people are so loth to die when they know that they will see such horrible creatures.' But, low as she spoke, the giantess caught the words, and began to laugh.

'Oh, don't be afraid; you are still alive, and perhaps, after all, you may be sorry for it. I am the Lion Fairy, and you are going to spend the rest of your days with me in my palace, which is quite near this. So come along.' But the queen shrank back in horror.

'Oh, Madam Lion, take me back, I pray you, to my castle; and fix what ransom you like, for my husband will pay it, whatever it is. But the giantess shook her head.

'I am rich enough already,' she answered, 'but I am often dull, and I think you may amuse me a little.' And, so saying, she changed her shape into that of a lion, and throwing the queen across her back, she went down the ten thousand steps that led to her palace. The lion had reached the centre of the earth before she stopped in front of a house, lighted with lamps, and built on the edge of a lake of quicksilver. In this lake various huge monsters might be seen playing or fighting—the queen did not know which—and around flew rooks and ravens, uttering dismal croaks. In the distance was a mountain down whose sides waters slowly coursed—these were the tears of unhappy lovers—and nearer the gate were trees without either fruit of flowers, while nettles and brambles covered the ground. If the castle had been gloomy, what did the queen feel about this?

For some days the queen was so much shaken by all she had gone through that she lay with her eyes closed, unable either to move or speak. When she got better, the Lion Fairy told her that if she liked she could build herself a cabin, as she would have to spend her life in that place. At these words the queen burst into tears, and implored her gaoler to put her to death rather than condemn her to such a life; but the Lion Fairy only laughed, and counselled her to try to make herself pleasant, as many worse things might befall her.

'Is there no way in which I can touch your heart?' asked the poor girl in despair.

'Well, if you really wish to please me you will make me a pasty out of the stings of bees, and be sure it is good.'

'But I don't see any bees,' answered the queen, looking round.

'Oh, no, there aren't any,' replied her tormentor; 'but you will have to find them all the same.' And, so saying, she went away.

'After all, what does it matter?' thought the queen to herself, 'I have only one life, and I can but lose it.' And not caring what she did, she left the palace and seating herself under a yew tree, poured out all her grief.

'Oh, my dear husband,' wept she, 'what will you think when you come to the castle to fetch me and find me gone? Rather a thousand times that you should fancy me dead than imagine that I had forgotten you! Ah, how fortunate that the broken chariot should be lying in the wood, for then you may grieve for me as one devoured by wild beasts. And if another should take my place in your heart—Well, at least I shall never know it.'

She might have continued for long in this fashion had not the voice of a crow directly overhead attracted her attention. Looking up to see what was the matter she beheld, in the dim light, a crow holding a fat frog in his claws, which he evidently intended for his supper. The queen rose hastily from the seat, and striking the bird sharply on the claws with the fan which hung from her side, she forced him to drop the frog, which fell to the round more dead than alive. The crow, furious at his disappointment, flew angrily away.

As soon as the frog had recovered her senses she hopped up to the queen, who was still sitting under the yew. Standing on her hind legs, and bowing low before her, she said gently:

'Beautiful lady, by what mischance do you come here? You are the only creature that I have seen do a kind deed since a fatal curiosity lured me to this place.'

'What sort of a frog can you be that knows the language of mortals?' asked the queen in her turn. 'But if you do, tell me, I pray, if I alone am a captive, for hitherto I have beheld no one but the monsters of the lake.'

'Once upon a time they were men and women like yourself,' answered the frog, 'but having power in their hands, they used it for their own pleasure.

Therefore fate has sent them here for a while to bear the punishment of their misdoings.'

'But you, friend frog, you are not one of these wicked people, I am sure?' asked the queen.

'I am half a fairy,' replied the frog; 'but, although I have certain magic gifts, I am not able to do all I wish. And if the Lion Fairy were to know of my presence in her kingdom she would hasten to kill me.'

'But if you are a fairy, how was it that you were so nearly slain by the crow?' said the queen, wrinkling her forehead.

'Because the secret of my power lies in my little cap that is made of rose leaves; but I had laid it aside for the moment, when that horrible crow pounced upon me. Once it is on my head I fear nothing. But let me repeat; had it not been for you I could not have escaped death, and if I can do anything to help you, or soften your hard fate, you have only to tell me.'

'Alas,' sighed the queen, 'I have been commanded by the Lion Fairy to make her a pasty out of the stings of bees, and, as far as I can discover, there are none here; as how should there be, seeing there are no flowers for them to feed on? And, even if there were, how could I catch them?'

'Leave it to me,' said the frog, 'I will manage it for you.' And, uttering a strange noise, she struck the ground thrice with her foot. In an instant six thousand frogs appeared before her, one of them bearing a little cap.

'Cover yourselves with honey, and hop round by the beehives,' commanded the frog, putting on the cap which her friend was holding in her mouth. And turning to the queen, he added:

'The Lion Fairy keeps a store of bees in a secret place near to the bottom of the ten thousand steps leading into the upper world. Not that she wants them for herself, but they are sometimes useful to her in punishing her victims. However, this time we will get the better of her.'

Just as she had finished speaking the six thousand frogs returned, looking so strange with bees sticking to every part of them that, sad as she felt, the poor queen could not help laughing. The bees were all so stupefied with what they had eaten that it was possible to draw their stings without hunting them. So, with the help of her friend, the queen soon made ready her pasty and carried it to the Lion Fairy.

'Not enough pepper,' said the giantess, gulping down large morsels, in order the hide the surprise she felt. 'Well, you have escaped this time, and I am glad to find I have got a companion a little more intelligent than the others I have tried. Now, you had better go and build yourself a house.'

So the queen wandered away, and picking up a small axe which lay near the door she began with the help of her friend the frog to cut down some cypress trees for the purpose. And not content with that the six thousand froggy servants were told to help also, and it was not long before they had built the prettiest little cabin in the world, and made a bed in one corner of dried ferns which they fetched from the top of the ten thousand steps. It looked soft and comfortable, and the queen was very glad to lie down upon it, so tired was she with all that had happened since the morning. Scarcely, however, had she fallen asleep when the lake monsters began to make the most horrible noises just outside, while a small dragon crept in and terrified her so that she ran away, which was just what the dragon wanted!

The poor queen crouched under a rock for the rest of the night, and the next morning, when she woke from her troubled dreams, she was cheered at seeing the frog watching by her.

'I hear we shall have to build you another palace,' said she. 'Well, this time we won't go so near the lake.' And she smiled with her funny wide mouth, till the queen took heart, and they went together to find wood for the new cabin.

The tiny palace was soon ready, and a fresh bed made of wild thyme, which smelt delicious. Neither the queen nor the frog said anything about it, but somehow, as always happens, the story came to the ears of the Lion Fairy, and she sent a raven to fetch the culprit.

'What gods or men are protecting you?' she asked, with a frown. 'This earth, dried up by a constant rain of sulphur and fire, produces nothing, yet I hear that YOUR bed is made of sweet smelling herbs. However, as you can get flowers for yourself, of course you can get them for me, and in an hour's time I must have in my room a nosegay of the rarest flowers. If not—! Now you can go.'

The poor queen returned to her house looking so sad that the frog, who was waiting for her, noticed it directly.

'What is the matter?' said she, smiling.

'Oh, how can you laugh!' replied the queen. 'This time I have to bring her in an hour a posy of the rarest flowers, and where am I to find them? If I fail I know she will kill me.'

'Well, I must see if I can't help you,' answered the frog. 'The only person I have made friends with here is a bat. She is a good creature, and always does what I tell her, so I will just lend her my cap, and if she puts it on, and flies into the world, she will bring back all we want. I would go myself, only she will be quicker.'

Then the queen dried her eyes, and waited patiently, and long before the hour had gone by the bat flew in with all the most beautiful and sweetest flowers that grew on the earth. The girl sprang up overjoyed at the sight, and hurried with them to the Lion Fairy, who was so astonished that for once she had nothing to say.

Now the smell and touch of the flowers had made the queen sick with longing for her home, and she told the frog that she would certainly die if she did not manage to escape somehow.

'Let me consult my cap,' said the frog; and taking it off she laid it in a box, and threw in after it a few sprigs of juniper, some capers, and two peas, which she carried under her right leg; she then shut down the lid of the box, and murmured some words which the queen did not catch.

In a few moments a voice was heard speaking from the box.

'Fate, who rules us all,' said the voice, 'forbids your leaving this place till the time shall come when certain things are fulfilled. But, instead, a gift shall be given you, which will comfort you in all your troubles.'

And the voice spoke truly, for, a few days after, when the frog peeped in at the door she found the most beautiful baby in the world lying by the side of the queen.

'So the cap has kept its word,' cried the frog with delight. 'How soft its cheeks are, and what tiny feet it has got! What shall we call it?'

This was a very important point, and needed much discussion. A thousand names were proposed and rejected for a thousand silly reasons. One was another reminded the queen of somebody she did not like; but at length an idea flashed into the queen's head, and she called out:

'I know! We will call her Muffette.'

'That is the very thing,' shouted the frog, jumping high into the air; and so it was settled.

The princess Muffette was about six months old when the frog noticed that the queen had begun to grow sad again.

'Why do you have that look in your eyes?' she asked one day, when she had come in to play with the baby, who could now crawl.

The way they played their game was to let Muffette creep close to the frog, and then for the frog to bound high into the air and alight on the child's head, or back, or legs, when she always sent up a shout of pleasure. There is no play fellow like a frog; but then it must be a fairy frog, or else you might hurt it, and if you did something dreadful might happen to you. Well, as I have said, our frog was struck with the queen's sad face, and lost no time in asking her what was the reason.

'I don't see what you have to complain of now; Muffette is quite well and quite happy, and even the Lion Fairy is kind to her when she sees her. What is it?'

'Oh! if her father could only see her!' broke forth the queen, clasping her hands. 'Or if I could only tell him all that has happened since we parted. But they will have brought him tidings of the broken carriage, and he will have thought me dead, or devoured by wild beasts. And though he will mourn for me long—I know that well—yet in time they will persuade him to take a wife, and she will be young and fair, and he will forget me.'

And in all this the queen guessed truly, save that nine long years were to pass before he would consent to put another in her place.

The frog answered nothing at the time, but stopped her game and hopped away among the cypress trees. Here she sat and thought and thought, and the next morning she went back to the queen and said:

'I have come, madam, to make you an offer. Shall I go to the king instead of you, and tell him of your sufferings, and that he has the most charming baby in the world for his daughter? The way is long, and I travel slowly; but, sooner or later, I shall be sure to arrive. Only, are you not afraid to be left without my protection? Ponder the matter carefully; it is for you to decide.'

'Oh, it needs no pondering,' cried the queen joyfully, holding up her clasped hands, and making Muffette do likewise, in token of gratitude. But in order that he may know that you have come from me I will send him a letter.' And pricking her arm, she wrote a few words with her blood on the corner of her handkerchief. Then tearing it off, she gave it to the frog, and they bade each other farewell.

It took the frog a year and four days to mount the ten thousand steps that led to the upper world, but that was because she was still under the spell of a wicked fairy. By the time she reached the top, she was so tired that she had to remain for another year on the banks of a stream to rest, and also to arrange the procession with which she was to present herself before the king. For she knew far too well what was due to herself and her relations, to appear at Court as if she was a mere nobody. At length, after many consultations with her cap, the affair was settled, and at the end of the second year after her parting with the queen they all set out.

First walked her bodyguard of grasshoppers, followed by her maids of honour, who were those tiny green frogs you see in the fields, each one mounted on a snail, and seated on a velvet saddle. Next came the water-rats, dressed as pages, and lastly the frog herself, in a litter borne by eight toads, and made of tortoiseshell. Here she could lie at her ease, with her cap on her head, for it was quite large and roomy, and could easily have held two eggs when the frog was not in it.

The journey lasted seven years, and all this time the queen suffered tortures of hope, though Muffette did her best to comfort her. Indeed, she would most likely have died had not the Lion Fairy taken a fancy that the child and her mother should go hunting with her in the upper world, and, in spite of her sorrows, it was always a joy to the queen to see the sun again. As for little Muffette, by the time she was seven her arrows seldom missed their mark. So, after all, the years of waiting passed more quickly than the queen had dared to hope.

The frog was always careful to maintain her dignity, and nothing would have persuaded her to show her face in public places, or even along the high road, where there was a chance of meeting anyone. But sometimes, when the procession had to cross a little stream, or go over a piece of marshy ground, orders would be given for a halt; fine clothes were thrown off, bridles were flung aside, and grasshoppers, water-rats, even the frog herself, spent a delightful hour or two playing in the mud.

But at length the end was in sight, and the hardships were forgotten in the vision of the towers of the king's palace; and, one bright morning, the cavalcade entered the gates with all the pomp and circumstance of a royal embassy. And surely no ambassador had ever created such a sensation! Door and windows, even the roofs of houses, were filled with people, whose cheers reached the ears of the king. However, he had no time to attend to such matters just then, as, after nine years, he had at last consented to the entreaties of his courtiers, and was on the eve of celebrating his second marriage.

The frog's heart beat high when her litter drew up before the steps of the palace, and leaning forward she beckoned to her side one of the guards who were standing in his doorway.

'I wish to see his Majesty,' said he.

'His Majesty is engaged, and can see no one,' answered the soldier.

'His Majesty will see ME,' returned the frog, fixing her eye upon him; and somehow the man found himself leading the procession along the gallery into the Hall of Audience, where the king sat surrounded by his nobles arranging the dresses which everyone was to wear at his marriage ceremony.

All stared in surprise as the procession advanced, and still more when the frog gave one bound from the litter on to the floor, and with another landed on the arm of the chair of state.

'I am only just in time, sire,' began the frog; 'had I been a day later you would have broken your faith which you swore to the queen nine years ago.'

'Her remembrance will always be dear to me,' answered the king gently, though all present expected him to rebuke the frog severely for her impertinence. But know, Lady Frog, that a king can seldom do as he wishes, but must be bound by the desires of his subjects. For nine years I have resisted them; now I can do so no longer, and have made choice of the fair young maiden playing at ball yonder.'

'You cannot wed her, however fair she may be, for the queen your wife is still alive, and sends you this letter written in her own blood,' said the frog, holding out the square of handkerchief as she spoke. 'And, what is more, you have a daughter who is nearly nine years old, and more beautiful than all the other children in the world put together.'

The king turned pale when he heard these words, and his hand trembled so that he could hardly read what the queen had written. Then he kissed the handkerchief twice or thrice, and burst into tears, and it was some minutes before he could speak. When at length he found his voice he told his councillors that the writing was indeed that of the queen, and now that he had the joy of knowing she was alive he could, of course, proceed no further with his second marriage. This naturally displeased the ambassadors who had conducted the bride to court, and one of them inquired indignantly if he meant to put such an insult on the princess on the word of a mere frog.

'I am not a "mere frog," and I will give you proof of it,' retorted the angry little creature. And putting on her cap, she cried: Fairies that are my friends, come hither!' And in a moment a crowd of beautiful creatures, each one with a crown on her head, stood before her. Certainly none could have guessed that they were the snails, water-rats, and grasshoppers from which she had chosen her retinue.

At a sign from the frog the fairies danced a ballet, with which everyone was so delighted that they begged to have to repeated; but now it was not youths and maidens who were dancing, but flowers. Then these again melted into fountains, whose waters interlaced and, rushing down the sides of the hall, poured out in a cascade down the steps, and formed a river found the castle, with the most beautiful little boats upon it, all painted and gilded.

'Oh, let us go in them for a sail!' cried the princess, who had long ago left her game of ball for a sight of these marvels, and, as she was bent upon it, the ambassadors, who had been charged never to lose sight of her, were obliged to go also, though they never entered a boat if they could help it.

But the moment they and the princess had seated themselves on the soft cushions, river and boats vanished, and the princess and the ambassadors vanished too. Instead the snails and grasshoppers and water-rats stood round the frog in their natural shapes.

'Perhaps,' said she, 'your Majesty may now be convinced that I am a fairy and speak the truth. Therefore lose no time in setting in order the affairs of your kingdom and go in search of your wife. Here is a ring that will admit you into the presence of the queen, and will likewise allow you to address unharmed the Lion Fairy, though she is the most terrible creature that ever existed.'

By this time the king had forgotten all about the princess, whom he had only chosen to please his people, and was as eager to depart on his journey as the frog was for him to go. He made one of his ministers regent of the kingdom, and gave the frog everything her heart could desire; and with her ring on his finger he rode away to the outskirts of the forest. Here he dismounted, and bidding his horse go home, he pushed forward on foot.

Having nothing to guide him as to where he was likely to find the entrance of the under-world, the king wandered hither and thither for a long while, till, one day, while he was resting under a tree, a voice spoke to him.

'Why do you give yourself so much trouble for nought, when you might know what you want to know for the asking? Alone you will never discover the path that leads to your wife.'

Much startled, the king looked about him. He could see nothing, and somehow, when he thought about it, the voice seemed as if it were part of himself. Suddenly his eyes fell on the ring, and he understood.

'Fool that I was!' cried he; 'and how much precious time have I wasted? Dear ring, I beseech you, grant me a vision of my wife and my daughter!' And even as he spoke there flashed past him a huge lioness, followed by a lady and a beautiful young maid mounted on fairy horses.

Almost fainting with joy he gazed after them, and then sank back trembling on the ground.

'Oh, lead me to them, lead me to them!' he exclaimed. And the ring, bidding him take courage, conducted him safely to the dismal place where his wife had lived for ten years.

Now the Lion Fairy knew beforehand of his expected presence in her dominions, and she ordered a palace of crystal to be built in the middle of the lake of quicksilver; and in order to make it more difficult of approach she let it float whither it would. Immediately after their return from the chase, where the king had seen them, she conveyed the queen and Muffette into the palace, and put them under the guard of the monsters of the lake, who one and all had fallen in love with the princess. They were horribly jealous, and ready to eat each other up for her sake, so they readily accepted the charge. Some stationed themselves round the floating palace, some sat by the door, while the smallest and lightest perched themselves on the roof.

Of course the king was quite ignorant of these arrangements, and boldly entered the palace of the Lion Fairy, who was waiting for him, with her tail lashing furiously, for she still kept her lion's shape. With a roar that shook the walls she flung herself upon him; but he was on the watch, and a blow from his sword cut off the paw she had put forth to strike him dead. She fell back, and with his helmet still on and his shield up, he set his foot on her throat.

'Give me back the wife and the child you have stolen from me,' he said, 'or you shall not live another second!'

But the fairy answered:

'Look through the window at that lake and see if it is in my power to give them to you.' And the king looked, and through the crystal walls he beheld his wife and daughter floating on the quicksilver. At that sight the Lion Fairy and all her wickedness was forgotten. Flinging off his helmet, he shouted to them with all his might. The queen knew his voice, and she and Muffette ran to the window and held out their hands. Then the king swore a solemn oath that he would never leave the spot without taking them if it should cost him his life; and he meant it, though at the moment he did not know what he was undertaking.

Three years passed by, and the king was no nearer to obtaining his heart's desire. He had suffered every hardship that could be imagined—nettles had been his bed, wild fruits more bitter than gall his food, while his days had been spent in fighting the hideous monsters which kept him from the palace. He had not advanced one single step, nor gained one solitary advantage. Now he was almost in despair, and ready to defy everything and throw himself into the lake.

It was at this moment of his blackest misery that, one night, a dragon who had long watched him from the roof crept to his side.

'You thought that love would conquer all obstacles,' said he; 'well, you have found it hasn't! But if you will swear to me by your crown and sceptre that you will give me a dinner of the food that I never grow tired of, whenever I choose to ask for it, I will enable you to reach your wife and daughter.'

Ah, how glad the king was to hear that! What oath would he not have taken so as to clasp his wife and child in is arms? Joyfully he swore whatever the dragon asked of him; then he jumped on his back, and in another instant would have been carried by the strong wings into the castle if the nearest monsters had not happened to awake and hear the noise of talking and swum to the shore to give battle. The fight was long and hard, and when the king at last beat back his foes another struggle awaited him. At the entrance gigantic bats, owls, and crows set upon him from all sides; but the dragon had teeth and claws, while the queen broke off sharp bits of glass and stabbed and cut in her anxiety to help her husband. At length the horrible creatures flew away; a sound like thunder was heard, the palace and the monsters vanished, while, at the same moment—no one knew how—the king found himself standing with his wife and daughter in the hall of his own home.

The dragon had disappeared with all the rest, and for some years no more was heard or thought of him. Muffette grew every day more beautiful, and when she was fourteen the kings and emperors of the neighbouring countries sent to ask her in marriage for themselves or their sons. For a long time the girl turned a deaf ear to all their prayers; but at length a young prince of rare gifts touched her heart, and though the king had left her free to choose what husband she would, he had secretly hoped that out of all the wooers this one might be his son-in-law. So they were betrothed that some day with great pomp, and then with many tears, the prince set out for his father's court, bearing with him a portrait of Muffette.

The days passed slowly to Muffette, in spite of her brave efforts to occupy herself and not to sadden other people by her complaints. One morning she was playing on her harp in the queen's chamber when the king burst into the room and clasped his daughter in his arms with an energy that almost frightened her.

'Oh, my child! my dear child! why were you ever born?' cried he, as soon as he could speak.

'Is the prince dead?' faltered Muffette, growing white and cold.

'No, no; but—oh, how can I tell you!' And he sank down on a pile of cushions while his wife and daughter knelt beside him.

At length he was able to tell his tale, and a terrible one it was! There had just arrived at court a huge giant, as ambassador from the dragon by whose help the king had rescued the queen and Muffette from the crystal palace. The dragon had been very busy for many years past, and had quite forgotten the princess till the news of her betrothal reached his ears. Then he remembered the bargain he had made with her father; and the more he heard of Muffette the more he felt sure she would make a delicious dish. So he had ordered the giant who was his servant to fetch her at once.

No words would paint the horror of both the queen and the princess as they listened to this dreadful doom. They rushed instantly to the hall, where the giant was awaiting them, and flinging themselves at his feet implored him to take the kingdom if he would, but to have pity on the princess. The giant looked at them kindly, for he was not at all hard-hearted, but said that he had no power to do anything, and that if the princess did not go with him quietly the dragon would come himself.

Several days went by, and the king and queen hardly ceased from entreating the aid of the giant, who by this time was getting weary of waiting.

'There is only one way of helping you,' he said at last, 'and that is to marry the princess to my nephew, who, besides being young and handsome, has been trained in magic, and will know how to keep her safe from the dragon.'

'Oh, thank you, thank you!' cried the parents, clasping his great hands to their breasts. 'You have indeed lifted a load from us. She shall have half the kingdom for her dowry.' But Muffette stood up and thrust them aside.

'I will not buy my life with faithlessness,' she said proudly; 'and I will go with you this moment to the dragon's abode.' And all her father's and mother's tears and prayers availed nothing to move her.

The next morning Muffette was put into a litter, and, guarded by the giant and followed by the king and queen and the weeping maids of honour, they started for the foot of the mountain where the dragon had his castle. The way, though rough and stony, seemed all too short, and when they reached the spot appointed by the dragon the giant ordered the men who bore the litter to stand still.

'It is time for you to bid farewell to your daughter,' said he; 'for I see the dragon coming to us.'

It was true; a cloud appeared to pass over the sun, for between them and it they could all discern dimly a huge body half a mile long approaching nearer and nearer. At first the king could not believe that this was the small beast who had seemed so friendly on the shore of the lake of quicksilver but then he knew very little of necromancy, and had never studied the art of expanding and contracting his body. But it was the dragon and nothing else, whose six wings were carrying him forward as fast as might be, considering his great weight and the length of his tail, which had fifty twists and a half.

He came quickly, yes; but the frog, mounted on a greyhound, and wearing her cap on her head, went quicker still. Entering a room where the prince was sitting gazing at the portrait of his betrothed, she cried to him:

'What are you doing lingering here, when the life of the princess is nearing its last moment? In the courtyard you will find a green horse with three heads and twelve feet, and by its side a sword eighteen yards long. Hasten, lest you should be too late!'

The fight lasted all day, and the prince's strength was well-nigh spent, when the dragon, thinking that the victory was won, opened his jaws to give a roar of triumph. The prince saw his chance, and before his foe could shut his mouth again had plunged his sword far down his adversary's throat. There was a desperate clutching of the claws to the earth, a slow flagging of the great wings, then the monster rolled over on his side and moved no more. Muffette was delivered.

After this they all went back to the palace. The marriage took place the following day, and Muffette and her husband lived happy for ever after.

The Adventures of Covan the Brown-Haired

[From Les Contes des Fees, par Madame d'Aulnoy.]

On the shores of the west, where the great hills stand with their feet in the sea, dwelt a goatherd and his wife, together with their three sons and one daughter. All day long the young men fished and hunted, while their sister took out the kids to pasture on the mountain, or stayed at home helping her mother and mending the nets.

For several years they all lived happily together, when one day, as the girl was out on the hill with the kids, the sun grew dark and an air cold as a thick white mist came creeping, creeping up from the sea. She rose with a shiver, and tried to call to her kids, but the voice died away in her throat, and strong arms seemed to hold her.

Loud were the wails in the hut by the sea when the hours passed on and the maiden came not. Many times the father and brothers jumped up, thinking they heard her steps, but in the thick darkness they could scarcely see their own hands, nor could they tell where the river lay, nor where the mountain. One by one the kids came home, and at every bleat someone hurried to open the door, but no sound broke the stillness. Through the night no one slept, and when morning broke and the mist rolled back, they sought the maiden by sea and by land, but never a trace of her could be found anywhere.

Thus a year and a day slipped by, and at the end of it Gorla of the Flocks and his wife seemed suddenly to have grown old. Their sons too were sadder than before, for they loved their sister well, and had never ceased to mourn for her. At length Ardan the eldest spoke and said:

'It is now a year and a day since our sister was taken from us, and we have waited in grief and patience for her to return. Surely some evil has befallen her, or she would have sent us a token to put our hearts at rest; and I have vowed to myself that my eyes shall not know sleep till, living or dead, I have found her.'

'If you have vowed, then must you keep your vow,' answered Gorla. 'But better had it been if you had first asked your father's leave before you made it. Yet, since it is so, your mother will bake you a cake for you to carry with you on your journey. Who can tell how long it may be?'

So the mother arose and baked not one cake but two, a big one and a little one.

'Choose, my son,' said she. 'Will you have the little cake with your mother's blessing, or the big one without it, in that you have set aside your father and taken on yourself to make a vow?'

'I will have the large cake,' answered the youth; 'for what good would my mother's blessing do for me if I was dying of hunger?' And taking the big cake he went his way.

Straight on he strode, letting neither hill nor river hinder him. Swiftly he walked—swiftly as the wind that blew down the mountain. The eagles and the gulls looked on from their nests as he passed, leaving the deer behind him; but at length he stopped, for hunger had seized on him, and he could walk no more. Trembling with fatigue he sat himself on a rock and broke a piece off his cake.

'Spare me a morsel, Ardan son of Gorla,' asked a raven, fluttering down towards him.

'Seek food elsewhere, O bearer of ill-news,' answered Ardan son of Gorla; 'it is but little I have for myself.' And he stretched himself out for a few moments, then rose to his feet again. On and on went he till the little birds flew to their nests, and the brightness died out of the sky, and a darkness fell over the earth. On and on, and on, till at last he saw a beam of light streaming from a house and hastened towards it.

The door was opened and he entered, but paused when he beheld an old man lying on a bench by the fire, while seated opposite him was a maiden combing out the locks of her golden hair with a comb of silver.

'Welcome, fair youth,' said the old man, turning his head. 'Sit down and warm yourself, and tell me how fares the outer world. It is long since I have seen it.'

'All my news is that I am seeking service,' answered Ardan son of Gorla; 'I have come from far since sunrise, and glad was I to see the rays of your lamp stream into the darkness.'

'I need someone to herd my three dun cows, which are hornless,' said the old man. 'If, for the space of a year, you can bring them back to me each evening before the sun sets, I will make you payment that will satisfy your soul.'

But here the girl looked up and answered quickly:

'Ill will come of it if he listens to your offer.'

'Counsel unsought is worth nothing,' replied, rudely, Ardan son of Gorla. 'It would be little indeed that I am fit for if I cannot drive three cows out to pasture and keep them safe from the wolves that may come down from the mountains. Therefore, good father, I will take service with you at daybreak, and ask no payment till the new year dawns.'

Next morning the bell of the deer was not heard amongst the fern before the maiden with the hair of gold had milked the cows, and led them in front of the cottage where the old man and Ardan son of Gorla awaited them.

'Let them wander where they will,' he said to his servant, 'and never seek to turn them from their way, for well they know the fields of good pasture. But take heed to follow always behind them, and suffer nothing that you see, and nought that you hear, to draw you into leaving them. Now go, and may wisdom go with you.'

As he ceased speaking he touched one of the cows on her forehead, and she stepped along the path, with the two others one on each side. As he had been bidden, behind them came Ardan son of Gorla, rejoicing in his heart that work so easy had fallen to his lot. At the year's end, thought he, enough money would lie in his pocket to carry him into far countries where his sister might be, and, in the meanwhile, someone might come past who could give him tidings of her.

Thus he spoke to himself, when his eyes fell on a golden cock and a silver hen running swiftly along the grass in front of him. In a moment the words that the old man had uttered vanished from his mind and he gave chase. They were so near that he could almost seize their tails, yet each time he felt sure he could catch them his fingers closed on the empty air. At length he could run no more, and stopped to breathe, while the cock and hen went on as before. Then he remembered the cows, and, somewhat frightened, turned back to seek them. Luckily they had not strayed far, and were quietly feeding on the thick green grass.

Ardan son of Gorla was sitting under a tree, when he beheld a staff of gold and a staff of silver doubling themselves in strange ways on the meadow in front of him, and starting up he hastened towards them. He followed them till he was tired, but he could not catch them, though they seemed ever within his reach. When at last he gave up the quest his knees trembled beneath him for very weariness, and glad was he to see a tree growing close by lade with fruits of different sorts, of which he ate greedily.

The sun was by now low in the heavens, and the cows left off feeding, and turned their faces home again, followed by Ardan son of Gorla. At the door of their stable the maiden stood awaiting them, and saying nought to their herd, she sat down and began to milk. But it was not milk that flowed into her pail; instead it was filled with a thin stream of water, and as she rose up from the last cow the old man appeared outside.

'Faithless one, you have betrayed your trust!' he said to Ardan son of Gorla. 'Not even for one day could you keep true! Well, you shall have your reward at once, that others may take warning from you.' And waving his wand he touched with it the chest of the youth, who became a pillar of stone.

Now Gorla of the Flocks and his wife were full of grief that they had lost a son as well as a daughter, for no tidings had come to them of Ardan their eldest born. At length, when two years and two days had passed since the maiden had led her kids to feed on the mountain and had been seen no more, Ruais, second son of Gorla, rose up one morning, and said:

'Time is long without my sister and Ardan my brother. So I have vowed to seek them wherever they may be.'

And his father answered:

'Better it had been if you had first asked my consent and that of your mother; but as you have vowed so must you do.' Then he bade his wife make a cake, but instead she made two, and offered Ruais his choice, as she had done to Ardan. Like Ardan, Ruais chose the large, unblessed cake, and set forth on his way, doing always, though he knew it not, that which Ardan had done; so, needless is it to tell what befell him till he too stood, a pillar of stone, on the hill behind the cottage, so that all men might see the fate that awaited those who broke their faith.

Another year and a day passed by, when Covan the Brown-haired, youngest son of Gorla of the Flocks, one morning spake to his parents, saying:

'It is more than three years since my sister left us. My brothers have also gone, no one know whither, and of us four none remains but I. No, therefore, I long to seek them, and I pray you and my mother to place no hindrance in my way.'

And his father answered:

'Go, then, and take our blessing with you.'

So the wife of Gorla of the Flocks baked two cakes, one large and one small; and Covan took the small one, and started on his quest. In the wood he felt hungry, for he had walked far, and he sat down to eat. Suddenly a voice behind him cried:

'A bit for me! a bit for me!' And looking round he beheld the black raven of the wilderness.

'Yes, you shall have a bit,' said Covan the Brown-haired; and breaking off a piece he stretched it upwards to the raven, who ate it greedily. Then Covan arose and went forward, till he saw the light from the cottage streaming before him, and glad was he, for night was at hand.

'Maybe I shall find some work there,' he thought, 'and at least I shall gain money to help me in my search; for who knows how far my sister and my brothers may have wandered?'

The door stood open and he entered, and the old man gave him welcome, and the golden-haired maiden likewise. As happened before, he was offered by the old man to herd his cows; and, as she had done to his brothers, the maiden counselled him to leave such work alone. But, instead of answering rudely, like both Ardan and Ruais, he thanked her, with courtesy, though he had no mind to heed her; and he listened to the warnings and words of his new master.

Next day he set forth at dawn with the dun cows in front of him, and followed patiently wherever they might lead him. On the way he saw the gold cock and silver hen, which ran even closer to him than they had done to his brothers. Sorely tempted, he longed to give them chase; but, remembering in time that he had been bidden to look neither to the right nor to the left, with a mighty effort he turned his eyes away. Then the gold and silver staffs seemed to spring from the earth before him, but this time also he overcame; and though the fruit from the magic tree almost touched his mouth, he brushed it aside and went steadily on.

That day the cows wandered father than ever they had done before, and never stopped till they had reached a moor where the heather was burning. The fire was fierce, but the cows took no heed, and walked steadily through it, Covan the Brown-haired following them. Next they plunged into a foaming river, and Covan plunged in after them, though the water came high above his waist. On the other side of the river lay a wide plain, and here the cows lay down, while Covan looked about him. Near him was a house built of yellow stone, and from it came sweet songs, and Covan listened, and his heart grew light within him.

While he was thus waiting there ran up to him a youth, scarcely able to speak so swiftly had he sped; and he cried aloud:

'Hasten, hasten, Covan the Brown-haired, for your cows are in the corn, and you must drive them out!'

'Nay,' said Covan smiling, 'it had been easier for you to have driven them out than to come here to tell me.' And he went on listening to the music.

Very soon the same youth returned and cried with panting breath:

'Out upon you, Covan son of Gorla, that you stand there agape. For our dogs are chasing your cows, and you must drive them off!'

'Nay, then,' answered Covan as before, 'it had been easier for you to call off your dogs than to come here to tell me.' And he stayed where he was till the music ceased.

Then he turned to look for the cows, and found them all lying in the place where he had left them; but when they saw Covan they rose up and walked homewards, taking a different path to that they had trod in the morning. This time they passed over a plain so bare that a pin could not have lain there unnoticed, yet Covan beheld with surprise a foal and its mother feeding there, both as fat as if they had pastured on the richest grass. Further on they crossed another plain, where the grass was thick and green, but on it were feeding a foal and its mother, so lean that you could have counted their ribs. And further again the path led them by the shores of a lake whereon were floating two boats; one full of gay and happy youths, journeying to the land of the Sun, and another with grim shapes clothed in black, travelling to the land of Night.

'What can these things mean?' said Covan to himself, as he followed his cows.

Darkness now fell, the wind howled, and torrents of rain poured upon them. Covan knew not how far they might yet have to go, or indeed if they were on the right road. He could not even see his cows, and his heart sank lest, after all, he should have failed to bring them safely back. What was he to do?

He waited thus, for he could go neither forwards nor backwards, till he felt a great friendly paw laid on his shoulder.

'My cave is just here,' said the Dog of Maol-mor, of whom Covan son of Gorla had heard much. 'Spend the night here, and you shall be fed on the flesh of lamb, and shall lay aside three-thirds of thy weariness.'

And Covan entered, and supped, and slept, and in the morning rose up a new man.

'Farewell, Covan,' said the Dog of Maol-mor. 'May success go with you, for you took what I had to give and did not mock me. So, when danger is your companion, wish for me, and I will not fail you.'

At these words the Dog of Maol-mor disappeared into the forest, and Covan went to seek his cows, which were standing in the hollow where the darkness had come upon them.

At the sight of Covan the Brown-haired they walked onwards, Covan following ever behind them, and looking neither to the right nor to the left. All that day they walked, and when night fell they were in a barren plain, with only rocks for shelter.

'We must rest here as best we can,' spoke Covan to the cows. And they bowed their heads and lay down in the place where they stood. Then came the black raven of Corri-nan-creag, whose eyes never closed, and whose wings never tired; and he fluttered before the face of Covan and told him that he knew of a cranny in the rock where there was food in plenty, and soft moss for a bed.

'Go with me thither,' he said to Covan, 'and you shall lay aside three-thirds of your weariness, and depart in the morning refreshed,' and Covan listened thankfully to his words, and at dawn he rose up to seek his cows.

'Farewell!' cried the black raven. 'You trusted me, and took all I had to offer in return for the food you once gave me. So if in time to come you need a friend, wish for me, and I will not fail you.'

As before, the cows were standing in the spot where he had left them, ready to set out. All that day they walked, on and on, and on, Covan son of Gorla walking behind them, till night fell while they were on the banks of a river.

'We can go no further,' spake Covan to the cows. And they began to eat the grass by the side of the stream, while Covan listened to them and longed for some supper also, for they had travelled far, and his limbs were weak under him. Then there was a swish of water at his feet, and out peeped the head of the famous otter Doran-donn of the stream.

'Trust to me and I will find you warmth and shelter,' said Doran-donn; 'and for food fish in plenty.' And Covan went with him thankfully, and ate and rested, and laid aside three-thirds of his weariness. At sunrise he left his bed of dried sea-weed, which had floated up with the tide, and with a grateful heart bade farewell to Doran-donn.

'Because you trusted me and took what I had to offer, you have made me your friend, Covan,' said Doran-donn. 'And if you should be in danger, and need help from one who can swim a river or dive beneath a wave, call to me and I will come to you.' Then he plunged into the stream, and was seen no more.

The cows were standing ready in the place where Covan had left them, and they journeyed on all that day, till, when night fell, they reached the cottage. Joyful indeed was the old man as the cows went into their stables, and he beheld the rich milk that flowed into the pail of the golden-haired maiden with the silver comb.

'You have done well indeed,' he said to Covan son of Gorla. 'And now, what would you have as a reward?'

'I want nothing for myself,' answered Covan the Brown-haired; 'but I ask you to give me back my brothers and my sister who have been lost to us for three years past. You are wise and know the lore of fairies and of witches; tell me where I can find them, and what I must do to bring them to life again.'

The old man looked grave at the words of Covan.

'Yes, truly I know where they are,' answered he, 'and I say not that they may not be brought to life again. But the perils are great—too great for you to overcome.'

'Tell me what they are,' said Covan again, 'and I shall know better if I may overcome them.'

'Listen, then, and judge. In the mountain yonder there dwells a roe, white of foot, with horns that branch like the antlers of a deer. On the lake that leads to the land of the Sun floats a duck whose body is green and whose neck is of gold. In the pool of Corri-Bui swims a salmon with a skin that shines like silver, and whose gills are red—bring them all to me, and then you shall know where dwell your brothers and your sister!'

'To-morrow at cock-crow I will begone!' answered Covan.

The way to the mountain lay straight before him, and when he had climbed high he caught sight of the roe with the white feet and the spotted sides, on the peak in front.

Full of hope he set out in pursuit of her, but by the time he had reached that peak she had left it and was to be seen on another. And so it always happened, and Covan's courage had well-nigh failed him, when the thought of the Dog of Maol-mor darted into his mind.

'Oh, that he was here!' he cried. And looking up he saw him.

'Why did you summon me?' asked the Dog of Maol-mor. And when Covan had told him of his trouble, and how the roe always led him further and further, the Dog only answered:

'Fear nothing; I will soon catch her for you.' And in a short while he laid the roe unhurt at Covan's feet.

'What will you wish me to do with her?' said the Dog. And Covan answered:

'The old man bade me bring her, and the duck with the golden neck, and the salmon with the silver sides, to his cottage; if I shall catch them, I know not. But carry you the roe to the back of the cottage, and tether her so that she cannot escape.'

'It shall be done,' said the Dog of Maol-mor.

Then Covan sped to the lake which led to the land of the Sun, where the duck with the green body and the golden neck was swimming among the water-lilies.

'Surely I can catch him, good swimmer as I am,' to himself. But, if he could swim well, the duck could swim better, and at length his strength failed him, and he was forced to seek the land.

'Oh that the black raven were here to help me!' he thought to himself. And in a moment the black raven was perched on his shoulder.

'How can I help you?' asked the raven. And Covan answered:

'Catch me the green duck that floats on the water.' And the raven flew with his strong wings and picked him up in his strong beak, and in another moment the bird was laid at the feet of Covan.

This time it was easy for the young man to carry his prize, and after giving thanks to the raven for his aid, he went on to the river.

In the deep dark pool of which the old man had spoken the silver-sided salmon was lying under a rock.

'Surely I, good fisher as I am, can catch him,' said Covan son of Gorla. And cutting a slender pole from a bush, he fastened a line to the end of it. But cast with what skill he might, it availed nothing, for the salmon would not even look at the bait.

'I am beaten at last, unless the Doran-donn can deliver me,' he cried. And as he spoke there was a swish of the water, and the face of the Doran-donn looked up at him.

'O catch me, I pray you, that salmon under the rock!' said Covan son of Gorla. And the Doran-donn dived, and laying hold of the salmon by his tail, bore it back to the place where Covan was standing.

'The roe, and the duck, and the salmon are here,' said Covan to the old man, when he reached the cottage. And the old man smiled on him and bade him eat and drink, and after he hungered no more, he would speak with him.

And this was what the old man said: 'You began well, my son, so things have gone well with you. You set store by your mother's blessing, therefore you have been blest. You gave food to the raven when it hungered, you were true to the promise you had made to me, and did not suffer yourself to be turned aside by vain shows. You were skilled to perceive that the boy who tempted you to leave the temple was a teller of false tales, and took with a grateful heart what the poor had to offer you. Last of all, difficulties gave you courage, instead of lending you despair.

And now, as to your reward, you shall in truth take your sister home with you, and your brothers I will restore to life; but idle and unfaithful as they are their lot is to wander for ever. And so farewell, and may wisdom be with you.'

'First tell me your name?' asked Covan softly.

'I am the Spirit of Age,' said the old man.

The Princess Bella-Flor

[Taken from a Celtic Story. Translated by Doctor Macleod Clarke.]

Once upon a time there lived a man who had two sons. When they grew up the elder went to seek his fortune in a far country, and for many years no one heard anything about him. Meanwhile the younger son stayed at home with his father, who died at last in a good old age, leaving great riches behind him.

For some time the son who stayed at home spent his father's wealth freely, believing that he alone remained to enjoy it. But, one day, as he was coming down stairs, he was surprised to see a stranger enter the hall, looking about as if the house belonged to him.

'Have you forgotten me?' asked the man.

'I can't forget a person I have never known,' was the rude answer.

'I am your brother,' replied the stranger, 'and I have returned home without the money I hoped to have made. And, what is worse, they tell me in the village that my father is dead. I would have counted my lost gold as nothing if I could have seen him once more.'

'He died six months ago,' said the rich brother, 'and he left you, as your portion, the old wooden chest that stands in the loft. You had better go there and look for it; I have no more time to waste.' And he went his way.

So the wanderer turned his steps to the loft, which was at the top of the storehouse, and there he found the wooden chest, so old that it looked as if it were dropping to pieces.

'What use is this old thing to me?' he said to himself. 'Oh, well, it will serve to light a fire at which I can warm myself; so things might be worse after all.'

Placing the chest on his back, the man, whose name was Jose, set out for his inn, and, borrowing a hatchet, began to chop up the box. In doing so he discovered a secret drawer, and in it lay a paper. He opened the paper, not knowing what it might contain, and was astonished to find that it was the acknowledgment of a large debt that was owing to his father. Putting the precious writing in his pocket, he hastily inquired of the landlord where he could find the man whose name was written inside, and he ran out at once in search of him.

The debtor proved to be an old miser, who lived at the other end of the village. He had hoped for many months that the paper he had written had been lost or destroyed, and, indeed, when he saw it, was very unwilling to pay what he owed. However, the stranger threatened to drag him before the king, and when the miser saw that there was no help for it he counted out the coins one by one. The stranger picked them up and put them in his pocket, and went back to his inn feeling that he was now a rich man.

A few weeks after this he was walking through the streets of the nearest town, when he met a poor woman crying bitterly. He stopped and asked her what was the matter, and she answered between her sobs that her husband was dying, and, to make matters worse, a creditor whom he could not pay was anxious to have him taken to prison.

'Comfort yourself,' said the stranger kindly; 'they shall neither send your husband to prison nor sell your goods. I will not only pay his debts but, if he dies, the cost of his burial also. And now go home, and nurse him as well as you can.'

And so she did; but, in spite of her care, the husband died, and was buried by the stranger. But everything cost more than he expected, and when all was paid he found that only three gold pieces were left.

'What am I to do now?' said he to himself. 'I think I had better go to court, and enter into the service of the king.'

At first he was only a servant, who carried the king the water for his bath, and saw that his bed was made in a particular fashion. But he did his duties so well that his master soon took notice of him, and in a short time he rose to be a gentleman of the bedchamber.

Now, when this happened the younger brother had spent all the money he had inherited, and did not know how to make any for himself. He then bethought him of the king's favourite, and went whining to the palace to beg that his brother, whom he had so ill-used, would give him his protection, and find him a place. The elder, who was always ready to help everyone spoke to the king on his behalf, and the next day the young man took up is work at court.

Unfortunately, the new-comer was by nature spiteful and envious, and could not bear anyone to have better luck than himself. By dint of spying through keyholes and listening at doors, he learned that the king, old and ugly though he was, had fallen in love with the Princess Bella-Flor, who would have nothing to say to him, and had hidden herself in some mountain castle, no one knew where.

'That will do nicely,' thought the scoundrel, rubbing his hands. 'It will be quite easy to get the king to send my brother in search of her, and if he returns without finding her, his head will be the forfeit. Either way, he will be out of MY path.'

So he went at once to the Lord High Chamberlain and craved an audience of the king, to whom he declared he wished to tell some news of the highest importance. The king admitted him into the presence chamber without delay, and bade him state what he had to say, and to be quick about it.

'Oh, sire! the Princess Bella-Flor—' answered the man, and then stopped as if afraid.

'What of the Princess Bella-Flor?' asked the king impatiently.

'I have heard—it is whispered at court—that your majesty desires to know where she lies in hiding.'

'I would give half my kingdom to the man who will bring her to me,' cried the king, eagerly. 'Speak on, knave; has a bird of the air revealed to you the secret?'

'It is not I, but my brother, who knows,' replied the traitor; 'if your majesty would ask him—' But before the words were out of his mouth the king had struck a blow with his sceptre on a golden plate that hung on the wall.

'Order Jose to appear before me instantly,' he shouted to the servant who ran to obey his orders, so great was the noise his majesty had made; and when Jose entered the hall, wondering what in the world could be the matter, the king was nearly dumb from rage and excitement.

'Bring me the Princess Bella-Flor this moment,' stammered he, 'for if you return without her I will have you drowned!' And without another word he left the hall, leaving Jose staring with surprise and horror.

'How can I find the Princess Bella-Flor when I have never even seen her?' thought he. 'But it is no use staying here, for I shall only be put to death.' And he walked slowly to the stables to choose himself a horse.

There were rows upon rows of fine beasts with their names written in gold above their stalls, and Jose was looking uncertainly from one to the other, wondering which he should choose, when an old white horse turned its head and signed to him to approach.

'Take me,' it said in a gentle whisper, 'and all will go well.'

Jose still felt so bewildered with the mission that the king had given him that he forgot to be astonished at hearing a horse talk. Mechanically he laid his hand on the bridle and led the white horse out of the stable. He was about to mount on his back, when the animal spoke again:

'Pick up those three loaves of bread which you see there, and put them in your pocket.'

Jose did as he was told, and being in a great hurry to get away, asked no questions, but swung himself into the saddle.

They rode far without meeting any adventures, but at length they came to an ant-hill, and the horse stopped.

'Crumble those three loaves for the ants,' he said. But Jose hesitated.

'Why, we may want them ourselves!' answered he.

'Never mind that; give them to the ants all the same. Do not lose a chance of helping others.' And when the loaves lay in crumbs on the road, the horse galloped on.

By-and-by they entered a rocky pass between two mountains, and here they saw an eagle which had been caught in a hunter's net.

'Get down and cut the meshes of the net, and set the poor bird free,' said the horse.

'But it will take so long,' objected Jose, 'and we may miss the princess.'

'Never mind that; do not lose a chance of helping others,' answered the horse. And when the meshes were cut, and the eagle was free, the horse galloped on.

The had ridden many miles, and at last they came to a river, where they beheld a little fish lying gasping on the sand, and the horse said:

'Do you see that little fish? It will die if you do not put it back in the water.'

'But, really, we shall never find the Princess Bella-Flor if we waste our time like this!' cried Jose.

'We never waste time when we are helping others,' answered the horse. And soon the little fish was swimming happily away.

A little while after they reached a castle, which was built in the middle of a very thick wood, and right in front was the Princess Bella-Flor feeding her hens.

'Now listen,' said the horse. 'I am going to give all sorts of little hops and skips, which will amuse the Princess Bella-Flor. Then she will tell you that she would like to ride a little way, and you must help her to mount. When she is seated I shall begin to neigh and kick, and you must say that I have never carried a woman before, and that you had better get up behind so as to be able to manage me. Once on my back we will go like the wind to the king's palace.'

Jose did exactly as the horse told him, and everything fell out as the animal prophesied; so that it was not until they were galloping breathlessly towards the palace that the princess knew that she was taken captive. She said nothing, however, but quietly opened her apron which contained the bran for the chickens, and in a moment it lay scattered on the ground.

'Oh, I have let fall my bran!' cried she; 'please get down and pick it up for me.' But Jose only answered:

'We shall find plenty of bran where we are going.' And the horse galloped on.

They were now passing through a forest, and the princess took out her handkerchief and threw it upwards, so that it stuck in one of the topmost branches of a tree.

'Dear me; how stupid! I have let my handkerchief blow away,' said she. 'Will you climb up and get it for me?' But Jose answered:

'We shall find plenty of handkerchiefs where we are going.' And the horse galloped on.

After the wood they reached a river, and the princess slipped a ring off her finger and let it roll into the water.

'How careless of me,' gasped she, beginning to sob. 'I have lost my favourite ring; DO stop for a moment and look if you can see it.' But Jose answered:

'You will find plenty of rings where you are going.' And the horse galloped on.

At last they entered the palace gates, and the king's heart bounded with joy at beholding his beloved Princess Bella-Flor. But the princess brushed him aside as if he had been a fly, and locked herself into the nearest room, which she would not open for all his entreaties.

'Bring me the three things I lost on the way, and perhaps I may think about it,' was all she would say. And, in despair, the king was driven to take counsel of Jose.

'There is no remedy that I can see,' said his majesty, 'but that you, who know where they are, should go and bring them back. And if you return without them I will have you drowned.'

Poor Jose was much troubled at these words. He thought that he had done all that was required of him, and that his life was safe. However, he bowed low, and went out to consult his friend the horse.

'Do not vex yourself,' said the horse, when he had heard the story; 'jump up, and we will go and look for the things.' And Jose mounted at once.

They rode on till they came to the ant-hill, and then the horse asked:

'Would you like to have the bran?'

'What is the use of liking?' answered Jose.

'Well, call the ants, and tell them to fetch it for you; and, if some of it has been scattered by the wind, to bring in its stead the grains that were in the cakes you gave them.' Jose listened in surprise. He did not much believe in the horse's plan; but he could not think of anything better, so he called to the ants, and bade them collect the bran as fast as they could.

Then he saw under a tree and waited, while his horse cropped the green turf.

'Look there!' said the animal, suddenly raising its head; and Jose looked behind him and saw a little mountain of bran, which he put into a bag that was hung over his saddle.

'Good deeds bear fruit sooner or later,' observed the horse; 'but mount again, as we have far to go.'

When they arrived at the tree, they saw the handkerchief fluttering like a flag from the topmost branch, and Jose's spirits sank again.

'How am I to get that handkerchief?' cried he; 'why I should need Jacob's ladder!' But the horse answered:

'Do not be frightened; call to the eagle you set free from the net, he will bring it to you.'

So Jose called to the eagle, and the eagle flew to the top of the tree and brought back the handkerchief in its beak. Jose thanked him, and vaulting on his horse they rode on to the river.

A great deal of rain had fallen in the night, and the river, instead of being clear as it was before, was dark and troubled.

'How am I to fetch the ring from the bottom of this river when I do not know exactly where it was dropped, and cannot even see it?' asked Jose. But the horse answered: 'Do not be frightened; call the little fish whose life you saved, and she will bring it to you.'

So he called to the fish, and the fish dived to the bottom and slipped behind big stones, and moved little ones with its tail till it found the ring, and brought it to Jose in its mouth.

Well pleased with all he had done, Jose returned to the palace; but when the king took the precious objects to Bella-Flor, she declared that she would never open her door till the bandit who had carried her off had been fried in oil.

'I am very sorry,' said the king to Jose, 'I really would rather not; but you see I have no choice.'

While the oil was being heated in the great caldron, Jose went to the stables to inquire of his friend the horse if there was no way for him to escape.

'Do not be frightened,' said the horse. 'Get on my back, and I will gallop till my whole body is wet with perspiration, then rub it all over your skin, and no matter how hot the oil may be you will never feel it.'

Jose did not ask any more questions, but did as the horse bade him; and men wondered at his cheerful face as they lowered him into the caldron of boiling oil. He was left there till Bella-Flor cried that he must be cooked enough. Then out came a youth so young and handsome, that everyone fell in love with him, and Bella-Flor most of all.

As for the old king, he saw that he had lost the game; and in despair he flung himself into the caldron, and was fried instead of Jose. Then Jose was proclaimed king, on condition that he married Bella-Flor which he promised to do the next day. But first he went to the stables and sought out the horse, and said to him: 'It is to you that I owe my life and my crown. Why have you done all this for me?'

And the horse answered: 'I am the soul of that unhappy man for whom you spent all your fortune. And when I saw you in danger of death I begged that I might help you, as you had helped me. For, as I told you, Good deeds bear their own fruit!'

The Bird of Truth

[From Cuentos, Oraciones, y Adivinas, por Fernan Caballero.]

Once upon a time there lived a poor fisher who built a hut on the banks of a stream which, shunning the glare of the sun and the noise of the towns, flowed quietly past trees and under bushes, listening to the songs of the birds overhead.

One day, when the fisherman had gone out as usual to cast his nets, he saw borne towards him on the current a cradle of crystal. Slipping his net quickly beneath it he drew it out and lifted the silk coverlet. Inside, lying on a soft bed of cotton, were two babies, a boy and a girl, who opened their eyes and smiled at him. The man was filled with pity at the sight, and throwing down his lines he took the cradle and the babies home to his wife.

The good woman flung up her hands in despair when she beheld the contents of the cradle.

'Are not eight children enough,' she cried, 'without bringing us two more? How do you think we can feed them?'

'You would not have had me leave them to die of hunger,' answered he, 'or be swallowed up by the waves of the sea? What is enough for eight is also enough for ten.'

The wife said no more; and in truth her heart yearned over the little creatures. Somehow or other food was never lacking in the hut, and the children grew up and were so good and gentle that, in time, their foster-parents loved them as well or better than their own, who were quarrelsome and envious. It did not take the orphans long to notice that the boys did not like them, and were always playing tricks on them, so they used to go away by themselves and spend whole hours by the banks of the river. Here they would take out the bits of bread they had saved from their breakfasts and crumble them for the birds. In return, the birds taught them many things: how to get up early in the morning, how to sing, and how to talk their language, which very few people know.

But though the little orphans did their best to avoid quarrelling with their foster-brothers, it was very difficult always to keep the peace. Matters got worse and worse till, one morning, the eldest boy said to the twins:

'It is all very well for you to pretend that you have such good manners, and are so much better than we, but we have at least a father and mother, while you have only got the river, like the toads and the frogs.'

The poor children did not answer the insult; but it made them very unhappy. And they told each other in whispers that they could not stay there any longer, but must go into the world and seek their fortunes.

So next day they arose as early as the birds and stole downstairs without anybody hearing them. One window was open, and they crept softly out and ran to the side of the river. Then, feeling as if they had found a friend, they walked along its banks, hoping that by-and-by they should meet some one to take care of them.

The whole of that day they went steadily on without seeing a living creature, till, in the evening, weary and footsore, they saw before them a small hut. This raised their spirits for a moment; but the door was shut, and the hut seemed empty, and so great was their disappointment that they almost cried. However, the boy fought down his tears, and said cheerfully:

'Well, at any rate here is a bench where we can sit down, and when we are rested we will think what is best to do next.'

Then they sat down, and for some time they were too tired even to notice anything; but by-and-by they saw that under the tiles of the roof a number of swallows were sitting, chattering merrily to each other. Of course the swallows had no idea that the children understood their language, or they would not have talked so freely; but, as it was, they said whatever came into their heads.

'Good evening, my fine city madam,' remarked a swallow, whose manners were rather rough and countryfied to another who looked particularly distinguished. 'Happy, indeed, are the eyes that behold you! Only think of your having returned to your long-forgotten country friends, after you have lived for years in a palace!'

'I have inherited this nest from my parents,' replied the other, 'and as they left it to me I certainly shall make it my home. But,' she added politely, 'I hope that you and all your family are well?'

'Very well indeed, I am glad to say. But my poor daughter had, a short time ago, such bad inflammation in her eyes that she would have gone blind had I not been able to find the magic herb, which cured her at once.'

'And how is the nightingale singing? Does the lark soar as high as ever? And does the linnet dress herself as smartly?' But here the country swallow drew herself up.

'I never talk gossip,' she said severely. 'Our people, who were once so innocent and well-behaved, have been corrupted by the bad examples of men. It is a thousand pities.'

'What! innocence and good behaviour are not to be met with among birds, nor in the country! My dear friend, what are you saying?'

'The truth and nothing more. Imagine, when we returned here, we met some linnets who, just as the spring and the flowers and the long days had come, were setting out for the north and the cold? Out of pure compassion we tried to persuade them to give up this folly; but they only replied with the utmost insolence.'

'How shocking!' exclaimed the city swallow.

'Yes, it was. And worse than that, the crested lark, that was formerly so timid and shy, is now no better than a thief, and steals maize and corn whenever she can find them.'

'I am astonished at what you say.'

'You will be more astonished when I tell you that on my arrival here for the summer I found my nest occupied by a shameless sparrow! "This is my nest," I said. "Yours?" he answered, with a rude laugh. "Yes, mine; my ancestors were born here, and my sons will be born here also." And at that my husband set upon him and threw him out of the nest. I am sure nothing of this sort ever happens in a town.'

'Not exactly, perhaps. But I have seen a great deal—if you only knew!'

'Oh! do tell us! do tell us!' cried they all. And when they had settled themselves comfortably, the city swallow began:

'You must know, then that our king fell in love with the youngest daughter of a tailor, who was as good and gentle as she was beautiful. His nobles hoped that he would have chosen a queen from one of their daughters, and tried to prevent the marriage; but the king would not listen to them, and it took place. Not many months later a war broke out, and the king rode away at the head of his army, while the queen remained behind, very unhappy at the separation. When peace was made, and the king returned, he was told that his wife had had two babies in his absence, but that both were dead; that she herself had gone out of her mind and was obliged to be shut up in a tower in the mountains, where, in time, the fresh air might cure her.'

'And was this not true?' asked the swallows eagerly.

'Of course not,' answered the city lady, with some contempt for their stupidity. 'The children were alive at that very moment in the gardener's cottage; but at night the chamberlain came down and put them in a cradle of crystal, which he carried to the river.

'For a whole day they floated safely, for though the stream was deep it was very still, and the children took no harm. In the morning—so I am told by my friend the kingfisher—they were rescued by a fisherman who lived near the river bank.'

The children had been lying on the bench, listening lazily to the chatter up to this point; but when they heard the story of the crystal cradle which their foster-mother had always been fond of telling them, they sat upright and looked at each other.

'Oh, how glad I am I learnt the birds' language!' said the eyes of one to the eyes of the other.

Meanwhile the swallows had spoken again.

'That was indeed good fortune!' cried they.

'And when the children are grown up they can return to their father and set their mother free.'

'It will not be so easy as you think,' answered the city swallow, shaking her head; 'for they will have to prove that they are the king's children, and also that their mother never went mad at all. In fact, it is so difficult that there is only one way of proving it to the king.'

'And what is that?' cried all the swallows at once. 'And how do you know it?'

'I know it,' answered the city swallow, 'because, one day, when I was passing through the palace garden, I met a cuckoo, who, as I need not tell you, always pretends to be able to see into the future. We began to talk about certain things which were happening in the palace, and of the events of past years. "Ah," said he, "the only person who can expose the wickedness of the ministers and show the king how wrong he has been, is the Bird of Truth, who can speak the language of men."

'"And where can this bird be found?" I asked.

'"It is shut up in a castle guarded by a fierce giant, who only sleeps one quarter of an hour out of the whole twenty-four," replied the cuckoo.

'And where is this castle?' inquired the country swallow, who, like all the rest, and the children most of all, had been listening with deep attention.

'That is just what I don't know,' answered her friend. 'All I can tell you is that not far from here is a tower, where dwells an old witch, and it is she who knows the way, and she will only teach it to the person who promises to bring her the water from the fountain of many colours, which she uses for her enchantments. But never will she betray the place where the Bird of Truth is hidden, for she hates him, and would kill him if she could; knowing well, however, that this bird cannot die, as he is immortal, she keeps him closely shut up, and guarded night and day by the Birds of Bad Faith, who seek to gag him so that his voice should not be heard.'

'And is there no one else who can tell the poor boy where to find the bird, if he should ever manage to reach the tower?' asked the country swallow.

'No one,' replied the city swallow, 'except an owl, who lives a hermit's life in that desert, and he knows only one word of man's speech, and that is "cross." So that even if the prince did succeed in getting there, he could never understand what the owl said. But, look, the sun is sinking to his nest in the depths of the sea, and I must go to mine. Good-night, friends, good-night!'

Then the swallow flew away, and the children, who had forgotten both hunger and weariness in the joy of this strange news, rose up and followed in the direction of her flight. After two hours' walking, they arrived at a large city, which they felt sure must be the capital of their father's kingdom. Seeing a good-natured looking woman standing at the door of a house, they asked her if she would give them a night's lodging, and she was so pleased with their pretty faces and nice manners that she welcomed them warmly.

It was scarcely light the next morning before the girl was sweeping out the rooms, and the boy watering the garden, so that by the time the good woman came downstairs there was nothing left for her to do. This so delighted her that she begged the children to stay with her altogether, and the boy answered that he would leave his sisters with her gladly, but that he himself had serious business on hand and must not linger in pursuit of it. So he bade them farewell and set out.

For three days he wandered by the most out-of-the-way paths, but no signs of a tower were to be seen anywhere. On the fourth morning it was just the same, and, filled with despair, he flung himself on the ground under a tree and hid his face in his hands. In a little while he heard a rustling over his head, and looking up, he saw a turtle dove watching him with her bright eyes.

'Oh dove!' cried the boy, addressing the bird in her own language, 'Oh dove! tell me, I pray you, where is the castle of Come-and-never-go?'

'Poor child,' answered the dove, 'who has sent you on such a useless quest?'

'My good or evil fortune,' replied the boy, 'I know not which.'

'To get there,' said the dove, 'you must follow the wind, which to-day is blowing towards the castle.'

The boy thanked her, and followed the wind, fearing all the time that it might change its direction and lead him astray. But the wind seemed to feel pity for him and blew steadily on.

With each step the country became more and more dreary, but at nightfall the child could see behind the dark and bare rocks something darker still. This was the tower in which dwelt the witch; and seizing the knocker he gave three loud knocks, which were echoed in the hollows of the rocks around.

The door opened slowly, and there appeared on the threshold an old woman holding up a candle to her face, which was so hideous that the boy involuntarily stepped backwards, almost as frightened by the troop of lizards, beetles and such creatures that surrounded her, as by the woman herself.

'Who are you who dare to knock at my door and wake me?' cried she. 'Be quick and tell me what you want, or it will be the worse for you.'

'Madam,' answered the child, 'I believe that you alone know the way to the castle of Come-and-never-go, and I pray you to show it to me.'

'Very good,' replied the witch, with something that she meant for a smile, 'but to-day it is late. To-morrow you shall go. Now enter, and you shall sleep with my lizards.'

'I cannot stay,' said he. 'I must go back at once, so as to reach the road from which I started before day dawns.'

'If I tell you, will you promise me that you will bring me this jar full of the many-coloured water from the spring in the court-yard of the castle?' asked she. 'If you fail to keep your word I will change you into a lizard for ever.'

'I promise,' answered the boy.

Then the old woman called to a very thin dog, and said to him:

'Conduct this pig of a child to the castle of Come-and-never-go, and take care that you warn my friend of his arrival.' And the dog arose and shook itself, and set out.

At the end of two hours they stopped in front of a large castle, big and black and gloomy, whose doors stood wide open, although neither sound nor light gave sign of any presence within. The dog, however, seemed to know what to expect, and, after a wild howl, went on; but the boy, who was uncertain whether this was the quarter of an hour when the giant was asleep, hesitated to follow him, and paused for a moment under a wild olive that grew near by, the only tree which he had beheld since he had parted from the dove. 'Oh, heaven, help me!' cried he.

'Cross! cross!' answered a voice.

The boy leapt for joy as he recognised the note of the owl of which the swallow had spoken, and he said softly in the bird's language:

'Oh, wise owl, I pray you to protect and guide me, for I have come in search of the Bird of Truth. And first I must fill this far with the many-coloured water in the courtyard of the castle.'

'Do not do that,' answered the owl, 'but fill the jar from the spring which bubbles close by the fountain with the many-coloured water. Afterwards, go into the aviary opposite the great door, but be careful not to touch any of the bright-plumaged birds contained in it, which will cry to you, each one, that he is the Bird of Truth. Choose only a small white bird that is hidden in a corner, which the others try incessantly to kill, not knowing that it cannot die. And, be quick!—for at this very moment the giant has fallen asleep, and you have only a quarter of an hour to do everything.'

The boy ran as fast as he could and entered the courtyard, where he saw the two spring close together. He passed by the many-coloured water without casting a glance at it, and filled the jar from the fountain whose water was clear and pure. He next hastened to the aviary, and was almost deafened by the clamour that rose as he shut the door behind him. Voices of peacocks, voices of ravens, voices of magpies, each claiming to be the Bird of Truth. With steadfast face the boy walked by them all, to the corner, where, hemmed in by a hand of fierce crows, was the small white bird he sought. Putting her safely in his breast, he passed out, followed by the screams of the birds of Bad Faith which he left behind him.

Once outside, he ran without stopping to the witch's tower, and handed to the old woman the jar she had given him.

'Become a parrot!' cried she, flinging the water over him. But instead of losing his shape, as so many had done before, he only grew ten times handsomer; for the water was enchanted for good and not ill. Then the creeping multitude around the witch hastened to roll themselves in the water, and stood up, human beings again.

When the witch saw what was happening, she took a broomstick and flew away.

Who can guess the delight of the sister at the sight of her brother, bearing the Bird of Truth? But although the boy had accomplished much, something very difficult yet remained, and that was how to carry the Bird of Truth to the king without her being seized by the wicked courtiers, who would be ruined by the discovery of their plot.

Soon—no one knew how—the news spread abroad that the Bird of Truth was hovering round the palace, and the courtiers made all sorts of preparations to hinder her reaching the king.

They got ready weapons that were sharpened, and weapons that were poisoned; they sent for eagles and falcons to hunt her down, and constructed cages and boxes in which to shut her up if they were not able to kill her. They declared that her white plumage was really put on to hide her black feathers—in fact there was nothing they did not do in order to prevent the king from seeing the bird or from paying attention to her words if he did.

As often happens in these cases, the courtiers brought about that which they feared. They talked so much about the Bird of Truth that at last the king heard of it, and expressed a wish to see her. The more difficulties that were put in his way the stronger grew his desire, and in the end the king published a proclamation that whoever found the Bird of Truth should bring her to him without delay.

As soon as he saw this proclamation the boy called his sister, and they hastened to the palace. The bird was buttoned inside his tunic, but, as might have been expected, the courtiers barred the way, and told the child that he could not enter. It was in vain that the boy declared that he was only obeying the king's commands; the courtiers only replied that his majesty was not yet out of bed, and it was forbidden to wake him.

They were still talking, when, suddenly, the bird settled the question by flying upwards through an open window into the king's own room. Alighting on the pillow, close to the king's head, she bowed respectfully, and said:

'My lord, I am the Bird of Truth whom you wished to see, and I have been obliged to approach you in the manner because the boy who brought me is kept out of the palace by your courtiers.'

'They shall pay for their insolence,' said the king. And he instantly ordered one of his attendants to conduct the boy at once to his apartments; and in a moment more the prince entered, holding his sister by the hand.

'Who are you?' asked the king; 'and what has the Bird of Truth to do with you?'

'If it please your majesty, the Bird of Truth will explain that herself,' answered the boy.

And the bird did explain; and the king heard for the first time of the wicked plot that had been successful for so many years. He took his children in his arms, with tears in his eyes, and hurried off with them to the tower in the mountains where the queen was shut up. The poor woman was as white as marble, for she had been living almost in darkness; but when she saw her husband and children, the colour came back to her face, and she was as beautiful as ever.

They all returned in state to the city, where great rejoicings were held. The wicked courtiers had their heads cut off, and all their property was taken away. As for the good old couple, they were given riches and honour, and were loved and cherished to the end of their lives.

The Mink and the Wolf

[From Cuentos, Oraciones y Adivinas, por Fernan Caballero.]

In a big forest in the north of America lived a quantity of wild animals of all sorts. They were always very polite when they met; but, in spite of that, they kept a close watch one upon the other, as each was afraid of being killed and eaten by somebody else. But their manners were so good that no one would ever had guessed that.

One day a smart young wolf went out to hunt, promising his grandfather and grandmother that he would be sure to be back before bedtime. He trotted along quite happily through the forest till he came to a favourite place of his, just where the river runs into the sea. There, just as he had hoped, he saw the chief mink fishing in a canoe.

'I want to fish too,' cried the wolf. But the mink said nothing and pretended not to hear.

'I wish you would take me into your boat!' shouted the wolf, louder than before, and he continued to beseech the mink so long that at last he grew tired of it, and paddled to the shore close enough for the wolf to jump in.

'Sit down quietly at that end or we shall be upset,' said the mink; 'and if you care about sea-urchins' eggs, you will find plenty in that basket. But be sure you eat only the white ones, for the red ones would kill you.'

So the wolf, who was always hungry, began to eat the eggs greedily; and when he had finished he told the mink he thought he would have a nap.

'Well, then, stretch yourself out, and rest your head on that piece of wood,' said the mink. And the wolf did as he was bid, and was soon fast asleep. Then the mink crept up to him and stabbed him to the heart with his knife, and he died without moving. After that he landed on the beach, skinned the wolf, and taking the skin to his cottage, he hung it up before the fire to dry.

Not many days later the wolf's grandmother, who, with the help of her relations, had been searching for him everywhere, entered the cottage to buy some sea-urchins' eggs, and saw the skin, which she at once guessed to be that of her grandson.

'I knew he was dead—I knew it! I knew it!' she cried, weeping bitterly, till the mink told her rudely that if she wanted to make so much noise she had better do it outside as he liked to be quiet. So, half-blinded by her tears, the old woman went home the way she had come, and running in at the door, she flung herself down in front of the fire.

'What are you crying for?' asked the old wolf and some friends who had been spending the afternoon with him.

'I shall never see my grandson any more!' answered she. 'Mink has killed him, oh! oh!' And putting her head down, she began to weep as loudly as ever.

'There! there!' said her husband, laying his paw on her shoulder. 'Be comforted; if he IS dead, we will avenge him.' And calling to the others they proceeded to talk over the best plan. It took them a long time to make up their minds, as one wolf proposed one thing and one another; but at last it was agreed that the old wolf should give a great feast in his house, and that the mink should be invited to the party. And in order that no time should be lost it was further agreed that each wolf should bear the invitations to the guests that lived nearest to him.

Now the wolves thought they were very cunning, but the mink was more cunning still; and though he sent a message by a white hare, that was going that way, saying he should be delighted to be present, he determined that he would take his precautions. So he went to a mouse who had often done him a good turn, and greeted her with his best bow.

'I have a favour to ask of you, friend mouse,' said he, 'and if you will grant it I will carry you on my back every night for a week to the patch of maize right up the hill.'

'The favour is mine,' answered the mouse. 'Tell me what it is that I can have the honour of doing for you.'

'Oh, something quite easy,' replied the mink. 'I only want you—between to-day and the next full moon—to gnaw through the bows and paddles of the wolf people, so that directly they use them they will break. But of course you must manage it so that they notice nothing.'

'Of course,' answered the mouse, 'nothing is easier; but as the full moon is to-morrow night, and there is not much time, I had better begin at once.' Then the mink thanked her, and went his way; but before he had gone far he came back again.

'Perhaps, while you are about the wolf's house seeing after the bows, it would do no harm if you were to make that knot-hole in the wall a little bigger,' said he. 'Not large enough to draw attention, of course; but it might come in handy.' And with another nod he left her.

The next evening the mink washed and brushed himself carefully and set out for the feast. He smiled to himself as he looked at the dusty track, and perceived that though the marks of wolves' feet were many, not a single guest was to be seen anywhere. He knew very well what that meant; but he had taken his precautions and was not afraid.

The house door stood open, but through a crack the mink could see the wolves crowding in the corner behind it. However, he entered boldly, and as soon as he was fairly inside the door was shut with a bang, and the whole herd sprang at him, with their red tongues hanging out of their mouths. Quick as they were they were too late, for the mink was already through the knot-hole and racing for his canoe.

The knot-hole was too small for the wolves, and there were so many of them in the hut that it was some time before they could get the door open. Then they seized the bows and arrows which were hanging on the walls and, once outside, aimed at the flying mink; but as they pulled the bows broke in their paws, so they threw them away, and bounded to the shore, with all their speed, to the place where their canoes were drawn up on the beach.

Now, although the mink could not run as fast as the wolves, he had a good start, and was already afloat when the swiftest among them threw themselves into the nearest canoe. They pushed off, but as they dipped the paddles into the water, they snapped as the bows had done, and were quite useless.

'I know where there are some new ones,' cried a young fellow, leaping on shore and rushing to a little cave at the back of the beach. And the mink's heart smote him when he heard, for he had not known of this secret store.

After a long chase the wolves managed to surround their prey, and the mink, seeing it was no good resisting any more, gave himself up. Some of the elder wolves brought out some cedar bands, which they always carried wound round their bodies, but the mink laughed scornfully at the sight of them.

'Why I could snap those in a moment,' said he; 'if you want to make sure that I cannot escape, better take a line of kelp and bind me with that.'

'You are right,' answered the grandfather; 'your wisdom is greater than ours.' And he bade his servants gather enough kelp from the rocks to make a line, as they had brought none with them.

'While the line is being made you might as well let me have one last dance,' remarked the mink. And the wolves replied: 'Very good, you may have your dance; perhaps it may amuse us as well as you.' So they brought two canoes and placed them one beside the other. The mink stood up on his hind legs and began to dance, first in one canoe and then in the other; and so graceful was he, that the wolves forgot they were going to put him to death, and howled with pleasure.

'Pull the canoes a little apart; they are too close for this new dance,' he said, pausing for a moment. And the wolves separated them while he gave a series of little springs, sometime pirouetting while he stood with one foot on the prow of both. 'Now nearer, now further apart,' he would cry as the dance went on. 'No! further still.' And springing into the air, amidst howls of applause, he came down head-foremost, and dived to the bottom. And through the wolves, whose howls had now changed into those of rage, sought him everywhere, they never found him, for he hid behind a rock till they were out of sight, and then made his home in another forest.

Adventures of an Indian Brave

[From the Journal of the Anthropological Institute.]

A long, long way off, right away in the west of America, there once lived an old man who had one son. The country round was covered with forests, in which dwelt all kinds of wild beasts, and the young man and his companions used to spend whole days in hunting them, and he was the finest hunter of all the tribe.

One morning, when winter was coming on, the youth and his companions set off as usual to bring back some of the mountain goats and deer to be salted down, as he was afraid of a snow-storm; and if the wind blew and the snow drifted the forest might be impassable for some weeks. The old man and the wife, however, would not go out, but remained in the wigwam making bows and arrows.

It soon grew so cold in the forest that at last one of the men declared they could walk no more, unless they could manage to warm themselves.

'That is easily done,' said the leader, giving a kick to a large tree. Flames broke out in the trunk, and before it had burnt up they were as hot as if it had been summer. Then they started off to the place where the goats and deer were to be found in the greatest numbers, and soon had killed as many as they wanted. But the leader killed most, as he was the best shot.

'Now we must cut up the game and divide it,' said he; and so they did, each one taking his own share; and, walking one behind the other, set out for the village. But when they reached a great river the young man did not want the trouble of carrying his pack any further, and left it on the bank.

'I am going home another way,' he told his companions. And taking another road he reached the village long before they did.

'Have you returned with empty hands?' asked the old man, as his son opened the door.

'Have I ever done that, that you put me such a question?' asked the youth. 'No; I have slain enough to feast us for many moons, but it was heavy, and I left the pack on the bank of the great river. Give me the arrows, I will finish making them, and you can go to the river and bring home the pack!'

So the old man rose and went, and strapped the meat on his shoulder; but as he was crossing the ford the strap broke and the pack fell into the river. He stooped to catch it, but it swirled past him. He clutched again; but in doing so he over-balanced himself and was hurried into some rapids, where he was knocked against some rocks, and he sank and was drowned, and his body was carried down the stream into smoother water when it rose to the surface again. But by this time it had lost all likeness to a man, and was changed into a piece of wood.

The wood floated on, and the river got bigger and bigger and entered a new country. There it was borne by the current close to the shore, and a woman who was down there washing her clothes caught it as it passed, and drew it out, saying to herself: 'What a nice smooth plank! I will use it as a table to put my food upon.' And gathering up her clothes she took the plank with her into her hut.

When her supper time came she stretched the board across two strings which hung from the roof, and set upon it the pot containing a stew that smelt very good. The woman had been working hard all day and was very hungry, so she took her biggest spoon and plunged it into the pot. But what was her astonishment and disgust when both pot and food vanished instantly before her!

'Oh, you horrid plank, you have brought me ill-luck!' she cried. And taking it up she flung it away from her.

The woman had been surprised before at the disappearance of her food, but she was more astonished still when, instead of the plank, she beheld a baby. However, she was fond of children and had none of her own, so she made up her mind that she would keep it and take care of it. The baby grew and throve as no baby in that country had ever done, and in four days he was a man, and as tall and strong as any brave of the tribe.

'You have treated me well,' he said, 'and meat shall never fail to your house. But now I must go, for I have much work to do.'

Then he set out for his home.

It took him many days to get there, and when he saw his son sitting in his place his anger was kindled, and his heart was stirred to take vengeance upon him. So he went out quickly into the forest and shed tears, and each tear became a bird. 'Stay there till I want you,' said he; and he returned to the hut.

'I saw some pretty new birds, high up in a tree yonder,' he remarked. And the son answered: 'Show me the way and I will get them for dinner.'

The two went out together, and after walking for about half an hour they old man stopped. 'That is the tree,' he said. And the son began to climb it.

Now a strange thing happened. The higher the young man climbed the higher the birds seemed to be, and when he looked down the earth below appeared no bigger than a star. Sill he tried to go back, but he could not, and though he could not see the birds any longer he felt as if something were dragging him up and up.

He thought that he had been climbing that tree for days, and perhaps he had, for suddenly a beautiful country, yellow with fields of maize, stretched before him, and he gladly left the top of the tree and entered it. He walked through the maize without knowing where he was going, when he heard a sound of knocking, and saw two old blind women crushing their food between two stones. He crept up to them on tiptoe, and when one old woman passed her dinner to the other he held out his hand and took it and ate if for himself.

'How slow you are kneading that cake,' cried the other old woman at last.

'Why, I have given you your dinner, and what more do you want?' replied the second.

'You didn't; at least I never got it,' said the other.

'I certainly thought you took it from me; but here is some more.' And again the young man stretched out his hand; and the two old women fell to quarrelling afresh. But when it happened for the third time the old women suspected some trick, and one of them exclaimed:

'I am sure there is a man here; tell me, are you not my grandson?'

'Yes,' answered the young man, who wished to please her, 'and in return for your good dinner I will see if I cannot restore your sight; for I was taught in the art of healing by the best medicine man in the tribe.' And with that he left them, and wandered about till he found the herb which he wanted. Then he hastened back to the old women, and begging them to boil him some water, he threw the herb in. As soon as the pot began to sing he took off the lid, and sprinkled the eyes of the women, and sight came back to them once more.

There was no night in that country, so, instead of going to bed very early, as he would have done in his own hut, the young man took another walk. A splashing noise near by drew him down to a valley through which ran a large river, and up a waterfall some salmon were leaping. How their silver sides glistened in the light, and how he longed to catch some of the great fellows! But how could he do it? He had beheld no one except the old women, and it was not very likely that they would be able to help him. So with a sigh he turned away and went back to them, but, as he walked, a thought struck him. He pulled out one of his hairs which hung nearly to his waist, and it instantly became a strong line, nearly a mile in length.

'Weave me a net that I may catch some salmon,' said he. And they wove him the net he asked for, and for many weeks he watched by the river, only going back to the old women when he wanted a fish cooked.

At last, one day, when he was eating his dinner, the old woman who always spoke first, said to him:

'We have been very glad to see you, grandson, but now it is time that you went home.' And pushing aside a rock, he saw a deep hole, so deep that he could not see to the bottom. Then they dragged a basket out of the house, and tied a rope to it. 'Get in, and wrap this blanket round your head,' said they; 'and, whatever happens, don't uncover it till you get to the bottom.' Then they bade him farewell, and he curled himself up in the basket.

Down, down, down he went; would he ever stop going? But when the basket did stop, the young man forgot what he had been told, and put his head out to see what was the matter. In an instant the basket moved, but, to his horror, instead of going down, he felt himself being drawn upwards, and shortly after he beheld the faces of the old women.

'You will never see your wife and son if you will not do as you are bid,' said they. 'Now get in, and do not stir till you hear a crow calling.'

This time the young man was wiser, and though the basket often stopped, and strange creatures seemed to rest on him and to pluck at his blanket, he held it tight till he heard the crow calling. Then he flung off the blanket and sprang out, while the basket vanished in the sky.

He walked on quickly down the track that led to the hut, when, before him, he saw his wife with his little son on her back.

'Oh! there is father at last,' cried the boy; but the mother bade him cease from idle talking.

'But, mother, it is true; father is coming!' repeated the child. And, to satisfy him, the woman turned round and perceived her husband.

Oh, how glad they all were to be together again! And when the wind whistled through the forest, and the snow stood in great banks round the door, the father used to take the little boy on his knee and tell him how he caught salmon in the Land of the Sun.

How the Stalos Were Tricked

[From the Journal of the Anthropological Institute.]

'Mother, I have seen such a wonderful man,' said a little boy one day, as he entered a hut in Lapland, bearing in his arms the bundle of sticks he had been sent out to gather.

'Have you, my son; and what was he like?' asked the mother, as she took off the child's sheepskin coat and shook it on the doorstep.

'Well, I was tired of stooping for the sticks, and was leaning against a tree to rest, when I heard a noise of 'sh-'sh, among the dead leaves. I thought perhaps it was a wolf, so I stood very still. But soon there came past a tall man—oh! twice as tall as father—with a long red beard and a red tunic fastened with a silver girdle, from which hung a silver-handled knife. Behind him followed a great dog, which looked stronger than any wolf, or even a bear. But why are you so pale, mother?'

'It was the Stalo,' replied she, her voice trembling; 'Stalo the man-eater! You did well to hide, or you might never had come back. But, remember that, though he is so tall and strong, he is very stupid, and many a Lapp has escaped from his clutches by playing him some clever trick.'

Not long after the mother and son had held this talk, it began to be whispered in the forest that the children of an old man called Patto had vanished one by one, no one knew whither. The unhappy father searched the country for miles round without being able to find as much as a shoe or a handkerchief, to show him where they had passed, but at length a little boy came with news that he had seen the Stalo hiding behind a well, near which the children used to play. The boy had waited behind a clump of bushes to see what would happen, and by-and-by he noticed that the Stalo had laid a cunning trap in the path to the well, and that anybody who fell over it would roll into the water and drown there.

And, as he watched, Patto's youngest daughter ran gaily down the path, till her foot caught in the strings that were stretched across the steepest place. She slipped and fell, and in another instant had rolled into the water within reach of the Stalo.

As soon as Patto heard this tale his heart was filled with rage, and he vowed to have his revenge. So he straightway took an old fur coat from the hook where it hung, and putting it on went out into the forest. When he reached the path that led to the well he looked hastily round to be sure that no one was watching him, then laid himself down as if he had been caught in the snare and had rolled into the well, though he took care to keep his head out of the water.

Very soon he heard a 'sh-'sh of the leaves, and there was the Stalo pushing his way through the undergrowth to see what chance he had of a dinner. At the first glimpse of Patto's head in the well he laughed loudly, crying:

'Ha! ha! This time it is the old ass! I wonder how he will taste?' And drawing Patto out of the well, he flung him across his shoulders and carried him home. Then he tied a cord round him and hung him over the fire to roast, while he finished a box that he was making before the door of the hut, which he meant to hold Patto's flesh when it was cooked. In a very short time the box was so nearly done that it only wanted a little more chipping out with an axe; but this part of the work was easier accomplished indoors, and he called to one of his sons who were lounging inside to bring him the tool.

The young man looked everywhere, but he could not find the axe, for the very good reason that Patto had managed to pick it up and hide it in his clothes.

'Stupid fellow! what is the use of you?' grumbled his father angrily; and he bade first one and then another of his sons to fetch him the tool, but they had no better success than their brother.

'I must come myself, I suppose!' said Stalo, putting aside the box. But, meanwhile, Patto had slipped from the hook and concealed himself behind the door, so that, as Stalo stepped in, his prisoner raised the axe, and with one blow the ogre's head was rolling on the ground. His sons were so frightened at the sight that they all ran away.

And in this manner Patto avenged his dead children.

But though Stalo was dead, his three sons were still living, and not very far off either. They had gone to their mother, who was tending some reindeer on the pastures, and told her that by some magic, they knew not what, their father's head had rolled from his body, and they had been so afraid that something dreadful would happen to them that they had come to take refuge with her. The ogress said nothing. Long ago she had found out how stupid her sons were, so she just sent them out to milk the reindeer, while she returned to the other house to bury her husband's body.

Now, three days' journey from the hut on the pastures two brothers Sodno dwelt in a small cottage with their sister Lyma, who tended a large herd of reindeer while they were out hunting. Of late it had been whispered from one to another that the three young Stalos were to be seen on the pastures, but the Sodno brothers did not disturb themselves, the danger seemed too far away.

Unluckily, however, one day, when Lyma was left by herself in the hut, the three Stalos came down and carried her and the reindeer off to their own cottage. The country was very lonely, and perhaps no one would have known in which direction she had gone had not the girl managed to tie a ball of thread to the handle of a door at the back of the cottage and let it trail behind her. Of course the ball was not long enough to go all the way, but it lay on the edge of a snowy track which led straight to the Stalos' house.

When the brothers returned from their hunting they found both the hut and the sheds empty. Loudly they cried: 'Lyma! Lyma!' But no voice answered them; and they fell to searching all about, lest perchance their sister might have dropped some clue to guide them. At length their eyes dropped on the thread which lay on the snow, and they set out to follow it.

On and on they went, and when at length the thread stopped the brothers knew that another day's journey would bring them to the Stalos' dwelling. Of course they did not dare to approach it openly, for the Stalos had the strength of giants, and besides, there were three of them; so the two Sodnos climbed into a big bushy tree which overhung a well.

'Perhaps our sister may be sent to draw water here,' they said to each other.

But it was not till the moon had risen that the sister came, and as she let down her bucket into the well, the leaves seemed to whisper 'Lyma! Lyma!'

The girl started and looked up, but could see nothing, and in a moment the voice came again.

'Be careful—take no notice, fill your buckets, but listen carefully all the while, and we will tell you what to do so that you may escape yourself and set free the reindeer also.'

So Lyman bent over the well lower than before, and seemed busier than ever.

'You know,' said her brother, 'that when a Stalo finds that anything has been dropped into his food he will not eat a morsel, but throws it to his dogs. Now, after the pot has been hanging some time over the fire, and the broth is nearly cooked, just rake up the log of wood so that some of the ashes fly into the pot. The Stalo will soon notice this, and will call you to give all the food to the dogs; but, instead, you must bring it straight to us, as it is three days since we have eaten or drunk. That is all you need do for the present.'

Then Lyma took up her buckets and carried them into the house, and did as her brothers had told her. They were so hungry that they ate the food up greedily without speaking, but when there was nothing left in the pot, the eldest one said:

'Listen carefully to what I have to tell you. After the eldest Stalo has cooked and eaten a fresh supper, he will go to bed and sleep so soundly that not even a witch could wake him. You can hear him snoring a mile off, and then you must go into his room and pull off the iron mantle that covers him, and put it on the fire till it is almost red hot. When that is done, come to us and we will give you further directions.'

'I will obey you in everything, dear brothers,' answered Lyman; and so she did.

It had happened that on this very evening the Stalos had driven in some of the reindeer from the pasture, and had tied them up to the wall of the house so that they might be handy to kill for next day's dinner. The two Sodnos had seen what they were doing, and where the beasts were secured; so, at midnight, when all was still, they crept down from their tree and seized the reindeer by the horns which were locked together. The animals were frightened, and began to neigh and kick, as if they were fighting together, and the noise became so great that even the eldest Stalo was awakened by it, and that was a thing which had never occurred before. Raising himself in his bed, he called to his youngest brother to go out and separate the reindeer or they would certainly kill themselves.

The young Stalo did as he was bid, and left the house; but no sooner was he out of the door than he was stabbed to the heart by one of the Sodnos, and fell without a groan. Then they went back to worry the reindeer, and the noise became as great as ever, and a second time the Stalo awoke.

'The boy does not seem to be able to part the beasts,' he cried to his second brother; 'go and help him, or I shall never get to sleep.' So the brother went, and in an instant was struck dead as he left the house by the sword of the eldest Sodno. The Stalo waited in bed a little longer for things to get quiet, but as the clatter of the reindeer's horns was as bad as ever, he rose angrily from his bed muttering to himself:

'It is extraordinary that they cannot unlock themselves; but as no one else seems able to help them I suppose I must go and do it.'

Rubbing his eyes, he stood up on the floor and stretched his great arms and gave a yawn which shook the walls. The Sodnos heard it below, and posted themselves, one at the big door and one at the little door at the back, for they did not know what their enemy would come out at.

The Stalo put out his hand to take his iron mantle from the bed, where it always lay, but the mantle was no there. He wondered where it could be, and who could have moved it, and after searching through all the rooms, he found it hanging over the kitchen fire. But the first touch burnt him so badly that he let it alone, and went with nothing, except a stick in his hand, through the back door.

The young Sodno was standing ready for him, and as the Stalo passed the threshold struck him such a blow on the head that he rolled over with a crash and never stirred again. The two Sodnos did not trouble about him, but quickly stripped the younger Stalos of their clothes, in which they dressed themselves. Then they sat still till the dawn should break and they could find out from the Stalos' mother where the treasure was hidden.

With the first rays of the sun the young Sodno went upstairs and entered the old woman's room. She was already up and dressed, and sitting by the window knitting, and the young man crept in softly and crouched down on the floor, laying his head on her lap. For a while he kept silence, then he whispered gently:

'Tell me, dear mother, where did my eldest brother conceal his riches?'

'What a strange question! Surely you must know,' answered she.

'No, I have forgotten; my memory is so bad.'

'He dug a hole under the doorstep and placed it there,' said she. And there was another pause.

By-and-by the Sodno asked again:

'And where may my second brother's money be?'

'Don't you know that either?' cried the mother in surprise.

'Oh, yes; I did once. But since I fell upon my head I can remember nothing.'

'It is behind the oven,' answered she. And again was silence.

'Mother, dear mother,' said the young man at last, 'I am almost afraid to ask you; but I really have grown so stupid of late. Where did I hide my own money?'

But at this question the old woman flew into a passion, and vowed that if she could find a rod she would bring his memory back to him. Luckily, no rod was within her reach, and the Sodno managed, after a little, to coax her back into good humour, and at length she told him that the youngest Stalo had buried his treasure under the very place where she was sitting.

'Dear mother,' said Lyman, who had come in unseen, and was kneeling in front of the fire. 'Dear mother, do you know who it is you have been talking with?'

The old woman started, but answered quietly:

'It is a Sodno, I suppose?'

'You have guessed right,' replied Lyma.

The mother of the Stalos looked round for her iron cane, which she always used to kill her victims, but it was not there, for Lyma had put it in the fire.

'Where is my iron cane?' asked the old woman.

'There!' answered Lyma, pointing to the flames.

The old woman sprang forwards and seized it, but her clothes caught fire, and in a few minutes she was burned to ashes.

So the Sodno brothers found the treasure, and they carried it, and their sister and the reindeer, to their own home, and were the richest men in all Lapland.

Andras Baive

[From Lapplandische Marchen, J. C. Poestion.]

Once upon a time there lived in Lapland a man who was so very strong and swift of foot that nobody in his native town of Vadso could come near him if they were running races in the summer evenings. The people of Vadso were very proud of their champion, and thought that there was no one like him in the world, till, by-and-by, it came to their ears that there dwelt among the mountains a Lapp, Andras Baive by name, who was said by his friends to be even stronger and swifter than the bailiff. Of course not a creature in Vadso believed that, and declared that if it made the mountaineers happier to talk such nonsense, why, let them!

The winter was long and cold, and the thoughts of the villagers were much busier with wolves than with Andras Baive, when suddenly, on a frosty day, he made his appearance in the little town of Vadso. The bailiff was delighted at this chance of trying his strength, and at once went out to seek Andras and to coax him into giving proof of his vigour. As he walked along his eyes fell upon a big eight-oared boat that lay upon the shore, and his face shone with pleasure. 'That is the very thing,' laughed he, 'I will make him jump over that boat.' Andras was quite ready to accept the challenge, and they soon settled the terms of the wager. He who could jump over the boat without so much as touching it with his heel was to be the winner, and would get a large sum of money as the prize. So, followed by many of the villagers, the two men walked down to the sea.

An old fisherman was chosen to stand near the boat to watch fair play, and to hold the stakes, and Andras, as the stranger was told to jump first. Going back to the flag which had been stuck into the sand to mark the starting place, he ran forward, with his head well thrown back, and cleared the boat with a mighty bound. The lookers-on cheered him, and indeed he well deserve it; but they waited anxiously all the same to see what the bailiff would do. On he came, taller than Andras by several inches, but heavier of build. He too sprang high and well, but as he came down his heel just grazed the edge of the boat. Dead silence reigned amidst the townsfolk, but Andras only laughed and said carelessly:

'Just a little too short, bailiff; next time you must do better than that.'

The bailiff turned red with anger at his rival's scornful words, and answered quickly: 'Next time you will have something harder to do.' And turning his back on his friends, he went sulkily home. Andras, putting the money he had earned in his pocket, went home also.

The following spring Andras happened to be driving his reindeer along a great fiord to the west of Vadso. A boy who had met him hastened to tell the bailiff that his enemy was only a few miles off; and the bailiff, disguising himself as a Stalo, or ogre, called his son and his dog and rowed away across the fiord to the place where the boy had met Andras.

Now the mountaineer was lazily walking along the sands, thinking of the new hut that he was building with the money that he had won on the day of his lucky jump. He wandered on, his eyes fixed on the sands, so that he did not see the bailiff drive his boat behind a rock, while he changed himself into a heap of wreckage which floated in on the waves. A stumble over a stone recalled Andras to himself, and looking up he beheld the mass of wreckage. 'Dear me! I may find some use for that,' he said; and hastened down to the sea, waiting till he could lay hold of some stray rope which might float towards him. Suddenly—he could not have told why—a nameless fear seized upon him, and he fled away from the shore as if for his life. As he ran he heard the sound of a pipe, such as only ogres of the Stalo kind were wont to use; and there flashed into his mind what the bailiff had said when they jumped the boat: 'Next time you will have something harder to do.' So it was no wreckage after all that he had seen, but the bailiff himself.

It happened that in the long summer nights up in the mountain, where the sun never set, and it was very difficult to get to sleep, Andras had spent many hours in the study of magic, and this stood him in good stead now. The instant he heard the Stalo music he wished himself to become the feet of a reindeer, and in this guise he galloped like the wind for several miles. Then he stopped to take breath and find out what his enemy was doing. Nothing he could see, but to his ears the notes of a pipe floated over the plain, and ever, as he listened, it drew nearer.

A cold shiver shook Andras, and this time he wished himself the feet of a reindeer calf. For when a reindeer calf has reached the age at which he begins first to lose his hair he is so swift that neither beast nor bird can come near him. A reindeer calf is the swiftest of all things living. Yes; but not so swift as a Stalo, as Andras found out when he stopped to rest, and heard the pipe playing!

For a moment his heart sank, and he gave himself up for dead, till he remembered that, not far off, were two little lakes joined together by a short though very broad river. In the middle of the river lay a stone that was always covered by water, except in dry seasons, and as the winter rains had been very heavy, he felt quite sure that not even the top of it could be seen. The next minute, if anyone had been looking that way, he would have beheld a small reindeer calf speeding northwards, and by-and-by giving a great spring, which landed him in the midst of the stream. But, instead of sinking to the bottom, he paused a second to steady himself, then gave a second spring which landed him on the further shore. He next ran on to a little hill where he saw down and began to neigh loudly, so that the Stalo might know exactly where he was.

'Ah! There you are,' cried the Stalo, appearing on the opposite bank; 'for a moment I really thought I had lost you.'

'No such luck,' answered Andras, shaking his head sorrowfully. By this time he had taken his own shape again.

'Well, but I don't see how I am to get to you,' said the Stalo, looking up and down.

'Jump over, as I did,' answered Andras; 'it is quite easy.'

'But I could not jump this river; and I don't know how you did,' replied the Stalo.

'I should be ashamed to say such things,' exclaimed Andras. 'Do you mean to tell me that a jump, which the weakest Lapp boy would make nothing of, is beyond your strength?'

The Stalo grew red and angry when he heard these words, just as Andras meant him to do. He bounded into the air and fell straight into the river. Not that that would have mattered, for he was a good swimmer; but Andras drew out the bow and arrows which every Lapp carries, and took aim at him. His aim was good, but the Stalo sprang so high into the air that the arrow flew between his feet. A second shot, directed at his forehead, fared no better, for this time the Stalo jumped so high to the other side that the arrow passed between his finger and thumb. Then Andras aimed his third arrow a little over the Stalo's head, and when he sprang up, just an instant too soon, it hit him between the ribs.

Mortally wounded as he was, the Stalo was not yet dead, and managed to swim to the shore. Stretching himself on the sand, he said slowly to Andras:

'Promise that you will give me an honourable burial, and when my body is laid in the grave go in my boat across the fiord, and take whatever you find in my house which belongs to me. My dog you must kill, but spare my son, Andras.'

Then he died; and Andras sailed in his boat away across the fiord and found the dog and boy. The dog, a fierce, wicked-looking creature, he slew with one blow from his fist, for it is well known that if a Stalo's dog licks the blood that flows from his dead master's wounds the Stalo comes to life again. That is why no REAL Stalo is ever seen without his dog; but the bailiff, being only half a Stalo, had forgotten him, when he went to the little lakes in search of Andras. Next, Andras put all the gold and jewels which he found in the boat into his pockets, and bidding the boy get in, pushed it off from the shore, leaving the little craft to drift as it would, while he himself ran home. With the treasure he possessed he was able to buy a great herd of reindeer; and he soon married a rich wife, whose parents would not have him as a son-in-law when he was poor, and the two lived happy for ever after.

The White Slipper

[From Lapplandische Mahrchen, J. C. Poestion.]

Once upon a time there lived a king who had a daughter just fifteen years old. And what a daughter!

Even the mothers who had daughters of their own could not help allowing that the princess was much more beautiful and graceful than any of them; and, as for the fathers, if one of them ever beheld her by accident he could talk of nothing else for a whole day afterwards.

Of course the king, whose name was Balancin, was the complete slave of his little girl from the moment he lifted her from the arms of her dead mother; indeed, he did not seem to know that there was anyone else in the world to love.

Now Diamantina, for that was her name, did not reach her fifteenth birthday without proposals for marriage from every country under heaven; but be the suitor who he might, the king always said him nay.

Behind the palace a large garden stretched away to the foot of some hills, and more than one river flowed through. Hither the princess would come each evening towards sunset, attended by her ladies, and gather herself the flowers that were to adorn her rooms. She also brought with her a pair of scissors to cut off the dead blooms, and a basket to put them in, so that when the sun rose next morning he might see nothing unsightly. When she had finished this task she would take a walk through the town, so that the poor people might have a chance of speaking with her, and telling her of their troubles; and then she would seek out her father, and together they would consult over the best means of giving help to those who needed it.

But what has all this to do with the White Slipper? my readers will ask.

Have patience, and you will see.

Next to his daughter, Balancin loved hunting, and it was his custom to spend several mornings every week chasing the boars which abounded in the mountains a few miles from the city. One day, rushing downhill as fast as he could go, he put his foot into a hole and fell, rolling into a rocky pit of brambles. The king's wounds were not very severe, but his face and hands were cut and torn, while his feet were in a worse plight still, for, instead of proper hunting boots, he only wore sandals, to enable him to run more swiftly.

In a few days the king was as well as ever, and the signs of the scratches were almost gone; but one foot still remained very sore, where a thorn had pierced deeply and had festered. The best doctors in the kingdom treated it with all their skill; they bathed, and poulticed, and bandaged, but it was in vain. The foot only grew worse and worse, and became daily more swollen and painful.

After everyone had tried his own particular cure, and found it fail, there came news of a wonderful doctor in some distant land who had healed the most astonishing diseases. On inquiring, it was found that he never left the walls of his own city, and expected his patients to come to see him; but, by dint of offering a large sum of money, the king persuaded the famous physician to undertake the journey to his own court.

On his arrival the doctor was led at once into the king's presence, and made a careful examination of his foot.

'Alas! your majesty,' he said, when he had finished, 'the wound is beyond the power of man to heal; but though I cannot cure it, I can at least deaden the pain, and enable you to walk without so much suffering.'

'Oh, if you can only do that,' cried the king, 'I shall be grateful to you for life! Give your own orders; they shall be obeyed.'

'Then let your majesty bid the royal shoemaker make you a shoe of goat-skin very loose and comfortable, while I prepare a varnish to paint over it of which I alone have the secret!' So saying, the doctor bowed himself out, leaving the king more cheerful and hopeful than he had been for long.

The days passed very slowly with him during the making of the shoe and the preparation of the varnish, but on the eighth morning the physician appeared, bringing with him the shoe in a case. He drew it out to slip on the king's foot, and over the goat-skin he had rubbed a polish so white that the snow itself was not more dazzling.

'While you wear this shoe you will not feel the slightest pain,' said the doctor. 'For the balsam with which I have rubbed it inside and out has, besides its healing balm, the quality of strengthening the material it touches, so that, even were your majesty to live a thousand years, you would find the slipper just as fresh at the end of that time as it is now.'

The king was so eager to put it on that he hardly gave the physician time to finish. He snatched it from the case and thrust his foot into it, nearly weeping for joy when he found he could walk and run as easily as any beggar boy.

'What can I give you?' he cried, holding out both hands to the man who had worked this wonder. 'Stay with me, and I will heap on you riches greater than ever you dreamed of.' But the doctor said he would accept nothing more than had been agreed on, and must return at once to his own country, where many sick people were awaiting him. So king Balancin had to content himself with ordering the physician to be treated with royal honours, and desiring that an escort should attend him on his journey home.

For two years everything went smoothly at court, and to king Balancin and his daughter the sun no sooner rose than it seemed time for it to set. Now, the king's birthday fell in the month of June, and as the weather happened to be unusually fine, he told the princess to celebrate it in any way that pleased her. Diamantina was very fond of being on the river, and she was delighted at this chance of delighting her tastes. She would have a merry-making such as never had been seen before, and in the evening, when they were tired of sailing and rowing, there should be music and dancing, plays and fireworks. At the very end, before the people went home, every poor person should be given a loaf of bread and every girl who was to be married within the year a new dress.

The great day appeared to Diamantina to be long in coming, but, like other days, it came at last. Before the sun was fairly up in the heavens the princess, too full of excitement to stay in the palace, was walking about the streets so covered with precious stones that you had to shade your eyes before you could look at her. By-and-by a trumpet sounded, and she hurried home, only to appear again in a few moments walking by the side of her father down to the river. Here a splendid barge was waiting for them, and from it they watched all sorts of races and feats of swimming and diving. When these were over the barge proceeded up the river to the field where the dancing and concerts were to take place, and after the prizes had been given away to the winners, and the loaves and the dresses had been distributed by the princess, they bade farewell to their guests, and turned to step into the barge which was to carry them back to the palace.

Then a dreadful thing happened. As the king stepped on board the boat one of the sandals of the white slipper, which had got loose, caught in a nail that was sticking out, and caused the king to stumble. The pain was great, and unconsciously he turned and shook his foot, so that the sandals gave way, and in a moment the precious shoe was in the river.

It had all occurred so quickly that nobody had noticed the loss of the slipper, not even the princess, whom the king's cries speedily brought to his side.

'What is the matter, dear father?' asked she. But the king could not tell her; and only managed to gasp out: 'My shoe! my shoe!' While the sailors stood round staring, thinking that his majesty had suddenly gone mad.

Seeing her father's eyes fixed on the stream, Diamantina looked hastily in that direction. There, dancing on the current, was the point of something white, which became more and more distant the longer they watched it. The king could bear the sight no more, and, besides, now that the healing ointment in the shoe had been removed the pain in his foot was as bad as ever; he gave a sudden cry, staggered, and fell over the bulwarks into the water.

In an instant the river was covered with bobbing heads all swimming their fastest towards the king, who had been carried far down by the swift current. At length one swimmer, stronger than the rest, seized hold of his tunic, and drew him to the bank, where a thousand eager hands were ready to haul him out. He was carried, unconscious, to the side of his daughter, who had fainted with terror on seeing her father disappear below the surface, and together they were place in a coach and driven to the palace, where the best doctors in the city were awaiting their arrival.

In a few hours the princess was as well as ever; but the pain, the wetting, and the shock of the accident, all told severely on the king, and for three days he lay in a high fever. Meanwhile, his daughter, herself nearly mad with grief, gave orders that the white slipper should be sought for far and wide; and so it was, but even the cleverest divers could find no trace of it at the bottom of the river.

When it became clear that the slipper must have been carried out to sea by the current, Diamantina turned her thoughts elsewhere, and sent messengers in search of the doctor who had brought relief to her father, begging him to make another slipper as fast as possible, to supply the place of the one which was lost. But the messengers returned with the sad news that the doctor had died some weeks before, and, what was worse, his secret had died with him.

In his weakness this intelligence had such an effect on the king that the physicians feared he would become as ill as before. He could hardly be persuaded to touch food, and all night long he lay moaning, partly with pain, and partly over his own folly in not having begged the doctor to make him several dozens of white slippers, so that in case of accidents he might always have one to put on. However, by-and-by he saw that it was no use weeping and wailing, and commanded that they should search for his lost treasure more diligently than ever.

What a sight the river banks presented in those days! It seemed as if all the people in the country were gathered on them. But this second search was no more fortunate than the first, and at last the king issued a proclamation that whoever found the missing slipper should be made heir to the crown, and should marry the princess.

Now many daughters would have rebelled at being disposed of in the manner; and it must be admitted that Diamantina's heart sank when she heard what the king had done. Still, she loved her father so much that she desired his comfort more than anything else in the world, so she said nothing, and only bowed her head.

Of course the result of the proclamation was that the river banks became more crowded than before; for all the princess's suitors from distant lands flocked to the spot, each hoping that he might be the lucky finder. Many times a shining stone at the bottom of the stream was taken for the slipper itself, and every evening saw a band of dripping downcast men returning homewards. But one youth always lingered longer than the rest, and night would still see him engaged in the search, though his clothes stuck to his skin and his teeth chattered.

One day, when the king was lying on his bed racked with pain, he heard the noise of a scuffle going on in his antechamber, and rang a golden bell that stood by his side to summon one of his servants.

'Sire,' answered the attendant, when the king inquired what was the matter, 'the noise you heard was caused by a young man from the town, who has had the impudence to come here to ask if he may measure your majesty's foot, so as to make you another slipper in place of the lost one.'

'And what have you done to the youth?' said the king.

'The servants pushed him out of the palace, and, added a few blows to teach him not to be insolent,' replied the man.

'Then they did very ill,' answered the king, with a frown. 'He came here from kindness, and there was no reason to maltreat him.'

'Oh, my lord, he had the audacity to wish to touch your majesty's sacred person—he, a good-for-nothing boy, a mere shoemaker's apprentice, perhaps! And even if he could make shoes to perfection they would be no use without the soothing balsam.'

The king remained silent for a few moments, then he said:

'Never mind. Go and fetch the youth and bring him to me. I would gladly try any remedy that may relieve my pain.'

So, soon afterwards, the youth, who had not gone far from the palace, was caught and ushered into the king's presence.

He was tall and handsome and, though he professed to make shoes, his manners were good and modest, and he bowed low as he begged the king not only to allow him to take the measure of his foot, but also to suffer him to place a healing plaster over the wound.

Balancin was pleased with the young man's voice and appearance, and thought that he looked as if he knew what he was doing. So he stretched out his bad foot which the youth examined with great attention, and then gently laid on the plaster.

Very shortly the ointment began to soothe the sharp pain, and the king, whose confidence increased every moment, begged the young man to tell him his name.

'I have no parents; they died when I was six, sire,' replied the youth, modestly. 'Everyone in the town calls me Gilguerillo, because, when I was little, I went singing through the world in spite of my misfortunes. Luckily for me I was born to be happy.'

'And you really think you can cure me?' asked the king.

'Completely, my lord,' answered Gilguerillo.

'And how long do you think it will take?'

'It is not an easy task; but I will try to finish it in a fortnight,' replied the youth.

A fortnight seemed to the king a long time to make one slipper. But he only said:

'Do you need anything to help you?'

'Only a good horse, if your majesty will be kind enough to give me one,' answered Gilguerillo. And the reply was so unexpected that the courtiers could hardly restrain their smiles, while the king stared silently.

'You shall have the horse,' he said at last, 'and I shall expect you back in a fortnight. If you fulfil your promise you know your reward; if not, I will have you flogged for your impudence.'

Gilguerillo bowed, and turned to leave the palace, followed by the jeers and scoffs of everyone he met. But he paid no heed, for he had got what he wanted.

He waited in front of the gates till a magnificent horse was led up to him, and vaulting into the saddle with an ease which rather surprised the attendant, rode quickly out of the town amidst the jests of the assembled crowd, who had heard of his audacious proposal. And while he is on his way let us pause for a moment and tell who he is.

Both father and mother had died before the boy was six years old; and he had lived for many years with his uncle, whose life had been passed in the study of chemistry. He could leave no money to his nephew, as he had a son of his own; but he taught him all he knew, and at his dead Gilguerillo entered an office, where he worked for many hours daily. In his spare time, instead of playing with the other boys, he passed hours poring over books, and because he was timid and liked to be alone he was held by everyone to be a little mad. Therefore, when it became known that he had promised to cure the king's foot, and had ridden away—no one knew where—a roar of laughter and mockery rang through the town, and jeers and scoffing words were sent after him.

But if they had only known what were Gilguerillo's thoughts they would have thought him madder than ever.

The real truth was that, on the morning when the princess had walked through the streets before making holiday on the river Gilguerillo had seen her from his window, and had straightway fallen in love with her. Of course he felt quite hopeless. It was absurd to imagine that the apothecary's nephew could ever marry the king's daughter; so he did his best to forget her, and study harder than before, till the royal proclamation suddenly filled him with hope. When he was free he no longer spent the precious moments poring over books, but, like the rest, he might have been seen wandering along the banks of the river, or diving into the stream after something that lay glistening in the clear water, but which turned out to be a white pebble or a bit of glass.

And at the end he understood that it was not by the river that he would win the princess; and, turning to his books for comfort, he studied harder than ever.

There is an old proverb which says: 'Everything comes to him who knows how to wait.' It is not all men who know hot to wait, any more than it is all men who can learn by experience; but Gilguerillo was one of the few and instead of thinking his life wasted because he could not have the thing he wanted most, he tried to busy himself in other directions. So, one day, when he expected it least, his reward came to him.

He happened to be reading a book many hundreds of years old, which told of remedies for all kinds of diseases. Most of them, he knew, were merely invented by old women, who sought to prove themselves wiser than other people; but at length he came to something which caused him to sit up straight in his chair, and made his eyes brighten. This was the description of a balsam—which would cure every kind of sore or wound—distilled from a plant only to be found in a country so distant that it would take a man on foot two months to go and come back again.

When I say that the book declared that the balsam could heal every sort of sore or wound, there were a few against which it was powerless, and it gave certain signs by which these might be known. This was the reason why Gilguerillo demanded to see the king's foot before he would undertake to cure it; and to obtain admittance he gave out that he was a shoemaker. However, the dreaded signs were absent, and his heart bounded at the thought that the princess was within his reach.

Perhaps she was; but a great deal had to be accomplished yet, and he had allowed himself a very short time in which to do it.

He spared his horse only so much as was needful, yet it took him six days to reach the spot where the plant grew. A thick wood lay in front of him, and, fastening the bridle tightly to a tree, he flung himself on his hands and knees and began to hunt for the treasure. Many time he fancied it was close to him, and many times it turned out to be something else; but, at last, when light was fading, and he had almost given up hope, he came upon a large bed of the plant, right under his feet! Trembling with joy, he picked every scrap he could see, and placed it in his wallet. Then, mounting his horse, he galloped quickly back towards the city.

It was night when he entered the gates, and the fifteen days allotted were not up till the next day. His eyes were heavy with sleep, and his body ached with the long strain, but, without pausing to rest, he kindled a fire on is hearth, and quickly filling a pot with water, threw in the herbs and left them to boil. After that he lay down and slept soundly.

The sun was shining when he awoke, and he jumped up and ran to the pot. The plant had disappeared and in its stead was a thick syrup, just as the book had said there would be. He lifted the syrup out with a spoon, and after spreading it in the sun till it was partly dry, poured it into a small flask of crystal. He next washed himself thoroughly, and dressed himself, in his best clothes, and putting the flask in his pocket, set out for the palace, and begged to see the king without delay.

Now Balancin, whose foot had been much less painful since Gilguerillo had wrapped it in the plaster, was counting the days to the young man's return; and when he was told Gilguerillo was there, ordered him to be admitted at once. As he entered, the king raised himself eagerly on his pillows, but his face fell when he saw no signs of a slipper.

'You have failed, then?' he said, throwing up his hands in despair.

'I hope not, your majesty; I think not,' answered the youth. And drawing the flask from his pocket, he poured two or three drops on the wound.

'Repeat this for three nights, and you will find yourself cured,' said he. And before the king had time to thank him he had bowed himself out.

Of course the news soon spread through the city, and men and women never tired of calling Gilguerillo an impostor, and prophesying that the end of the three days would see him in prison, if not on the scaffold. But Gilguerillo paid no heed to their hard words, and no more did the king, who took care that no hand but his own should put on the healing balsam.

On the fourth morning the king awoke and instantly stretched out his wounded foot that he might prove the truth or falsehood of Gilguerillo's remedy. The wound was certainly cured on that side, but how about the other? Yes, that was cured also; and not even a scar was left to show where it had been!

Was ever any king so happy as Balancin when he satisfied himself of this?

Lightly as a deer he jumped from his bed, and began to turn head over heels and to perform all sorts of antics, so as to make sure that his foot was in truth as well as it looked. And when he was quite tired he sent for his daughter, and bade the courtiers bring the lucky young man to his room.

'He is really young and handsome,' said the princess to herself, heaving a sigh of relief that it was not some dreadful old man who had healed her father; and while the king was announcing to his courtiers the wonderful cure that had been made, Diamantina was thinking that if Gilguerillo looked so well in his common dress, how much improved by the splendid garments of a king' son. However, she held her peace, and only watched with amusement when the courtiers, knowing there was no help for it, did homage and obeisance to the chemist's boy.

Then they brought to Gilguerillo a magnificent tunic of green velvet bordered with gold, and a cap with three white plumes stuck in it; and at the sight of him so arrayed, the princess fell in love with him in a moment. The wedding was fixed to take place in eight days, and at the ball afterwards nobody danced so long or so lightly as king Balancin.

The Magic Book

[From Capullos de Rosa, por D. Enrique Ceballos Quintana.]
[From AEventyr fra Zylland samlede og optegnede af Tang Kristensen. Translated from the Danish by Mrs. Skavgaard-Pedersen.]

There was once an old couple named Peder and Kirsten who had an only son called Hans. From the time he was a little boy he had been told that on his sixteenth birthday he must go out into the world and serve his apprenticeship. So, one fine summer morning, he started off to seek his fortune with nothing but the clothes he wore on his back.

For many hours he trudged on merrily, now and then stopping to drink from some clear spring or to pick some ripe fruit from a tree. The little wild creatures peeped at him from beneath the bushes, and he nodded and smiled, and wished them 'Good-morning.' After he had been walking for some time he met an old white-bearded man who was coming along the footpath. The boy would not step aside, and the man was determined not to do so either, so they ran against one another with a bump.

'It seems to me,' said the old fellow, 'that a boy should give way to an old man.'

'The path is for me as well as for you,' answered young Hans saucily, for he had never been taught politeness.

'Well, that's true enough,' answered the other mildly. 'And where are you going?'

'I am going into service,' said Hans.

'Then you can come and serve me,' replied the man.

Well, Hans could do that; but what would his wages be?

'Two pounds a year, and nothing to do but keep some rooms clean,' said the new-comer.

This seemed to Hans to be easy enough; so he agreed to enter the old man's service, and they set out together. On their way they crossed a deep valley and came to a mountain, where the man opened a trapdoor, and bidding Hans follow him, he crept in and began to go down a long flight of steps. When they got to the bottom Hans saw a large number of rooms lit by many lamps and full of beautiful things. While he was looking round the old man said to him:

'Now you know what you have to do. You must keep these rooms clean, and strew sand on the floor every day. Here is a table where you will always find food and drink, and there is your bed. You see there are a great many suits of clothes hanging on the wall, and you may wear any you please; but remember that you are never to open this locked door. If you do ill will befall you. Farewell, for I am going away again and cannot tell when I may return.

No sooner had the old man disappeared than Hans sat down to a good meal, and after that went to bed and slept until the morning. At first he could not remember what had happened to him, but by-and-by he jumped up and went into all the rooms, which he examined carefully.

'How foolish to bid me to put sand on the floors,' he thought, 'when there is nobody here by myself! I shall do nothing of the sort.' And so he shut the doors quickly, and only cleaned and set in order his own room. And after the first few days he felt that that was unnecessary too, because no one came there to see if the rooms where clean or not. At last he did no work at all, but just sat and wondered what was behind the locked door, till he determined to go and look for himself.

The key turned easily in the lock. Hans entered, half frightened at what he was doing, and the first thing he beheld was a heap of bones. That was not very cheerful; and he was just going out again when his eye fell on a shelf of books. Here was a good way of passing the time, he thought, for he was fond of reading, and he took one of the books from the shelf. It was all about magic, and told you how you could change yourself into anything in the world you liked. Could anything be more exciting or more useful? So he put it in his pocket, and ran quickly away out of the mountain by a little door which had been left open.

When he got home his parents asked him what he had been doing and where he had got the fine clothes he wore.

'Oh, I earned them myself,' answered he.

'You never earned them in this short time,' said his father. 'Be off with you; I won't keep you here. I will have no thieves in my house!'

'Well I only came to help you,' replied the boy sulkily. 'Now I'll be off, as you wish; but to-morrow morning when you rise you will see a great dog at the door. Do not drive it away, but take it to the castle and sell it to the duke, and they will give you ten dollars for it; only you must bring the strap you lead it with, back to the house.'

Sure enough the next day the dog was standing at the door waiting to be let in. The old man was rather afraid of getting into trouble, but his wife urged him to sell the dog as the boy had bidden him, so he took it up to the castle and sold it to the duke for ten dollars. But he did not forget to take off the strap with which he had led the animal, and to carry it home. When he got there old Kirsten met him at the door.

'Well, Peder, and have you sold the dog?' asked she.

'Yes, Kirsten; and I have brought back ten dollars, as the boy told us,' answered Peder.

'Ay! but that's fine!' said his wife. 'Now you see what one gets by doing as one is bid; if it had not been for me you would have driven the dog away again, and we should have lost the money. After all, I always know what is best.'

'Nonsense!' said her husband; 'women always think they know best. I should have sold the dog just the same whatever you had told me. Put the money away in a safe place, and don't talk so much.'

The next day Hans came again; but though everything had turned out as he had foretold, he found that his father was still not quite satisfied.

'Be off with you!' said he, 'you'll get us into trouble.'

'I haven't helped you enough yet,' replied the boy. 'To-morrow there will come a great fat cow, as big as the house. Take it to the king's palace and you'll get as much as a thousand dollars for it. Only you must unfasten the halter you lead it with and bring it back, and don't return by the high road, but through the forest.'

The next day, when the couple rose, they saw an enormous head looking in at their bedroom window, and behind it was a cow which was nearly as big as their hut. Kirsten was wild with joy to think of the money the cow would bring them.

'But how are you going to put the rope over her head?' asked she.

'Wait and you'll see, mother,' answered her husband. Then Peder took the ladder that led up to the hayloft and set it against the cow's neck, and he climbed up and slipped the rope over her head. When he had made sure that the noose was fast they started for the palace, and met the king himself walking in his grounds.

'I heard that the princess was going to be married,' said Peder, 'so I've brought your majesty a cow which is bigger than any cow that was ever seen. Will your majesty deign to buy it?'

The king had, in truth, never seen so large a beast, and he willingly paid the thousand dollars, which was the price demanded; but Peder remembered to take off the halter before he left. After he was gone the king sent for the butcher and told him to kill the animal for the wedding feast. The butcher got ready his pole-axe; but just as he was going to strike, the cow changed itself into a dove and flew away, and the butcher stood staring after it as if he were turned to stone. However, as the dove could not be found, he was obliged to tell the king what had happened, and the king in his turn despatched messengers to capture the old man and bring him back. But Peder was safe in the woods, and could not be found. When at last he felt the danger was over, and he might go home,

Kirsten nearly fainted with joy at the sight of all the money he brought with him.

'Now that we are rich people we must build a bigger house,' cried she; and was vexed to find that Peder only shook his head and said: 'No; if they did that people would talk, and say they had got their wealth by ill-doing.'

A few mornings later Hans came again.

'Be off before you get us into trouble,' said his father. 'So far the money has come right enough, but I don't trust it.'

'Don't worry over that, father,' said Hans. 'To-morrow you will find a horse outside by the gate. Ride it to market and you will get a thousand dollars for it. Only don't forget to loosen the bridle when you sell it.'

Well, in the morning there was the horse; Kirsten had never seen so find an animal. 'Take care it doesn't hurt you, Peder,' said she.

'Nonsense, wife,' answered he crossly. 'When I was a lad I lived with horses, and could ride anything for twenty miles round.' But that was not quite the truth, for he had never mounted a horse in his life.

Still, the animal was quiet enough, so Peder got safely to market on its back. There he met a man who offered nine hundred and ninety-nine dollars for it, but Peder would take nothing less than a thousand. At last there came an old, grey-bearded man who looked at the horse and agreed to buy it; but the moment he touched it the horse began to kick and plunge. 'I must take the bridle off,' said Peder. 'It is not to be sold with the animal as is usually the case.'

'I'll give you a hundred dollars for the bridle,' said the old man, taking out his purse.

'No, I can't sell it,' replied Hans's father.

'Five hundred dollars!'

'No.'

'A thousand!'

At this splendid offer Peder's prudence gave way; it was a shame to let so much money go. So he agreed to accept it. But he could hardly hold the horse, it became so unmanageable. So he gave the animal in charge to the old man, and went home with his two thousand dollars.

Kirsten, of course, was delighted at this new piece of good fortune, and insisted that the new house should be built and land bought. This time Peder consented, and soon they had quite a fine farm.

Meanwhile the old man rode off on his new purchase, and when he came to a smithy he asked the smith to forge shoes for the horse. The smith proposed that they should first have a drink together, and the horse was tied up by the spring whilst they went indoors. The day was hot, and both men were thirsty, and, besides, they had much to say; and so the hours slipped by and found them still talking. Then the servant girl came out to fetch a pail of water, and, being a kind-hearted lass, she gave some to the horse to drink. What was her surprise when the animal said to her: 'Take off my bridle and you will save my life.'

'I dare not,' said she; 'your master will be so angry.'

'He cannot hurt you,' answered the horse, 'and you will save my life.'

At that she took off the bridle; but nearly fainted with astonishment when the horse turned into a dove and flew away just as the old man came out of the house. Directly he saw what had happened he changed himself into a hawk and flew after the dove. Over the woods and fields they went, and at length they reached a king's palace surrounded by beautiful gardens. The princess was walking with her attendants in the rose garden when the dove turned itself into a gold ring and fell at her feet.

'Why, here is a ring!' she cried, 'where could it have come from?' And picking it up she put it on her finger. As she did so the hill-man lost his power over Hans—for of course you understand that it was he who had been the dog, the cow, the horse and the dove.

'Well, that is really strange,' said the princess. 'It fits me as though it had been made for me!'

Just at that moment up came the king.

'Look at what I have found!' cried his daughter.

'Well, that is not worth much, my dear,' said he. 'Besides, you have rings enough, I should think.'

'Never mind, I like it,' replied the princess.

But as soon as she was alone, to her amazement, the ring suddenly left her finger and became a man. You can imagine how frightened she was, as, indeed, anybody would have been; but in an instant the man became a ring again, and then turned back to a man, and so it went on for some time until she began to get used to these sudden changes.

'I am sorry I frightened you,' said Hans, when he thought he could safely speak to the princess without making her scream. 'I took refuge with you because the old hill-man, whom I have offended, was trying to kill me, and here I am safe.'

'You had better stay here then,' said the princess. So Hans stayed, and he and she became good friends; though, of course, he only became a man when no one else was present.

This was all very well; but, one day, as they were talking together, the king happened to enter the room, and although Hans quickly changed himself into a ring again it was too late.

The king was terribly angry.

'So this is why you have refused to marry all the kings and princes who have sought your hand?' he cried.

And, without waiting for her to speak, he commanded that his daughter should be walled up in the summer-house and starved to death with her lover.

That evening the poor princess, still wearing her ring, was put into the summer-house with enough food to last for three days, and the door was bricked up. But at the end of a week or two the king thought it was time to give her a grand funeral, in spite of her bad behaviour, and he had the summer-house opened. He could hardly believe his eyes when he found that the princess was not there, nor Hans either. Instead, there lay at his feet a large hole, big enough for two people to pass through.

Now what had happened was this.

When the princess and Hans had given up hope, and cast themselves down on the ground to die, they fell down this hole, and right through the earth as well, and at last they tumbled into a castle built of pure gold at the other side of the world, and there they lived happily. But of this, of course, the king knew nothing.

'Will anyone go down and see where the passage leads to?' he asked, turning to his guards and courtiers. 'I will reward splendidly the man who is brave enough to explore it.'

For a long time nobody answered. The hole was dark and deep, and if it had a bottom no one could see it. At length a soldier, who was a careless sort of fellow, offered himself for the service, and cautiously lowered himself into the darkness. But in a moment he, too, fell down, down, down. Was he going to fall for ever, he wondered! Oh, how thankful he was in the end to reach the castle, and to meet the princess and Hans, looking quite well and not at all as if they had been starved. They began to talk, and the soldier told them that the king was very sorry for the way he had treated his daughter, and wished day and night that he could have her back again.

Then they all took ship and sailed home, and when they came to the princess's country, Hans disguised himself as the sovereign of a neighbouring kingdom, and went up to the palace alone. He was given a hearty welcome by the king, who prided himself on his hospitality, and a banquet was commanded in his honour. That evening, whilst they sat drinking their wine, Hans said to the king:

'I have heard the fame of your majesty's wisdom, and I have travelled from far to ask your counsel. A man in my country has buried his daughter alive because she loved a youth who was born a peasant. How shall I punish this unnatural father, for it is left to me to give judgment?'

The king, who was still truly grieved for his daughter's loss, answered quickly:

'Burn him alive, and strew his ashes all over the kingdom.'

Hans looked at him steadily for a moment, and then threw off his disguise.

'You are the man,' said he; 'and I am he who loved your daughter, and became a gold ring on her finger. She is safe, and waiting not far from here; but you have pronounced judgment on yourself.'

Then the king fell on his knees and begged for mercy; and as he had in other respects been a good father, they forgave him. The wedding of Hans and the princess was celebrated with great festivities which lasted a month. As for the hill-man he intended to be present; but whilst he was walking along a street which led to the palace a loose stone fell on his head and killed him. So Hans and the princess lived in peace and happiness all their days, and when the old king died they reigned instead of him.

The End